# OXYGEN

SETH RAIN

Published by Human Fiction

ISBN: 978-1-915211-04-0

Editing: Jane Hammett

Cover Design: Books Covered

*YOUR FREE NOVELLA AND SHORT STORY ARE WAITING!*

Visit **sethrain.com** to download your free digital copy of the prequel novella: *The Rogue Watcher,* a free short story called *Dawn,* and sign up to Seth's emails.

## *A BRIEF NOTE*

Fellow reader,

I use British English spelling throughout this series. I'm a Brit and so find it more natural to use this. I hope it doesn't detract from your enjoyment.

All the best,

Seth.

# OXYGEN

## *CHAPTER 1*

### JAKE

JAKE SHOULDERED through the banged-up front door. Shuk's place always had the same stench – like something stale, or maybe dying. The trick was to breathe through your mouth.

Someone spoke from inside the darkness. 'You got some nerve coming back here.'

Jake squinted, trying to make out who it was. 'I don't want any trouble.'

Coming close enough for Jake to see his silhouette, Shuk wiped his mouth with the back of a hand, then raised his chin. 'You sure don't act like you don't want no trouble. Selling to Whistler.'

Jake raised his hands in surrender. 'She was offering over the odds. It was only business.'

Shuk angled his thin body away from Jake, his dark eyes narrowed. 'Only business, huh?'

'Sure,' Jake said. Whistler had gone missing, and now Shuk was the only Blue dealer in the village. Not that Jake was going to tell Shuk. He reached into his bag. At the same time, Shuk reached into his coat pocket and took out a gun.

'Hey, hey,' Jake said, holding out a tube of Blue Oxygen. 'It's just Blue.'

Shuk slid a step closer. 'I can't be too careful. Things are desperate out there.' He came even closer, pushing his gun back into his pocket.

'Hell, Shuk. What makes you think I'm here to cause trouble? You know me.'

'Yeah, I know you. Trouble follows you like a dog, kid. And I'm reaching that time in life when trouble ain't what I'm looking for.'

'Me neither, Shuk. Me neither.' Jake offered him the Blue. 'Take a look. I have more.'

Shuk took the tube, his lips pressed flat as he squinted at it.

'That's the one I owe you,' Jake said.

Shuk nodded and pushed the tube into his coat pocket. 'It hasn't been synced, has it?' His long brown hair was a mess – some loose, some tied up. He often, as he did now, took his straggly curls in both hands and pushed them back over his shoulders, only for it to fall back a moment later.

'Of course not,' Jake said. 'Totally unused.'

'How much more do you have?' Shuk asked, staring at Jake's bag.

'Do you have the motherboard and processor I need?' Jake asked.

Shuk folded his arms and nodded slowly.

'How much Blue is it going to take?' Jake asked.

Shuk snorted. 'How much do you have?'

Jake turned around, ready to leave. It was the same old routine with Shuk – the usual cat-and-mouse games.

'Wait,' Shuk said. Jake had him where he wanted him. 'Twenty.'

Jake let out a quick laugh and shook his head. 'I don't

think so.' He patted the top of the bag and turned away a second time.

Shuk snarled. 'Then how many?'

'I have what you want,' Jake said. 'It's supply and demand. The cornerstone of any culture. Who am I to rail against the fundamental drivers of our dearly held mercantile system?'

'Alright, kid,' Shuk said. 'I don't want to hear any of your bullshit.' He cleared his throat. 'Come on. How many you got?'

Jake opened the flap on the small leather bag and showed him. 'Twelve.'

Shuk took a big gulp of air. 'Hell, kid. The raiding will get you killed.'

'You want it or not?' Jake asked. The tubes of Blue illuminated the inside of the bag, then Shuk's face.

Just as Shuk was about to take the bag, Jake closed the flap and held it close to his stomach.

Shuk recoiled. A sheen of sweat covered his face. He took a deep breath, then turned to go back to the rear of the shack. 'Come with me.'

Jake followed him into the darkness.

At the rear of Shuk's place was what he called his shop. It was a metre-deep counter covered with all kinds of microchips, processors and shells of computers. To the right of the counter was a small table where two guys were playing chess. Neither looked up at Jake.

Shuk pushed through a gap in the counter, then turned to Jake.

Jake stared at him, waiting. It was hard work doing business with the likes of Shuk.

'Show me the processor,' Jake said. Shuk was the only one who dealt in Blue and who had the parts he needed.

Threatening to leave without making a deal was all a bluff. He could never work out whether Shuk knew that or not.

Shuk rummaged around in a box beneath the counter, now and then glancing up at Jake and his bag.

Jake looked over at the two men playing chess. The guy playing white smirked at his opponent as he moved his right flanking knight.

Shuk placed the motherboard and processor on the counter. Jake did all he could to not look pleased. He'd waited a long time to get his hands on such a quality processor. Shuk rubbed his chin, his lips moving as though he was doing maths in his head. 'You have twelve, you say?'

Jake nodded.

Shuk seemed to zone out for a moment. Then he gave Jake a serious look. 'You ever think about where it comes from?'

'The Blue?' Jake asked, wary of where Shuk was going with the questioning. 'From the city.'

'No,' Shuk said. 'Where it *actually* comes from. Do you think what they say is true?'

Jake had heard many stories about where Blue came from. But he'd given up trying to work it out. The truth, if it existed, was hidden somewhere inside the city. Shuk, like many others, figured the Blue came from those who died before their time. Any oxygen left over was taken from the overall Oxygen blockchain and repurposed as Blue Oxygen. That meant those who could afford it didn't use up their own quota of oxygen, but used the Blue Oxygen taken from the unlucky ones.

'Who knows?' Jake said, shrugging.

'Don't you wonder where they go? All those folks who go missing?' Shuk asked, with what looked like genuine surprise. '*They* take them.' He glanced over his shoulder. 'And kill them for their quota. It's the only explanation.'

'People leave the village,' Jake said. 'It's no big deal. I'm working on it myself.'

'No way,' Shuk said, shaking his head. 'They're being taken for their oxygen. Don't believe what they tell you.'

'Do we have a deal or what?' Jake said, tired of the conversation.

'You can take the processor,' Shuk said, pushing it across the counter. 'But I want three more tubes when you get them.'

Jake sighed. He couldn't be bothered to argue.

'This is where you counter my offer, kid.'

'I'm tired of the same old crap,' Jake said, turning to leave.

'Come on,' Shuk moaned. 'You know how this works.'

Jake clutched the leather bag. 'I'll take it to Whistler.' He was bluffing, but he figured Shuk wouldn't work that out.

Shuk hesitated. For a moment, Jake wondered whether Shuk was actually smarter than he looked.

'You win,' Shuk said.

Jake stopped, but didn't turn around. No. Shuk wasn't that smart.

'Twelve tubes,' Jake said. 'No more bullshit.' He patted his bag, then slowly turned and placed the bag on the counter.

Shuk opened the flap of the bag and looked inside, his eyes wide. 'Got to hand it to you, kid. You're one hell of a raider.'

Jake reached for the processor.

'What do you do with them, anyway?' Shuk asked.

Jake raised an eyebrow. 'That would be telling.'

'Top-secret, huh?' Shuk said, tapping his nose.

Jake inspected the motherboard and processor.

Shuk shrugged. 'Don't you trust me, kid?'

'No,' Jake said.

'I don't know what I have to do to prove I'm legit.'

Jake was ready to leave.

'Let me know when you get more,' Shuk said, looking more closely at one tube of Blue.

Then the guy playing white at the table in the corner jumped up, sending the chessboard and pieces flying. He was a short, skinny guy with all sorts of gold jewellery sticking out from his ears and nose.

Jake spun around.

'You're a goddamn cheat!' the skinny guy screamed, reaching across and grabbing the guy sitting opposite by his collar. The guy playing black was the huge, lumbering sort. He swung a slow-moving arm and missed the skinny guy by a mile.

'Now come on, gents,' Shuk said, edging sideways through the gap in the counter. The two men had stood and lunged at one another, and were now wrestling.

The huge one pushed into Shuk, sending him careening backwards. Shuk smacked his head against one of the stanchions holding up the counter. Shuk collapsed to the ground and didn't move. A tube rolled out of the bag on the counter and fell to the ground.

The two other guys stopped fighting and stared at Jake, who knelt down, picked up the tube that had fallen off the counter and pushed it into his coat pocket.

Shuk was out of it.

The two chess players helped one another up and, taking advantage of the opportunity, rolled Shuk onto his back and went through his pockets. The skinny guy took Shuk's gun.

Jake took his own gun out of his pocket.

'We don't have no problem with you,' the skinny guy said. He held the gun loosely by his side.

'Maybe you should leave?' Jake said. 'Probably for the best.'

Sheepishly, the guy with the gun edged towards the counter and picked up the bag.

'I can't let you take that,' Jake said.

'I'm taking this bag,' the skinny guy said. 'I'm not going to hurt you. But I'm taking this bag.'

'Shoot him,' the big guy said.

Jake gave him an impatient look. 'Really? Shoot him?'

Jake opened fire, shooting the skinny guy in the foot, who fell, his gun skidding across the floor towards Jake. The big guy ran to the door, stumbling and falling against the wall before finding the broken door and smashing through it.

'What the fuck?' the skinny guy said, staring in horror at his bloody foot.

Jake reached down, offering to help him up.

The skinny guy grimaced, refusing Jake's help. 'My fucking foot. You shot my foot!'

Jake picked up the bag and returned it to the counter, closing the flap carefully. At his feet, Shuk rocked his head from side to side.

'You'd better leave before he comes to his senses,' Jake said.

Still swearing, the skinny guy crawled to the door.

Jake lifted the semi-conscious Shuk, dragged him over to the wall and propped him up. Blood oozed from a deep gash on his forehead.

Jake took the tube of Blue from his pocket and stared at it. It weighed hardly anything at all. Most people said it tasted no different to normal oxygen. But Jake didn't agree.

'What ... happened?' Shuk asked groggily.

'You took a bit of a tumble,' Jake said.

Shuk squinted at him.

Jake took the leather bag from the counter and pushed it towards Shuk, who embraced it, still staring at Jake with confusion.

'Catch you later,' Jake said.

Shuk looked around, dazed.

'One of your buddies took a tube,' Jake said.

Shuk appeared to wake, as if from a dream, then checked inside the leather bag.

'Didn't you stop them?' he asked.

'They had your gun,' Jake said.

'Goddamn!' Shuk said.

Jake raised a hand to say goodbye and edged through the doorway, expecting to find the chess players outside waiting for him, but they were gone. Jake looked both ways, pushed his hands into his pockets, then strode through the village towards the tram stop.

On the tram, he leaned his head against the headrest. The tram rumbled and clattered over the steel junctions towards Ash Hills. Jake held the tube of Blue Oxygen. He should have taken it to his sister. But it didn't contain a lot – barely a few hundred litres. It was nothing compared to their quota of ten million litres. But still...

With a screech, the tram stopped and shunted backwards, ready to head back into the village. He hopped off. Somewhere deep inside the tram's workings, parts whirred and jolted.

He was alone. He enjoyed being alone.

The Ash Hills were all that remained after building Luxor City. The capital of Two North and the head of the Five Republics, Luxor City was the phoenix that had risen out of the destruction caused by the wars of 2029, almost a century before. The fields of industrial debris left behind, combined with the soot that had settled on the ground, gave the vast expanse between the villages and the city its name. Like sand dunes in the desert, which rose and fell in waves, the wreckage of the world that had once been known as Britain had been flattened, burned and left to settle. It took years, but out of the devastation, survivors constructed two new cities. In between, and scattered throughout the country, were the villages.

Luxor City loomed on the horizon, distant and unreachable. The high-rise apartment blocks, the towers, the cathedrals. What was it about humans that made them build cities? Like bees and hives.

Jake turned over the tube of Blue Oxygen in his hand. His sister wouldn't know he'd had a tube of oxygen. She wouldn't miss what she didn't know she'd had.

When he was a child, he ran whenever he could. No one ran any longer. It used up the quota too quickly. He missed running. He knelt and tied his shoelaces, the black ash staining his knees.

Lifting the tube to his mouth, he pressed the release button and inhaled. Now the Blue synced his lungs to the Oxygen blockchain. It didn't matter what anyone told him; he was convinced it tasted different. He set off at a jog, his arms and legs working together, propelling him. Then he was sprinting, his body leaning forward into the air and the world. The soles of his feet pounded the ash, throwing plumes of black dust into the air. If his sister had seen him, he'd have been in all sorts of trouble. What a waste...

It didn't take long for his desperate breathing to slow him down. His chest burned, his legs and shoulders ached. But it felt good. Better than good. Blue Oxygen was freedom … a way of escaping the constraints of his designated quota.

He took another hit of Blue, inhaling deeply.

Now and then he glanced over at the city on the horizon. That's where the oxygen-rich lived. The oxygen quota – ten million litres – meant nothing to them because they inhaled Blue Oxygen all the time. They slept in rooms into which it was pumped all night long. Why did they get it all, when people in the villages had to make do with their quota? It wasn't fair.

He inhaled the tube and began to jog again. As he ran, he told himself he would never stop, even though it was a lie.

## *CHAPTER 2*

### ASTRID

THE AIR PUMPED into the room from above blew strands of Astrid's hair from her shoulders. She stopped brushing her hair and peered up at the air vents. The small discs of white vented plastic filled her bedroom and the entire building with Blue. She thought about it often, knowing how important it was. Her mother told her repeatedly how fortunate they were to live in the city and to have so much of it.

She placed her brush on the table. Her face, reflected in the mirror, was serious. Her father and his guest were in the next room, and the dull cadence of their conversation vibrated through the wall.

There was no reason to be suspicious. Yet that was the word that came to mind as she crept towards her door. Perhaps she had subconsciously heard some words the two men had said, and had come to a kind of understanding. Whatever it was, she found herself creeping through her doorway, trying not to open the door any wider, fearing it would creak and give her away. Her father hadn't attempted to hide anything from her; even so, she wanted to listen without him knowing.

She peeked around the edge of the wall into the main living room. It was a foolish thought, but memories of being a child, creeping through the apartment, came to her. Here she was again. But she was not a child any longer. At least, that was what she had told her parents so many times. Nineteen was not a child.

The man standing opposite her father shook his enormous head, making the loose skin beneath his chin wobble. Her father reached over to the man and placed a hand gently on his shoulder. The man recoiled and folded his arms across his large belly.

'You must understand,' her father said. 'There is no alternative.'

'You know very well there *is* an alternative,' the man said, leaning in closer to her father. 'We help them. How's that for an alternative? There are tens of thousands of people out there, outside the city walls, living day to day, waiting for their letter.'

'Bartholomew, please, listen to reason,' her father said. 'The quota will work in time, but until then we must manage the process. It's the only way to control our numbers. You must see that.'

Astrid listened intently.

'There are thousands of us,' Bartholomew pleaded, 'locked away in our apartments, in this city, each supplied with almost limitless Blue Oxygen. Not only do we make money from selling Blue Oxygen, but we live on it too.'

Her father's face reddened in a way Astrid knew meant he was losing his patience. He inhaled deeply. 'They are different from us. You know that.'

'I don't know that at all,' Bartholomew snarled. 'You're claiming something that we know is untrue. Don't do that.'

Her father clenched his fists. 'Do not question me. I

have spent years working hard to provide for my family. What I have, I have earned.'

Bartholomew opened his mouth, as if ready to speak, then hesitated.

Astrid's father could be intimidating.

'If they die, why shouldn't we use what remains of their quota?' her father said. 'Blue Oxygen is simply a way of using what otherwise would be wasted.'

Bartholomew's tone was conciliatory. 'I know how hard you have worked and how much your family means to you. But those people in the villages are hard-working people too. They have families, they have dreams, they have ambitions.' He peered around the room, making Astrid duck down even lower. 'But I think you know what I'm talking about. Don't you? People dying is one thing, but if people are being killed ... then that's a different matter.'

Astrid covered her mouth. Who was being killed? Blue Oxygen was made using the oxygen people no longer needed. She had no idea that there were those who would kill for oxygen.

'I think you should leave,' her father said sternly.

'Gordon, please. I came here to talk to you, to help you see reason.'

Her father waved his hands and let out a loud, dismissive huff. 'You accuse me of such a thing and expect me to react reasonably?'

'Who said anything about accusing you?' Bartholomew said.

'I have somewhere to be,' her father said. 'You should leave.'

'Gordon. You and I have been friends for a long time. We have both made our fortune from Blue Oxygen. Maybe now is the time to give back. Those people in the villages across the country – what remains of the world's population – are the same as us. It is only luck, happenstance, fate, call it what you will, that has put you and me in the position we find ourselves.'

'You're wrong,' her father said, in a tone Astrid recognised; it was the voice he used when his mind was made up.

Bartholomew narrowed his eyes. 'Do you know someone called the Engineer?'

'What?' her father asked. 'Who?'

'The Engineer. Have you heard of him?'

Her father shook his head in annoyance. 'I don't know who you're talking about.'

'He's killing people,' Bartholomew said. 'Do you know that? I had my suspicions, but I have it on good authority that this is happening. I've tried to be reasonable with you. But you're not listening. He's killing people and selling what's left of their quota. That's the Blue Oxygen we are using.' The man pointed to the ceiling. 'The oxygen pumped into our homes comes from the people the Engineer, and God knows who else, have killed.'

'You've lost your mind,' her father said, ushering Bartholomew to the door.

Bartholomew spoke so quietly, Astrid had to strain to hear him. 'You have changed, my old friend.'

'I really must insist,' her father said, pointing at the door. 'I have an important appointment.'

Bartholomew left and her father closed the door. He walked back into the room, his head bowed. For a moment, Astrid thought he might change his mind and go after Bartholomew. But he took a deep breath, pushed back his shoulders and strode across the room as defiantly as she had ever seen him.

# CHAPTER 3

## JAKE

JAKE TOOK the final turn leading to his sister's shack. Rows and rows of them, all made from whatever people could get their hands on. Most were made from brick, some concrete, others of timber, a few from steel. Maybe people thought there was safety in numbers.

A shack door opened quickly, slamming against the wall. It was O'Leary.

'Jake!' the old man shouted.

Maybe Jake could pretend he hadn't heard.

'Hey! Jake!'

There was no chance of ignoring him.

'It's getting late,' Jake said, pointing towards his sister's shack. 'My sister won't be happy if I'm late again.'

But O'Leary wasn't listening. He never did. Wearing only a fleece dressing gown and muddied slippers, he ambled towards Jake.

Jake slowed down, sighed and told himself to be patient. O'Leary was a good man. Oblivious to another person's time, but a good man nonetheless.

'Did you hear about Marigold and Mr Hopkins?' O'Leary asked, hugging himself.

'No,' Jake said. He wished he had, because then he might have cut the conversation short.

'They're gone,' O'Leary said, raising his hands and looking around as though the missing people might be hiding close by. 'They've taken them.'

'What do you mean?' Jake asked. 'Who's taken them?'

O'Leary shook his head with annoyance and tutted.

Mr Hopkins must have been pretty close to his quota running out, but Marigold was younger than he was, and would have had a healthy amount of oxygen left. The two of them didn't leave their shack often.

O'Leary crept closer to Jake and looked both ways before whispering, 'They took them.'

Jake didn't know what to say. O'Leary had always been pretty crazy, but Shuk had said the same thing. He'd also heard other rumours over the past few weeks...

'Who is *they*?' Jake asked him. 'Who's doing it?'

Just as O'Leary looked as though he was about to answer, Mrs O'Leary appeared at the door.

'James!' she shouted. 'What have I told you about going outside in your dressing gown?'

At any other time, Jake would have been relieved to be saved from O'Leary's craziness. But this time, he wanted to hear more. O'Leary sounded genuine, as though he knew something.

O'Leary spun around immediately and, without speaking to Jake, jogged back to his shack. Mrs O'Leary scowled at Jake, who headed off towards his sister's shack, going over what O'Leary had said.

. . .

His sister's place stood apart from the rest. Out front were towers of old cars. His brother-in-law, Bailey, dismantled them and sold parts to those in the villages. He used the parts in ingenious ways to power all kinds of tools. He even used the bonnets and roofs to make walls for more shacks. People used the car seats as chairs indoors, and the glass for windows. Now the skeletons of these cars were stacked up, stripped of everything that could be stripped, of everything that had made them a car. Now, like extinct animals, motor cars only existed as fossils. Jake had seen functioning cars in the city, but even there they were scarce. He'd driven cars when he was younger – when his sister first got together with Bailey. But fuel soon became far too expensive, with much of the world's resources destroyed in the war, and finally it disappeared from the villages altogether.

At the far end of this car graveyard was his sister's shack, hunkered down with a backdrop of more stacked cars. A light shone from inside, reminding Jake how welcoming his sister's place always was, no matter what was happening outside.

It was evening, and the sun was going down. In the distance, the city glowed a dark red, the dim light of the sun reflecting off the glass skyscrapers and towers. The same hatred, or maybe it was envy, always came over Jake when he thought of the city. What made the people who lived there different from him or his sister or his niece? He knew the answer. The difference was money. They were all on the credit system, something those in villages hated using. Digital currency was yet another form of control, recording where you went and all your purchases. Gold had become the new currency in the villages. There was no way of tracking that.

He reached into his pocket and touched the empty tube

of Blue. Now he regretted using it. It had been reckless. But it had also been liberating.

Jake jumped onto the bonnet of an old car close to his sister's shack, climbed across it, and jumped down. Even something as simple as this made him think about how much oxygen it cost him. Whatever he did, his quota was always on his mind.

The door to his sister's shack opened, slamming against one of the columns holding up the porch. It was Jess, his niece.

'Uncle Jake!' she yelled and ran across the porch, her tiny feet flying across the wooden flooring as if she would take flight. She had recently turned seven, which seemed inconceivable. It felt like only weeks ago he'd first met and held her.

Jake jogged towards her and held out his arms. She leapt at him.

'If your mum catches you running, she'll blame me.'

But she wasn't listening. She held him tight, her arms wrapped around his shoulders and neck.

'You're going to strangle me, Jess,' he said, laughing lightly. He reached into his coat pocket and took out a bar of chocolate. 'Here you go.'

Jess's eyes lit up and she moved to grab it, before hesitating.

'What's wrong?' he asked her.

'Mother said I shouldn't eat chocolate because of my teeth.' She bared her teeth.

'They're beautiful.' He offered her the bar of chocolate.

She shook her head. 'Can't. Mother would be cross.'

Jake pushed the bar back into his pocket. 'Let me talk to your mother.' He carried her up the porch steps and into the shack.

'What have I told you about running?' his sister said to Jess, at the same time as she placed two plates on the table at the far end of the room. She turned her attention to Jake. 'And you said you'd be here an hour ago.'

'Sorry, Grace,' he said, not just apologising for being late, but also for wasting the Blue Oxygen.

His sister ignored his apology. She returned to the tiny kitchen, a few paces from the dining-room table, and came back with two more plates.

Finally, Jess let go of his neck and climbed down.

'Go and wash up,' her mother told her.

Jess sulked her way into the bathroom.

Bailey, Jake's brother-in-law, raised his head above the back of the settee at the other end of the shack, stretching his arms as though he'd only just woken up. He rolled off the settee and stumbled across the shack. 'How's it going, Jakey?' He punched Jake on the arm.

Jake took a swing back at Bailey, who dodged and winked simultaneously. Bailey was a big guy, but he could move fast when he wanted.

'Better than you, I reckon,' Jake said, pointing to the bandage around Bailey's arm.

'It's nothing,' he said, sitting at the table in front of the steaming plate of food Jess had placed down.

'Nothing?' Grace huffed. 'He nearly brought down one of those towers of useless cars out there.' She gestured towards the front of the shack. 'I've told him time and again it's over. He sells parts for hardly anything now. He's sold all the best parts.'

'It only takes a little imagination to work out what to do with the rest of them,' Bailey said, grabbing his knife and fork then pointing them at Grace. 'Mark my words. As soon as I figure out what to do with what's left, we'll be buying canisters of Blue Oxygen. Not just tubes. You'll see.'

'Yeah,' Grace said, shaking her head. 'Sure.'

Jess came out of the bathroom and moved her chair and plate so she was as close to Jake as possible.

Jake's attention was fixed on his plate of food. It was one of Grace's pies. They always looked good, but the synthetic meat inside never lived up to the promise of the golden pastry on the outside. Not that he would ever complain to his sister. The truth was, there wasn't much food around that tasted good. It kept you alive, and that was all you could ask for.

Jake tucked into his pie, trying to make the right sounds of enjoyment. It was only his sister who was allowed to sigh at the taste of the meat.

'It didn't always taste like this,' she said. 'I'm sure of it.'

'Tastes good to me,' Bailey said, shovelling another huge forkful into his mouth.

Jake was never sure whether Bailey actually meant it. But none of them would have dared to say anything different, even if Grace knew it was lies. It was only fair.

They finished dinner and moved on to bowls of fruit for dessert. Again, it was only Grace who complained about the size of the apple slices, or about the sourness of the oranges. Jake, like everyone else, was thankful for the vitamins. That was all that mattered.

After washing up, Bailey jerked his head at Jake, motioning for Jake to follow him outside.

'I'll put her to bed,' Grace said, picking up Jess, who had fallen asleep on a chair in the living room.

'Night, night,' Jess said to Jake sleepily, her head resting on her mother's shoulder.

Jake kissed the top of her head and, in one quick movement, without her knowing, slipped the bar of chocolate inside Jess's dressing-gown pocket. 'Night, princess.'

Jess closed her eyes and went back to sleep.

Bailey held the door open for Jake and they headed out onto the porch, each with a bottle of beer. 'The city gets brighter each night,' Bailey said, pointing into the distance towards the hazy red horizon.

Jake could only think of the Blue Oxygen being pumped into those towers. Every part of him tightened when he thought about everything *they* had, compared to him and his family.

'It's so unfair,' he said. 'Why should they get it all?'

'Because they have the credits.' Bailey shrugged, then downed what remained of his beer.

'They shouldn't have all the credits. That's my point.' Jake stared at the city skyline. 'I talked to O'Leary today. He was saying that Marigold and Mr Hopkins have gone missing. Had you heard that? Or about anyone else going missing? He said they were taking people for their oxygen.'

Bailey turned his head slowly and smiled. 'Another conspiracy theory, huh?'

'How do you explain them disappearing?'

'You've said yourself that you're going to leave the village as soon as you can. Maybe they did the same.'

'But they disappeared without anyone knowing where they've gone. Without saying goodbye.'

'Probably the best way to do it,' Bailey said, his expression downcast. 'If you ask me.'

Jake hated when Bailey spoke in that way ... like he'd already given up. He wanted to tell Bailey that he, Gambit and the other coders were going to take down the Oxygen blockchain someday. But Bailey wouldn't understand. He was like most other people. Bailey believed, like everyone else, that because of the nanotechnology inside them, which made them almost immortal, their life expectancy had to be managed. Jake had never believed this.

'I don't understand why you just accept it,' Jake said.

Bailey smiled. 'Where's this coming from, Jakey?'

It was pointless saying anything, but he couldn't stop himself. 'We're supposed to believe them that we can only have ten million litres of oxygen each. That Earth can't sustain more people.'

'And what? You think they're wrong?' Bailey asked.

'Yes,' Jake said. Wasn't it obvious?

'Why would they lie about something like that?' Bailey asked.

'Control,' Jake said. 'Carlisle wants to control everything and everybody.'

'Cameron Carlisle is the only thing standing between us and another nuclear war,' Bailey said, far more seriously than Jake had expected.

'You don't really think that,' Jake said. 'Do you?'

Bailey stared at him with a more serious expression than Jake had ever seen him muster. 'We can't let it happen again. We're doing this for future generations. For Jess and her children, and their children. We can't make the same mistakes.'

'They're brainwashing everyone,' Jake said, then immediately regretted it. The more he said, the more crazy he sounded. But he couldn't stop. 'Don't you see? There hasn't been a genuine vote for years. Across all five republics. Two North is the only republic that has nuclear weapons. Carlisle has all the power, and he's not letting go of it any time soon. He has more Blue than anyone else. He could stay alive forever if he wants. The quota is a way of controlling the people.'

Bailey placed a hand on Jake's shoulder and smiled. 'You need to stay off that computer. Stop talking to Gambit and your coding buddies.'

Jake sighed. It was no use. No one saw what was right there in front of them.

They stood on the porch, facing the towers of dismantled cars.

Bailey moved closer. 'I need to talk to you,' he whispered.

Jake didn't like Bailey's tone. 'What is it?'

Checking that Jess was not in sight, Bailey took a crumpled piece of paper from his trouser pocket.

At the sight of it, Jake's stomach twisted with fear. 'No.'

Bailey pushed the letter into Jake's hand. 'I guess this is what we've been talking about. I knew it would be here soon. I'm older than your sister. But it still caught me off guard.'

'No,' Jake said again, unfolding the paper. He read the words, knowing full well what they would say. He checked Bailey's eyes; They hadn't changed colour yet. It wasn't enough that the nanotechnology used to control the quota of oxygen was ever present, working to protect the body from diseases and ageing, but there was also a physical reminder visible in the eyes of everyone nearing the end.

'It's time,' Bailey said. 'I'm okay with it. I lost a chunk of oxygen when we bought the permit for Jess.'

Jake had tried to talk Grace and Bailey out of giving up half their quota for the permit to have Jess. He never spoke about that now, though. As soon as Jess was born, he understood why they had done it. Still, it was a huge sacrifice; one that he couldn't imagine making.

'You're okay with it?' Jake asked. 'What are you talking about?'

'Don't say anything to Jess. Not yet. I have to work out how to tell her.'

'When you get close to the last few hundred litres, she'll see it in your eyes.' Jake pushed the letter back into Bailey's hand. 'You're not doing anything. I'm going to get more Blue Oxygen.'

'Have you been raiding again?' Bailey gave him a stern look.

'Give me a few hours. I'll get it.'

'I have half a day,' Bailey said. 'A tube of Blue won't make any difference.'

'It will keep you alive while I get more.'

'No!' Bailey said. He never got angry. But now his eyes took on a darkness that frightened Jake.

Jake climbed down the porch steps.

'Wait,' Bailey said, his anger disappearing. 'Stay here. Help me talk to your sister.'

'Don't tell her anything,' Jake said. 'I'll be back here by morning with a canister of Blue Oxygen.'

'Jake, you can't—'

'Promise me you won't say anything,' Jake said, taking a step closer to the porch and Bailey. 'Say nothing to Grace until I'm back in the morning.'

Bailey glanced into the shack, then down at Jake. 'It's too late.'

Jake held up his hands. 'Just wait. I can do this.' Bailey had given up so much for his sister, for Jess, and for him. It was time to pay him back.

Bailey shifted his weight from one foot to the other, and again checked on Grace inside the shack. 'Don't do this. If you get into trouble, your sister won't forgive either of us.'

Jake strode away across the yard. 'I'll be back,' he shouted again and turned the corner, heading for the tram.

# CHAPTER 4

## ASTRID

Astrid sat opposite her mother at the table. To her right, her father stood and raised his glass, acknowledging Tom Carlisle, who sat at the other end of the table, to Astrid's left.

Her father cleared his throat.

'I would like to propose a toast. To Tom and his family. They are without doubt the most loyal, the most gracious, and the most wonderful people. We are blessed to call them our friends.'

Tom flushed. Astrid lowered her gaze momentarily. Her father thought nothing of embarrassing people.

Tom raised his glass. 'Please, Mr Solomon. You're too kind.'

Her father made a gruff sound in his throat. 'Not a bit of it. I'm thrilled that your father has invested in our company. Our families coming together in this way will benefit us all. It will enable us to propel the inhabitants of Luxor City and Two North to new heights.'

Tom tugged at his tie and collar, then half-heartedly raised his glass a second time.

'Let's eat!' Astrid's father shouted over to the two maids waiting by the door. The maids opened the doors and in came four servants, each holding a plate, which they set down on the table.

'This looks marvellous,' her father said. 'Simply marvellous. Don't you think, Tom? Only the best for the son of Cameron Carlisle.'

Tom bowed his head at the mention of his father.

'You're embarrassing him,' Astrid's mother said. She turned to Tom and smiled softly. 'Take no notice, my dear. My husband is excited, that's all.'

'Of course I'm excited,' her father said. 'This is historical. The Solomons and the Carlisles joining forces. With this deal, we can control the price of Blue. Control it to benefit the people.'

'You mean, benefit *you*,' Astrid said under her breath.

'What was that?' her father asked.

'Nothing.' She smiled. 'I was just agreeing.'

The four of them took up their forks and knives. An uncomfortable hush fell over the table as they dined.

When the sound of eating became almost unbearable, Astrid's mother broke the silence. 'So, Tom, how *are* your mother and father? Well, I hope?'

'They are well, thank you.' Tom finished chewing and put down his fork. 'They send their best and apologise for being unable to attend.'

'Not a bit of it,' her father said. 'They're busy people. They can't be expected to attend every dinner to which they are invited.'

Tom took up his fork and nodded apologetically.

Astrid did the best she could to get through the rest of the meal without giving away what she thought of her father's deal with Cameron Carlisle.

'Tell the cook to send in the dessert,' her father said to the maid waiting by the table.

'Before we have dessert,' Tom said, 'I would like to say something.' He fumbled with his wine glass, nearly spilling the little that remained. 'If that is okay with you, Mr Solomon.'

Astrid's father clapped his hands. 'By all means, my good man. And do call me Gordon.'

As Tom pushed back his chair and stood, his knee knocked the table, tipping over Astrid's glass.

'I'm so sorry,' Tom said, reaching for it.

'It was nearly finished,' Astrid said, righting the glass. 'Don't apologise.'

'I think Tom has had a little too much wine,' her father said, laughing loudly.

'I must say,' Tom said. 'I am a little nervous.' He glanced at Astrid.

She frowned, unsure what he meant.

'Let's hear it, then,' her father said.

'Dear,' her mother said. 'Please, give him a moment. You can see that the young man isn't used to this kind of thing.'

Embarrassment warmed Astrid's cheeks.

'I have thought carefully about what I'm about to say,' Tom said, 'and I hope it doesn't come as a shock to any of you.'

Astrid's mother and father shared a knowing look. Astrid frowned even more heavily.

'Astrid,' Tom said.

She stared at him.

'Our families have known each other for a very long time. Now, times are changing. We will control the sale of Blue Oxygen to benefit both our families and the people of this city and Two North.'

'Hear hear!' her father shouted. 'Bravo!'

Tom took a deep breath and walked around the table to Astrid. He fumbled in his trouser pocket and eventually pulled out a small box.

'No,' she muttered, shaking her head, wanting to escape from what she feared was about to happen.

Tom dropped to one knee.

'I say,' her father said.

'Oh my,' her mother said.

With an expression more of fear than of expectation, Tom opened the ring box to reveal a ring with an enormous diamond. He raised his head. 'Astrid, I have admired you for a long time. Would you do me the honour of marrying me?'

Astrid couldn't speak, couldn't breathe. She'd had no idea that Tom felt this way about her, or that marriage was something she would have to consider. Her father and mother stared at her, their mouths open, their eyes wide.

'I don't know what to say,' she blurted out.

She did, in fact, know what she wanted to say. But if she said any of the words that came to mind, she would have crushed Tom. She didn't love him, but she didn't want to hurt him either.

The room was silent, all eyes on her.

# CHAPTER 5

## JAKE

JAKE TOOK the tram through West Gate and into the market. Day trading had ended and the busier evening trade was beginning. Gambit lived over on the east side of the market, selling herbs he said helped with meditation. If anyone knew how Jake could get his hands on enough Blue Oxygen to keep Bailey around long enough for Jake to find a bigger haul, it was Gambit. If he didn't have any, then Jake would have to risk raiding again.

There were all kinds of rumours about Gambit. He'd been around longer than anyone could remember, yet he claimed he had never used Blue Oxygen. He had to be lying. Jake was sure of it. The meditation was a cover-up. Some said Gambit was ex-military. Others said he'd lived in the city. That made no sense to Jake. Why would he, if he had the choice, live in the villages? No way. Gambit was hiding something.

Jake weaved through the market. He took a handful of hot chestnuts from the woman on the corner, wincing at the heat and juggling them in his hand.

'Hey!' the woman shouted after him. 'Jake! You owe me for those.'

'I'll fix you up on my way back through. Promise!'

'You said that yesterday. And the day before that...'

He threw the nuts into his mouth and took a sharp right into the tunnel that led to Gambit's garden. That's where Gambit spent most of his time. In fact, Jake couldn't remember ever seeing Gambit anywhere other than in his garden.

Jake's footsteps echoed through the tunnel. He imagined running, but of course did not.

He stepped out of the tunnel and climbed the steep incline to Gambit's garden. There were few trees in West Gate, and definitely no trees in the market. Space was at a premium. But Gambit's place was a green oasis. Seven trees, each a different colour, spread their branches high and wide. Gambit told him they were Japanese. Red, yellow, orange and all the shades in between. Jake had asked once how he'd managed to grow them and keep them alive. Gambit explained how he'd travelled through the villages, to the outskirts of Moscov City to find soil good enough, filled with the nutrients the trees would need. Jake was impressed, but he was only ever interested in what Gambit could tell him about coding and building computers.

The city spires and towers peeked through the shady trees, and for a moment seemed less imposing, less superior. Gambit sat cross-legged at the far end of the garden, close to a small shed. Bowls of water of different sizes surrounded him. His eyes closed, he sat deathly still, his chest not appearing to move at all. He was the oldest-looking person Jake knew – much older than the fifty years most people got out of their quota. There was no hair on Gambit's head, but he had a bushy beard, black sprinkled with grey.

'What can I do for you?' Gambit asked without opening his eyes.

'I need your help.'

'What did you do to the last processor?' Gambit smiled. 'Or did you finally hack into the oxygen blockchain?'

Jake hated the way Gambit mocked him, but he bit his tongue.

Gambit opened his eyes and tilted his head in sympathy. 'Jake. You look troubled. What is it?'

'It's my brother-in-law. Bailey.'

Gambit sighed, his face downcast. 'He has received the letter?'

Jake nodded. 'I need Blue Oxygen. Just enough to help him through the next few days.'

Gambit looked confused.

'Come on, Gambit. I know you use it. You have to. Help me out. I can give you gold. Just tell me how much you need.'

'I can't help you,' Gambit said calmly.

Jake was running out of patience. 'Everyone knows you use it.'

'Do they? Well, that's strange, because I have never used Blue Oxygen.'

'I don't have time to play games,' Jake said. 'Please. You have to help me. Bailey doesn't have long. He has a kid. My niece.'

Gambit stood and strolled towards Jake. 'I can't help you. I don't use Blue Oxygen.'

Jake's brow wrinkled. 'So where's your letter?'

'My letter?'

'You must have used up your quota. What makes you different from the rest of us?'

Gambit raised an eyebrow. 'Before you interrupted me, I was meditating. Do you remember what I told you?'

'Don't give me that. There's no way that's enough.'

'You just don't want to hear the truth. You're like the rest of them. Lowering your heart rate, moving slowly, maintaining a steady rhythm is the only way to prolong your quota. They gave me the same ten million litres as you, Jake. The same as everyone else.'

'Topped up with Blue Oxygen,' Jake said.

Gambit sighed. 'If you'll excuse me, I must continue—'

'Goddamn!' Jake said, turning away.

Gambit laughed gently.

'What?' Jake asked.

'You have no idea how much oxygen you're using being so angry, do you? You only have so much. Use it wisely.'

'You sound like my brother-in-law. He's given up too.'

'It's not giving up. It's making the best of what you have.'

Jake huffed. 'What I have? A death sentence, you mean?'

'No. You have a life. You're looking at it the wrong way. They gave you enough oxygen to live a good, beautiful life.'

It was Jake's turn to laugh. 'You're deluded.' He looked towards the dim light given off by the city. 'Given by *them*? By those in control. Who the hell even are they? What right do they have to give us a quota? And all the time they're using Blue Oxygen, never eating into their own.'

'It is the way it is,' Gambit muttered. 'For now.'

'I hate them,' Jake said. 'Carlisle and those in the city take what they want, do what they want, leaving us to die out here when our quota runs out.'

'There are too many people,' Gambit said.

'You don't believe that. Why help me take down the Oxygen blockchain if you really think that?'

Gambit shrugged and gave Jake a wry smile. 'What can I say? I'm a contrarian. Besides, it's too much of a challenge to turn down.'

'But you believe there are too many people?'

Gambit considered the question. 'Maybe. When we cured illness and disease, it soon became apparent that we had to figure out a fair way to take our turn on this planet. And this is the way.'

'They've brainwashed you like they've brainwashed everybody else. It's all bullshit. I hate them!'

Gambit ambled through the garden towards the tallest tree. He clasped his hands behind his back. 'Hate is a strong word, Jake. Such a strong word to describe your feelings for people you don't even know.'

'I know them, and I know how I feel.' His heart raced, and he was breathing more quickly. He told himself to calm down, knowing the cost.

'I am aware of the many rumours about me,' Gambit said. 'One rumour is that I was a soldier. It is true.' Gambit crossed his arms. 'I have seen too often where hatred leads people. You should hate no one, Jake. It is a path to ruin.'

'How else should I feel? They live freely. They could give us Blue Oxygen – share it with us. But they choose not to. Why are you defending them?'

'I don't know the people who live in the city. But what I do know is that they will be more like us than you know. Once you see other people as different to yourself, then all kinds of evil will surely follow.'

Jake hesitated. 'If you know where I can get the Blue Oxygen, tell me.'

Gambit bowed his head. 'I'm sorry. As I told you, I cannot help.'

Jake took the motherboard and processor from his pocket and holding them in his cupped hands, offered them to Gambit.

'That is a powerful processor,' Gambit said.

'It cost me a lot.' Jake glanced at Gambit's front door. 'Will you install it for me? I have to find more Blue for Bailey.'

Gambit looked around, as if to check that no one could hear him. 'We still need more routers. There are around thirty coders who have a connection, but there are more waiting to get hooked up.'

Jake and Gambit had worked on their internet for close to three years, and every time Jake thought they were close to actually doing it, Gambit seemed to stamp on the brakes. The idea of escaping from state interference and being able to converse freely with people all across the villages was intoxicating to Jake. In time, he knew they would take down the Oxygen blockchain for good.

'We'll get them,' Jake said, frustrated.

'This is very risky,' Gambit said.

Jake wanted Gambit to tell him how to succeed, not give him problems that needed solving. But he kept his composure. 'The more nodes and data points we create, the more chance we have of creating something truly out of Carlisle's reach. We can finally free the people in the villages. Then take down the blockchain.'

Gambit took the motherboard and processor and slid them beneath his sweater. 'It is still only a rudimentary structure.'

'We will create more,' Jake said. 'But I have to help Bailey first.'

'There's more to life than constantly fighting those in charge.' Gambit's voice was more urgent than Jake was used to. 'Live the life you have. Stop trying to live a different one.'

Jake ignored him, turned, and entered the tunnel that led back towards the market.

# CHAPTER 6

## ASTRID

Astrid bit the side of a fingernail, drawing blood, then winced. She was waiting for her mother and father to come back into the room. Her refusal of Tom's proposal hung in the air like a fog.

Her father was saying goodbye to Tom, telling him that he would talk to Astrid. That *she wasn't herself ... she needed some time ... she would see reason.*

Astrid sucked her bleeding fingernail. She was not marrying Tom. The more she thought about it, the crazier it was that her father had even considered it.

The door closed with a thump.

Astrid steeled herself and sat up straight in her chair. She considered getting up so she was standing when he came for her. He had never hit her, but the look he'd given her when she refused Tom was the closest she had seen to him losing control. His stern expression had scared her.

A cold waft of air followed her father into the room. Her mother followed, not making eye contact with Astrid.

'So,' her father said, 'I suppose you think that was appropriate? That you have won?'

'No,' Astrid said, shaking her head frantically. It was a strange thing for him to say, and it caught her off guard. Something told her she would remember his words and the tone of his voice for as long as she lived. 'Of course not. It's not about winning or losing. But I don't want to marry him.'

Her father breathed in deeply. He rubbed his stubbled chin with finger and thumb.

Astrid wanted him to speak. She hated the way he could say so much with no words. His silence was always more frightening.

'Please,' Astrid said. 'I didn't want to be disrespectful. But I can't marry him.'

Her father sat in his chair at the head of the table. He reached into his jacket pocket and took out a cigar. He glanced over his shoulder at Astrid's mother who, realising what her husband wanted, rushed over to the table beneath the window and brought the lighter to him. She ignited it and held it to his cigar. He puffed, expelling swirls of silver smoke.

Astrid's chest pounded.

Her father leaned forward slowly. 'Tom is a good man. His family is successful. Tom is hard-working, clever, and – well, I am no judge, but I would say he is handsome.' He glanced at Astrid's mother, who nodded.

Astrid swallowed, air sticking in her throat. 'I don't want to marry him.'

Her father flicked ash into the ashtray, then sat back in his chair and crossed his legs. 'Tom's father is Cameron Carlisle. The governor of this city. The leader of the Five Republics.'

He wasn't hearing anything she was saying. His eyes were blank, devoid of feelings for her. She wanted to tell him that Carlisle was a dictator, a horrible man. She clenched her fists. 'You can't use me like an asset in a business deal.' A part of her was glad she had said it, but another part of her immediately regretted it. She froze. Her mother still wouldn't look at her.

'I can't use you like an asset in a business deal?' he said, mimicking her. 'That's what you think I'm doing? I arrange for the most eligible bachelor in the city to dine with us and offer you his hand in marriage, and you think I am interested in closing a business deal?'

Swallowing was impossible, but she tried all the same.

'You have always been an ungrateful girl,' he said, with genuine disappointment. He pushed his chair backwards, its screech making her jump.

'Father, please.'

'You *are* spoiled. It is our fault. Your mother and I have done everything we could to ensure you had everything you needed. Not once did we refuse to give you what you needed. I was foolish to think you would turn out differently.'

Astrid stood too.

Her father froze for a moment before facing her.

'I am immensely grateful for everything you have done for me,' she said, her voice more pleading with each word. 'I have always tried to express my gratitude. But I have never asked for anything. I know how lucky I am. I have all the Blue Oxygen I could ever wish for, unlike most of the people alive today. For that, I can never repay you.'

Her father snorted.

'But what you ask is too much,' she said, hoping this would be enough of a reason.

Her father shifted the cigar between his teeth, and with folded arms, strolled towards her.

Astrid looked at her mother, who still would not meet her eyes.

'It is too much?' her father asked, getting closer.

Astrid took a step back, stumbling, part of her preparing for him to hit her; his demeanour was more threatening than she had seen before. He took the cigar from his mouth. 'Listen carefully.' He stood with his legs slightly apart, the smoking end of the cigar pointing towards her. 'You have a choice. Either you agree to marry Tom or your world is going to change. Substantially.'

'Change?' she asked.

Her father inhaled deeply. 'It tastes different, you know?'

Astrid didn't know what he meant.

'You wouldn't know, because this is all you have ever known,' he continued. 'Blue Oxygen tastes different. It's clean. That's the difference.' He stabbed his cigar into the ashtray on the table. 'You will leave here. No more Blue Oxygen. I will give you enough money to rent a place in the city, but you will not have the means to buy Blue Oxygen. You will live on your quota like those in the villages. You will see for yourself what it is like to breathe away your life.'

Finally, her mother raised her head. Astrid waited for her to speak, to defend her, but she was silent.

'You want me to leave?' Astrid asked.

'I want you to marry Tom,' he said. Then his stern expression returned. 'I want you to pay this family back for all you have received. It is your duty.'

'But, Father, I can't marry him. I don't love—'

'Do not say that word!' he said. 'I have held my patience long enough. That would only push me to the limit.' His face was red. His hands trembled. 'I do not care for that word. And I do not care for disloyalty.' He turned and walked away.

She wanted to call him back, but knew better.

Her father left the room, leaving Astrid alone with her mother.

'Mother, please,' Astrid said, ready to go to her.

Her mother raised both hands. She was fighting back tears. 'It is your choice. But make sure you understand the repercussions.'

'Speak to him for me. You must.'

Her mother shook her head, then wiped delicately beneath each eye with the side of a finger. 'It would do no good. You have to choose.' She followed her husband out of the room.

Astrid stared at the dining table. She searched her mind for something she could say that would convince her father – that would prove to him she was serious. But nothing came to mind. All her life she had been forced to do as she was told, eventually agreeing to everything her father asked – or, rather, demanded – of her. There was no way out. The walls and ceilings were closing in, suffocating her.

A door opened on the opposite side of the room. A maid entered, took one look at Astrid, and closed the door again.

## *CHAPTER 7*

### JAKE

JAKE HAD RAIDED the city many times. Few others had the guts to do it. Being caught in the city cost you all your oxygen. Except for the standard programmed ten thousand litres that remained, triggering the letter. Seeing the Oxygen postman appear in your village was frightening; many children had nightmares about him. Reaching your final thousand litres meant that your eyes began to turn a darker shade of blue. Most people who lived in the villages had been brainwashed: they believed that it was only right that they take their turn on this earth and depart willingly. After the final war, when over half of the earth had been scorched by nuclear war, there hadn't been enough room for everyone, and certainly no room for children unless you were prepared to pay the price. The exchange of oxygen for new life. It was only right.

It seemed to Jake that he was the only person who saw how perverse it all was.

If he was found inside the city, they would take his oxygen. It would just mean pressing a few buttons. But after he'd done it the first time, after he'd raided a house for Blue

Oxygen and made it back, he couldn't stop himself. Each time, Jake told himself he wouldn't do it again. That was, until he'd used up all the Blue Oxygen and he remembered how much of it was available in the city. He sold some of the Blue he raided to buy processors and other parts. Most of it, he used himself.

Soon, though, Jake's friends brave enough to raid began to go missing. He didn't know exactly what had happened to them, but he knew *why* it had happened. They had tried raiding too, but they weren't as good as Jake. The clamp-down on raiders had begun. Jake had visited the city only once in months. It was foolish to do so. But now he had to. For Bailey.

He'd have gone to Shuk if there was a chance he could buy enough. But he had no gold, and that was all Shuk wanted.

The tram stopped south of Ash Hills, as close to the city as Jake could reach. Another reason no one from outside entered the city was the price it exacted, the oxygen it required for people to climb up the hill to the wall.

But Jake knew of a way into the city that avoided the main rails and entrances. During the night, there were brief windows of opportunity when the waste pipes that emptied the reservoirs on the other side of the wall flooded Ash Hills. The route through wasn't easy: crawling through was a smelly way into the city. But as far as he knew, Jake was the only person who had the technology to open the gates at each end. The security on the pipes was dated and pretty basic; the people who planned the city assumed no one would be stupid or maybe desperate enough to crawl through them. Jake was. He called the small boxes he used to open the gates, disruptors. They had been the first piece of kit he'd made that had actually worked and did what he intended. The magnetic boxes were simple but effective.

He marched up the incline, mindful of his laboured breathing. He thought of Gambit and how he'd lived so long through meditating and controlling his breathing. But Jake didn't care about any of that. He'd given up dwelling on it a long time ago.

The ash beneath his feet was now more like mud; the water from the pipe had dampened the ground for hundreds of metres in each direction. A foetid stench filled the air and a purplish mist hovered above the ground.

The moon had risen, and the sky was dark. Jake had spent all his life learning to control his breathing, and now was no different. Composing himself, he focused on his inhalations. He would be no good to his sister, Bailey or his niece if he used up all his quota before getting hold of more Blue. But it wasn't easy to take control of his heart rate and breathing when he was in danger and faced being caught.

Water gushed out of the pipe, which stuck out of the wall. The water came up over his shoes. He splashed through it, kicking through the scum-covered surface.

He checked his watch. The last time he'd used the pipe, it had stopped pumping water at hourly intervals. It was time. The hill rose to a plateau, where the water collected at his feet. He was so close that the water falling into the pool beneath the pipe splashed over him. He checked his watch again. When he looked up, the rush and splash of water had eased. Only a trickle of water fell from the pipe. This was his window. Taking the disruptor from his inside pocket, he pushed it against the rusted controls beneath the pipe. He slid the box from side to side, its magnetic surface clinging to the control box, until a flashing red light on the box turned green. He checked over his shoulder, then pressed the numbers on the keypad. A second later, the grate made a clunking sound and opened.

He took several steps backwards. The pipe was around two metres high up the wall, and protruded around half a metre. He jumped up to grab the pipe, then used his upper-body strength to pull himself inside the pipe. It was just about wide enough for him to crawl, which meant his hands and knees were submerged in the slimy water and gunge that lay at the bottom. He held his breath, not just to conserve his quota of oxygen, but also to avoid inhaling the stench. He crawled ahead frantically, the sound of his movements echoing along the pipe. Finally, he had to gasp for air. He told himself to remember why he was doing this.

The pipe turned to the right slightly, and Jake could see a faint light from the other end. Once the water emptied, rats appeared – clearly they used the pipe as a thoroughfare. The squeaking behind, then up ahead, made him shuffle through the pipe even faster.

At last he reached the end of the tunnel. Taking another disruptor from his coat pocket, he reached through the grate and felt for the control box beneath the pipe. This was the hardest part. He peered through the grate until he could see the light on the box flash red. As carefully as he could, he moved the box until he heard the beep that told him the light had turned green. The keypad was just out of sight, so he had to find the numbers with a finger. He'd practised enough; nevertheless, being stuck inside the pipe made it ten times harder. After three attempts, the grate released and opened outwards, taking Jake with it. He fell out of the pipe into a pool of water.

The water was already rising, ready to fill the pipe once again. Jake's feet touched the bottom of the pool, but it was easier to swim than walk. He swam as gently as he could, desperate not to be seen. But he'd never come across anyone so far from the city centre. In the darkness, he reached a concrete platform that rose out of the pool and led into a wooded area. He stayed on his hands and knees, crawling through the undergrowth so no one would spot him. Standing up, he caught his breath, then began to walk through the woods towards the first concrete wall that signalled the boundary of the city.

He regretted the oxygen he'd used up. He still had to make it back. This was why no one else did what he was doing. He still had years of oxygen remaining ... he hoped. He was only twenty. Still, whenever he found himself out of breath, he thought of receiving his letter. It haunted him. It was always there in the back of his mind. Those in the city knew that nobody on the outside would want to risk what Jake was risking. The only way to make it worthwhile was to find a substantial hoard of Blue Oxygen.

Taking deep breaths, he followed the wall around the edge of the wooded area and out into the city. Within minutes, the city's skyscrapers and towers dwarfed him. The streets were quiet; the city was nothing like West Gate. There, people came out at night. Here, they vanished into their homes.

He reached down to pick up a brick and used it to scratch a cross on the corner of the building. If he wasn't careful, he wouldn't find his way back. He'd been raiding for years, and through experience, knew there was always the risk of losing his way. Besides, much of the newly developed streets, squares and apartments throughout the city were way too similar.

A small truck turned the corner and drove towards him. Jake ducked behind the wall and waited for it to pass. The thin blue circle on the side of the truck told him there was

Blue Oxygen inside. The truck took a right at the end of the street. Jake followed it. The truck moved out of view, and he had to rely on his hearing to follow it. The truck engine stopped. Jake guessed which final two turnings to take, before finding it parked outside an enormous tower. The driver stepped out of the cab, walked along the side of the truck then opened the back door.

So much Blue Oxygen. Canister after canister. There was enough for ten lifetimes. Jake covered his mouth with his hand and told himself to stay calm.

## *CHAPTER 8*

### ASTRID

Astrid sat on her bed and stared at the wall. What had just happened? She'd gone to dinner that evening knowing that Tom would be there, but she had no idea what her father was planning. It was insane to think that all the visits Tom had made over the years had all been leading to that night ... to his proposal. The look on Tom's face when he asked her flashed through her mind. He'd expected her to say yes. How could he have misjudged the situation so badly? Her father too. She gripped the duvet in her fists. Why would her father think she thought of Tom in that way? Maybe he didn't care about her feelings. But to marry a man as part of a business deal was ridiculous. Yet to her father it clearly seemed a reasonable thing to ask of her.

She reached over to her vidi-screen and called Lucy. There were only a few people she was allowed to talk with regularly. Lucy was always top of the class, and Astrid's father wanted Astrid to learn from Lucy's example. At first, Astrid had fought her father when he pushed them together. He already controlled her day-to-day life – now he wanted to choose her friends? But once Astrid got to know

Lucy, they became best friends. She made an effort to hide this from her father, not wanting him to have the satisfaction of being right.

'Astrid?' Lucy said, her face appearing on the vidi-screen. 'Are you okay?'

That was the thing with Lucy – Astrid couldn't hide a thing from her. She frowned. 'What is it?'

'Tom just proposed,' Astrid said. Saying the words out loud made them even more unbelievable.

'Proposed?' Lucy asked, wide-eyed. 'Tom?'

'My father must have put him up to it.' The anger she felt towards her father returned.

'Wait a minute,' Lucy said. 'Let me get this straight. Tom Carlisle, the son of Cameron Carlisle, proposed to you? To marry you?'

'Believe me, I know how crazy it sounds.'

'What did you say?' Lucy asked.

Had Lucy thought she'd agreed?

'No. Of course. Why would I marry Tom?'

Lucy shook her head. 'No ... of course not. But still ... I don't know. I can't believe it.'

'My father isn't taking no for an answer. He wants me to marry him.'

Lucy's concerned expression returned. 'Oh, Astrid.'

'I'm not going to marry him,' she said, but her voice wavered.

'He can't make you,' Lucy said. 'That would be wrong.'

Lucy's naivety made Astrid see how pointless it was to fight it. It was wrong. But that wouldn't stop her father.

'I have to get out of here,' Astrid said.

'What? Home?' Lucy asked.

'The city. I have to get out of this damn city.'

'But there's nowhere else to go,' Lucy said, frowning. 'You can't leave the city. You can't.' She sounded desperate.

There was a loud rattle from above as the air conditioning system shifted gears and blew more forcefully.

'I have to,' Astrid said.

'Wait,' Lucy said, leaning in closer to the vidi-screen. 'Promise me you won't do anything stupid.'

Astrid regretted calling Lucy. She was her best friend, but there was no way she could understand what was happening to her. 'I promise,' she said, and ended the call.

She reached over to the table beside her bed and picked up a porcelain elephant. Looped over its trunk was a gold ring. Her grandmother had left the ring to her. She'd lived in Moscov City, some hundred miles to the east. There was no travelling between the cities these days; making it through the villages was too dangerous.

She took the ring and pushed it onto her finger. It was far too loose. If she wore it, it would fall off.

There were voices outside her window. She recognised the man's voice. A delivery of Blue Oxygen.

Placing the ring back on the elephant's trunk, she stood at the window and parted the blinds. She opened the window and looked down at the truck parked below. From four storeys up, she watched her father come out to greet the delivery man.

Her father thought so little of her.

She opened her wardrobe, snatched her rucksack and began stuffing clothes inside it. Then she stopped, breathless. Where would she go? She was being foolish. Maybe even childish. She needed to think. Her father wouldn't let her disappear. The moment she left, he would send people to bring her back. No. If she was going to leave, she had to think it through and do it properly. She threw the rucksack into the wardrobe and slammed the door.

Outside, her father laughed with the delivery man as though nothing had happened that night. Her father didn't care about her. She was pretty sure he didn't care about her mother, either.

The rear door of the truck screeched open. Gradually the metal door rose, the slatted metal sections rolling up into the truck's roof. The truck was filled with canisters of Blue Oxygen. It was obscene. But she was a hypocrite. For years she'd used Blue Oxygen without questioning where it came from. She knew no better. She had barely used any of her quota. All because of her father.

She recalled the conversation her father and Bartholomew had had earlier. It made no sense – that Blue Oxygen came from people who had been killed for it. She'd never heard of such a thing. Bartholomew had mentioned someone called the Engineer, who he thought was responsible for the killings.

Astrid held her head in her hands and gripped her hair. No. There was no way her father would be involved with anything like that. It was impossible. He was greedy ... and single-minded about business ... but he was no killer.

But where did the Blue Oxygen come from?

Down on the street, her father smoked a cigar and watched the delivery man lower the first six canisters from the back of the truck onto a trolley, then wheel them towards the vault door set into the wall. The delivery man glanced away as her father punched in his security number. The vault door opened. The man pushed the canisters inside the vault then backed away. The vault closed and the canisters of oxygen disappeared up the narrow pipe towards the Blue Oxygen filling station. The delivery man went back to the truck for more canisters.

Someone walked past Astrid's room, disturbing the square of light creeping beneath the door. It must have been her mother. Astrid wanted to go after her. Maybe if she could reason with her, she could get out of marrying Tom. But her mother wouldn't help her. She was as powerless as Astrid. The only way out was to leave – and not be found. A fresh wave of anger swept through her. She turned to the window – and something caught her attention. Something was moving on the other side of the street, among the undergrowth beneath the trees. She held her breath and leaned in closer to the window. What was that? Then it moved again. It was a person, wearing something over their head. From their build and height, she figured it was a man. He was hunched over, checking behind then to both sides. There was no way he should be there, that was certain. He was a villager. Had to be. His clothes were dishevelled, wet and dirty. Even hunched over, he looked well built, his shoulders wide, his arms tensed by his side, ready to take action.

Neither her father nor the delivery man seemed to know that the stranger was there. She couldn't take her eyes off him. What was he going to do? There was no way he'd risk raiding the truck where it was. Would he? That would be suicide. The moment they caught him, they'd take away his quota. She was ready to call out to her father, but something stopped her.

The man moved quickly, loping across the ground, hiding behind a tree so only his feet and some of his black hood were visible.

Astrid fled to her door, ran out into the hallway, then over to the front door. She waited for the lift. It arrived quickly and she got in. The lift took her to the ground floor.

What would she say to her father? The thought crossed her mind that maybe he deserved someone taking his oxygen. But there was also a chance that the man was armed.

She reached the main doors to the tower and stepped outside. Her father spun around, surprised. His hand holding the cigar stopped just short of his mouth. 'Astrid? What are you doing here?'

She scanned the undergrowth for the man, but there was no sign of him.

'You'll eat into your quota out here, young lady,' the delivery man said. 'If I were you, I'd never come outside.'

Astrid ignored him, taking three, then four steps outside, peering into the darkness.

'Astrid?' her father said, this time with the tone of authority she had learned to hate.

'It's nothing,' she said, staring into the blackness.

'You should go inside,' her father said.

She wanted to refuse. More than anything, she wanted to say no.

'Go inside,' he said.

'Yes, Father,' she said, and turned back towards the main doors.

## CHAPTER 9

### JAKE

JAKE MANOEUVRED around the side of the O delivery truck to get a look inside. He was only metres away. He could have his hands on the canisters within seconds. How many could he carry? Maybe half a dozen? But that would slow him down. There was no way he'd get back to the pipeline and through before someone set off the alarm. Six canisters would keep Bailey alive for years, though. Maybe he could take two – one under each arm. They wouldn't slow him down too much. His heart thumped, his legs tensing with the desire to run. The delivery guy spoke to a man smoking a cigar. There was a young woman there, too. The man spoke to the young woman in a harsh tone. Jake guessed he was her father. She bowed her head and turned to go back inside.

Jake held his breath.

The man purchasing the Blue Oxygen stood in front of the keypad. Jake took the binoculars from his pocket and peered through them. He read the digits the man entered, then repeated them to himself in a whisper over and over. Maybe he'd have a chance to use the code.

The delivery guy was some distance from the truck. Jake was ready to go for it. He'd take two canisters then head for the pipe. As long as they didn't follow him, by the time they notified the police, he'd be long gone. There was no way they'd follow him into the villages. Hell, there was so much Blue Oxygen in the truck, if he did it without them seeing, they might not even miss the canisters. They'd be none the wiser.

Or maybe he could simply explain why he needed it. There was life in those silver canisters. He'd explain to them that, by morning, his brother-in-law would be dead because he'd used up his quota, having spent half of it on his daughter. They would understand. He could tell them that Grace and Bailey only decided to have a child because they knew Jake would be there to look after Jess when they ran out of oxygen. He was doing this for Jess. Maybe they'd give him more canisters if he could explain.

'Go inside!' the man shouted at the young woman, throwing his cigar to the ground. It bounced on the path, sending a swirl of sparks into the air.

The young woman stared at her father. It was a cold, defiant stare. But it didn't last long before she bowed her head and turned towards the doorway.

The exchange refuelled the hatred Jake felt towards everyone inside the city. This man, shouting, throwing away his cigar, barking orders, filled him with even more rage. He'd take this man's oxygen and give it to someone who deserved it. Crouching behind a tree, he clenched his fists, his legs tensed, ready to spring into action.

Then something made him stop. He'd been spotted. It was an abstract sensation, hard to describe, but there all the same. The young woman was staring straight at him. How was that possible? One hand on the door to the tower, she had stopped and was looking straight at him, wide-eyed and motionless. Her eyes were dark. Her hair was tied in plaits, some loose strands falling across her shoulders. She was a young woman, but there was something girlish in her demeanour. He had never felt more different from those who lived in the city. He was a different species, a different being to the one staring back at him.

Jake was just as wide-eyed as the young woman. He shook his head, telling her not to give him away. Slowly, he raised his hands, signalling that he was no threat to her. And he wasn't. That was the truth. He didn't want to hurt anyone. All he wanted was the Blue Oxygen. If he could explain it to her, she would understand.

'Astrid!' her father said, pointing to the doorway. 'If I have to tell you again, I will not be pleased.'

The young woman didn't move.

Jake continued to shake his head, pleading with her not to say anything. Crouching, he backed away, showing her he was leaving. He couldn't help glancing over to the truck and the canisters one more time. Did he really have to go back empty-handed?

He looked again at the young woman. Now she was shaking her head, telling him not to do it. But if he left now, without it, Bailey would be dead by morning. If they caught him, his sister would have a dead brother on her hands too. It paralysed him.

He continued to back away. It was no good. He needed to think it through. Maybe he'd raid somewhere else.

The delivery guy dragged his trolley back to the van then unloaded another lot of canisters onto it. It was no good ... Jake had to leave. He retreated, his gaze on the young woman, who watched him the entire time. Her stance signalled she wouldn't tell anyone as long as he kept moving. Even so, he was filled with frustration and disappointment.

Jake took a step backwards and trod on a branch. He froze.

The delivery guy spun around and looked towards where Jake was hidden. 'Did you hear that?'

Jake waited, hidden in darkness, crouched behind a tree. He was helpless.

The young woman's father, his hands in his pockets, walked slowly down the steps, peering into the darkness. 'I'll take a look.'

Jake would have to make a run for it.

'Father, why can't I stay out here?' the young woman said.

'What did I tell you?' her father said, turning back to her.

The young woman glanced over at Jake. She was signalling to him – telling him to go.

The delivery guy continued to unload the Blue Oxygen, plainly not wanting to get involved in their argument.

With a flurry of violent gesticulations, the young woman's father ushered her into the tower. Jake would have thanked her if he could. She had bought him time. Why? He didn't know. But he was thankful.

## *CHAPTER 10*

ASTRID

ASTRID ENTERED THE APARTMENT, waiting for her father to appear and tell her again how disobedient ... insolent ... disrespectful she was. She stormed through the living room and into her bedroom before he said a word. That didn't stop him complaining to her mother about her, though.

'She's your daughter,' he said to her mother, as though she wasn't his too. 'You should tell her how to behave. I have to speak to her several times before she listens.'

'I'll talk to her,' her mother said.

'She must learn to respect my wishes. If she wants to live here, in my home, she will respect me. Do you hear me?'

'Yes,' her mother said. 'I will speak with her.'

'She showed me up. In front of the delivery man, for goodness' sake.'

Astrid threw herself onto her bed and screamed into her pillow. Who did he think he was? She was old enough to make her own decisions. She was an adult. She had her own mind. Why couldn't he see that? She rolled onto her back and stared up at the ceiling. The small plastic vents hummed as they expelled Blue Oxygen. That's what the hooded man had been after. But why would he risk it? If her father had known he was there, he'd have lost his oxygen. There were no two ways about it.

On the other side of her door, her father and mother continued to bicker until eventually her mother's bedroom door closed with a bang. Even she had heard enough. The clinking of glasses and ice being dropped into a glass meant her father was making a drink.

Astrid tiptoed across her room over to the window. It was dark outside – far too dark to see anything definitive. There was no way the man in the black hood would still be there. He wouldn't risk it. She'd made it clear that he needed to leave. Why had she done that? She should have told her father. If anyone found out she had known he was there and had done nothing about it, she would be in a world of trouble. But why should she tell anyone? The man had done nothing wrong. He had been thinking about it, though; she was sure of that. He was going to take canisters of Blue Oxygen.

She leaned in closer to the window, hoping he would appear again. His eyes, piercing the dark hood, locked on hers, flashed in the darkness, drawing her towards him. Even from so far away, his stare had been so assured.

On the horizon stars shimmered and blinked – crystal white against the expanse of sky, which seemed to go on forever. Her city was so sterile ... so organised. She'd heard little about the villages on the other side of the city walls. It was impossible to get anyone to talk about them. The people in the city ignored the outsiders as much as possible. She had met people who had visited the villages, but it would have been impolite to ask them about their experience. It was not the done thing for a young woman to wonder about such things.

What she knew about the villages, she had learned from books. Such books were hard to get hold of, but Sandy, the old man who owned the vintage bookshop in the retail park, turned a blind eye. He knew what she was doing when she disappeared down the aisle of old books. She was fascinated by the books that had been written the year the war ended – before they dropped the bombs. The winter of 2029. The tension and fear of nuclear war were there in the prose. For many years after the bombs were dropped, there had been no more literature. What could anyone write about? And who would have wanted to read it?

When her father asked what she was doing in the bookshop, the old man distracted him, even told him that Astrid had been reading about science or politics. These were the subjects her father wanted her to pursue.

Astrid had heard of the internet. The internet lived on computers and contained all kinds of useful knowledge that people could access. Her own knowledge had been garnered from books, as her father and every other inhabitant of the city insisted upon. The internet, her father would say, was filled with lies, fiction and pornography. Books, he said, were the only place to find the truth. She'd always loved reading, fiction and non-fiction. She devoured all the books her father had given her. Each day she asked to go to the bookshop. It took a long time before her father allowed her to go alone. Sandy asked her to do simple chores around the shop. In return, he allowed her to take as many books as she wished home with her. She would take books she knew her father would approve of, take off their dust jackets, then hide books he wouldn't want her to read inside them. It was risky, but after she had done this several times, it became a straightforward task, and she felt little guilt.

There was a knock at her bedroom door.

She walked across the room and opened her door. It was her father, a near empty glass in his hand. He let out a deep sigh.

'Astrid,' he said, walking into her room, forcing her to back away. 'I hate it when we argue. But you must listen to reason.'

Astrid waited, a plan forming in her mind. She wanted out of Luxor City. More than anything, she longed to be free. She'd travel to her grandmother's city – to Moscov City. This was no way to live. She wanted to escape the restrictions.

'I'm sorry, Father.' She edged towards him, her head downcast, conciliatory. When she glanced up at him, he wore a shocked smile.

'That's all I want to hear,' he said. 'I want you to be happy, my dear. You understand that, don't you?'

'Yes, Father. Of course.'

'Tom is a good man. He will make you happy.'

The urge to argue came and went. She needed to buy more time. She nodded slowly. 'I will marry him.'

Her father gasped, then laughed with what appeared to be relief.

'But I want to tell him myself,' she said.

'Of course, of course.' Her father walked out of the room, then back in again. 'You are a wonderful daughter. We argue, I know. But you are a good girl, Astrid.'

Again, the urge to tell him what she really thought filled her until it was almost impossible to keep it inside.

Her father left the room.

Astrid reached for her grandmother's ring and pushed it into her bra. She opened her wardrobe and took out her rucksack. There was no way she was staying. Her father was a tyrant, and she hated him.

## CHAPTER 11

JAKE

Jake tried to ignore the disgusted looks he received from his fellow passengers on the tram back to West Gate. The stale aroma coming off his clothes filled the carriage. But that wasn't the worst thing. He had been so close to getting his hands on the Blue Oxygen. He should have grabbed it. But the look in the woman's eyes told him he wouldn't get away with it. He had no choice. Even so, it was tough to take.

He couldn't go back to Bailey empty-handed. The thought filled him with dread. He couldn't stop imagining how distraught Jess would be when Bailey's oxygen ran out. He had failed. Now he was sitting in a tram car, stinking it up, and it had all been for nothing.

At his stop he jumped off the tram then watched it rattle along the street, heading north towards the opposite end of the Village.

If only he had more time. But time was against him.

It had always been just him and his sister – until Bailey came along. The three of them were all Jake had. Ever since his sister had hooked up with Bailey, his brother-in-law had looked out for him. Jake owed him everything.

The lights of Heaven Bar glowed purple at the end of the street. He should have stayed on the tram and gone home. But he couldn't face walking past his sister's place, knowing what would be happening inside.

'You stink,' Jez, the doorman, said to Jake, pinching his nose. He was the shorter one of the two. Doormen, Jake thought, always came in pairs. One was smaller but broader than the other, who was taller and thinner.

'You won't get a woman tonight, not with that whiff following you around.'

'That's not what your sister said,' Jake said.

Gable, the second doorman, slapped Jez on the back and laughed. 'You're not going to stand for that are you big man?'

'You owe me,' Jez said, pretending to punch Jake.

'Add it to the list,' Jake said, ignoring Jez's slow-moving fist.

Jake headed into the bar and ordered a drink, ready to make it the first of many. He needed to forget. Quickly finishing his drink, he ordered a second then scanned the bar. Over in the corner, where he usually sat, was Cray, along with his crew. Jake huffed and turned back to the bar to accept his second drink from Julian, the barman.

'He's been looking for you,' Julian said, nodding over at Cray.

'Don't tell him I've been here,' Jake said. 'I'm leaving after this one.'

But it was too late. When Jake turned back, Cray was on his way over.

'Shit,' Jake said, downing his drink and turning to go.

'Leaving already?' Cray asked him.

'Can't stay,' Jake said.

'Hey. Hang on!' Cray put a hand on Jake's shoulder and pulled him back. 'What's the rush?' Then Cray's face wrinkled with disgust. 'What have you been doing? You stink!'

'Like I said, I'm leaving. Need to get cleaned up.'

Cray shook his head. 'Forget that. We need to talk.'

Jake sighed, disappointed that he'd not ducked out earlier. Cray put a reluctant arm around Jake's shoulder. Cray had always been taller than Jake, and he reminded him of this fact whenever they were together.

'I really have to go,' Jake said, pointing to the door.

Cray glanced around to check that no one was listening. 'Oxygen.' His eyes were wide open. 'Blue Oxygen.'

'What are you talking about?' Jake asked, wondering if Cray knew the situation with Bailey.

'I'm going to raid,' Cray said. 'I can get my hands on it.'

'How much?'

Cray leaned in closer. 'A lot.'

Jake stopped and waited. There was a look in Cray's eyes that told Jake he was serious.

'I've been talking to the Engineer.'

'Oh, hell, no!' Jake shrugged off Cray's arm and walked towards the exit.

'It's not what you think,' Cray said, following him.

'Are you crazy?' Jake snapped. 'Stay away from him. He's trouble.'

'It's okay,' Cray said. 'He's on our side. He wants the Blue Oxygen as much as we do. We're going to take it back, divide it up among those who really need it. Not those in the city. They don't deserve it.'

'Bullshit!' Jake said. 'Don't believe him. He's going to take what he can and keep it for himself. Sell it for gold.'

'No. That's not what he wants. He's ready to take it all back and bring it here to the villages.'

Jake stared into Cray's eyes. Cray clearly believed what he was saying.

'I knew you could be stupid,' Jake said. 'But not gullible.'

Cray glanced away, looking unsure. 'I heard about Bailey. He has his letter.'

Jake wanted to punch Cray for making it real again. He should have known better – everyone knew everyone else's business in the villages.

'How long has he got?' Cray asked.

'Hours,' Jake said.

Cray lowered his voice, then leaned in eagerly. 'We can get more. The Engineer will help us. He wants his cut. But we can get enough for Bailey. Enough for everyone. Why should they have it all?'

He was right. But still. There was no way Cray was going to get into the city and back again without getting caught. It was never going to happen.

Cray held Jake's arm. 'How long have we known each other? Since school. Buddy. Come on.' He tilted his head. 'I know you can get in. I need your help.'

Jake should have left. But something was stopping him. 'Where is it? The Blue?'

Cray's eyes shone. 'The Engineer is going to tell us. Give us the coordinates.'

'No way,' Jake said, pulling away from Cray's grip. 'It's too risky. The police on the other side of the wall are getting beefed up again. Ways in are vanishing all the time. The days of raiding the city are over.'

'You don't believe that.' Cray looked Jake up and down. 'I'd say your stench tells me the opposite.'

'Stay away from the city. You're going to get yourself killed. Along with those suckers who are ready to follow you.'

'We're tired of waiting around,' Cray said. 'Tired of waiting for the letter. We're going in. With or without you.'

'Don't,' Jake said, walking towards the door.

'I'd rather you came with us,' Cray said. 'I'd feel more comfortable if you were there. Go on – you can get all the Blue you and Bailey need.'

Jake wanted to turn back, to work out together how they were going to do it. But it was no good. There was no way he was dealing with the Engineer. He reached the door and pushed it open.

'You'll be back!' Cray shouted after him.

## *CHAPTER 12*

ASTRID

ALL WAS quiet on the other side of Astrid's door. She crept across her bedroom and opened her door as gently as possible. Taking her time, she noted her mother's closed bedroom door. Her father's bedroom door was ajar. The urge to leave was overwhelming. But then she froze. Her father was lying on the settee, his eyes closed, an empty glass held loosely in his left hand. On the low table at his feet was his computer, its screen illuminating her father's face with a solemn blue light. He had been more and more secretive about his computer for some time, and Astrid rarely found the opportunity to use it. She crept through the living room, watching her father to check he didn't stir. She stood behind the settee, leaning over her father, checking out the computer. He was still logged on. Messages littered the right-hand side of the screen. Some of them were from his friend who had visited earlier that day: Bartholomew. She scanned the messages. He was still pleading for her father to listen to reason.

Her father stirred, grumbling something. He let go of the glass, which fell to the ground and tumbled on the rug.

Astrid froze. She waited, inventing all kinds of reasons why she was there. But her father did not stir again. He was out of it.

She crept around the settee and reached for the computer. What was she thinking? Her hands moved without thinking, doing something she would never have done if she'd had time to think it through. But there was no time. She wanted to know what her father was up to. Bartholomew had spoken with desperation ... even fear.

She backed away from her father, holding the computer tightly. Turning, she crept to her bedroom, then closed her door as much as she could without making a noise. She sat on the bed and placed the computer in front of her. It took a while to figure out what she was doing. If her father found her using his laptop while he was logged on, she would lose all privileges for close to forever. But she had to find out what her father was planning.

The screen flashed with another message from Bartholomew.

*This has to stop. More information has come to light. It's wrong. I have an appointment with the governor. With Carlisle. We can't keep doing this. I'm sorry, but I'm going to tell him everything.*

Astrid checked the previous messages Bartholomew had sent her father, as well as her father's responses. One of them read:

. . .

*It's almost done. We have enough Blue Oxygen to last us many years. With Carlisle's help, we will have dominance over the market. There is nothing to concern you or anyone else.*

Astrid's eyes narrowed as she read. And *she* was part of the deal. How could he treat her that way? Like a possession to barter with? The more messages she read, the angrier she became.

She opened another thread of messages. There was no name of the recipient or sender listed. The exchanges were abrupt, opaque. They made little sense. Many of the messages were simply numbers. Others could have been related to the exchange of payments. She read through the messages until she finally reached the most recent. It was from her father.

*Bartholomew knows who you are. It is time.*

Astrid covered her mouth. She recalled their conversation. Bartholomew had asked her father if he knew someone called the Engineer. This was who her father was messaging. It had to be. She closed her eyes and squinted, trying to remember what they had said. Her father had denied knowing him. Bartholomew had said the Engineer was killing people.

Astrid pushed away the laptop and held her head in her hands. *No.* Her father couldn't be involved in any of that. It was impossible.

She pushed the heels of her palms into her eye sockets

and took a deep breath. The Blue Oxygen that man had spoken about was all around her. Her heart thumped wildly. Where had all this Blue Oxygen come from? If what Bartholomew had said was true, then her father was involved in killing people outside the city walls, and turning their remaining quota into Blue Oxygen. She shook her head. It was ridiculous. Yes, her father was a ruthless businessman, but he was no killer.

She scrolled through his inbox. Most of the messages were between him and the Engineer. One of them made her stop scrolling and read. The message had a government seal at the top. She skimmed the message until she saw a sentence that stood out:

*The oxygen blockchain is under the direct control of the World Oxygen Federation. As you are aware, this blockchain is centralised and cannot be altered without direct input from its creator, Burhan Saifedean. Your suggestion of reducing the O quota for certain groups has been noted and passed on to the federation committee. There are many who support the bill, and we will treat your suggestion with careful consideration.*

Astrid's head spun. There was so much to take in. Why would they consider reducing the quota of oxygen for certain groups? Who were these groups? Why would they do that? It had to be connected to her father's Blue Oxygen company. She should have known better. Her father never stopped – nothing was ever good enough for him.

She had to return the computer before he woke up. A part of her didn't care if he found out what she had done.

Maybe it would be better if he did. Then she could confront him.

She needed to think. As she walked back through the living room with the laptop, she considered waking him. But that would be stupid. There was little she could do now.

When she placed the laptop on the table, her father stirred, his mouth falling open. He gave a deep, rattling snore. Something about the expulsion of air from his dry lips made her sneer with distaste.

# CHAPTER 13

## JAKE

JAKE STRODE past his sister's shack without looking directly at it. He couldn't face Bailey until he'd got hold of more Blue.

He pulled open his own shack door and went inside. He winced at the stench of the rubbish bin; it needed taking out. Dirty pans, bowls and mugs filled the kitchen sink, spilling over onto the kitchen worktop. Every time he washed up, he told himself that he wouldn't let it get that way again. But he didn't care enough. It was easier to let it stack up. What was the point in washing up or having a tidy place? It wasn't as though he was sharing it with anyone. It was only himself he was letting down.

He threw himself onto the settee and grabbed his guitar. As a kid, he'd spent years learning to play. The fingers on his left hand took their familiar shape along the frets. He picked at the strings with his right hand. What was it about the guitar and sad tunes? His sister had got him the guitar; she'd wanted him to do something else other than run around. When he was younger, running was all he wanted to do, just because it felt good. Maybe subconsciously he knew it was defiance. It took a long time and a lot of persistence before his sister got through to him.

As he plucked at the guitar strings, her words came back to him. He recalled how she had explained the quota of oxygen they gave each person, as though this was a gift. There was a gauge inside him that measured ten million litres of oxygen. Everyone had the same. It was only fair. Running, she'd told him, was a sure way to use up his quota. She'd explained, over and over, how this worked, and how he must take care of his oxygen. But the moment she turned her back, he would run.

He stopped playing the guitar. His sister's plan had worked. He'd been fascinated by the guitar for some time, and had stopped running. But it didn't last forever.

He rested the guitar against the arm of the settee, then reached over to open a drawer in the unit beside him. Inside were three tubes of Blue Oxygen, each one empty. When he'd started raiding, it had felt like he could get hold of as much Blue Oxygen as he wanted. Nothing held him back. He'd raided delivery trucks in the city, stealing the odd box here and there. In one haul, he'd taken thirty tubes. His plan was to sell them and get money for his sister. But before he could figure out how to sell it, he'd used it all. It was liberating, thrilling, using Blue Oxygen to run. He ran faster when he used Blue Oxygen. No doubt it was an illusion. But that's how it felt. Using Blue Oxygen was freedom. It was as simple as that. He wanted to be free to waste as much oxygen as he could.

What if Cray was on to something? What if he could find the Blue Oxygen Bailey needed?

But it would be a mistake to get involved with the Engineer. He'd heard way too many stories about him. The Engineer was ruthless. He meant business. People in the city stayed out of his way. The majority of the Blue Oxygen that had made its way out of the city and into the villages had been thanks to the Engineer. If there was such thing as a governor of the villages, then the Engineer was it.

Cray was playing with fire. Maybe Jake should help him. But he had never trusted Cray. Way back, even at school, Cray had been devious.

Maybe he could tell Cray what he'd done earlier in the city. Jake knew how to get into the city and now he had the code to get into the tower. With help, Jake could bring more of the Blue back to the village. If they could get inside, there were canisters of Blue Oxygen waiting to be taken. With Cray's crew, it would be a straightforward job. They could get in and out before anyone knew they'd been there. There was no need to include the Engineer. Jake would convince Cray that they could take it for themselves. Jake could still help his brother-in-law. His mind raced with the thrill of helping Bailey – and of taking what was rightfully his.

He remembered the woman outside the tower. She had watched him, ready to shout out. But she hadn't. She'd simply watched him. Why? Why had she let him leave?

Outside it was as cool a night as only those in the villages experienced. Bailey would run out of oxygen by morning. Maybe Jake should tell him he was going to help. He should be there with his family. But what use would that be? He was going to help them and get the oxygen his brother-in-law needed. Bailey wasn't going anywhere.

He took the tram down through the mini strip out into Carnival Square. All the times he had been in the square came back to him. He, Cray and many others he'd gone to school with had spent almost all their time there. After school, they'd catch the tram and head to the square. They sat around talking; there was nothing else to do. But that didn't stop them talking about all the things they would do when they had enough Blue Oxygen. They imagined sleeping in rooms filled with it, like people did in the city. They could spend days running, playing sports, riding bikes, skateboarding ... all the things they'd heard that young people had done once. Cray had always insisted that someday they'd have more oxygen than they could inhale. Jake had never really believed him. Not deep down. If it was in Cray's nature to be optimistic, it was in Jake's to be cynical.

The tram trundled through the square and swept to the right, heading for the south of the village and Cray's park.

Jake stepped off the tram before it came to a stop. Here, the shacks were newer and better quality than those in his own park. Jake was never one to be envious; even so, it didn't stop him from noticing the differences.

Visiting Cray's park reminded him of school. Sometimes they had left school early and, because Cray's place was closer, headed there. Cray's mum had worked at the rice store in the village during the day, giving Cray and Jake the shack to themselves. They'd watch sports played in the city. Those in the villages hated these sports. If anyone found them watching them, they'd be in big trouble. The men and women playing tennis, or football, or basketball, were reckless. That they could run around, sweating, breathless, seemed crazy. And yet there they were, doing just that. It mesmerised Jake. He had dreamed of running in competitions like those they had in the city. There were no crowds at any of these sporting events. There simply weren't that many people in the city. For sporting events with crowds, he and Cray had to watch recorded events – like the Olympics, or a football World Cup, or Wimbledon, or the baseball playoffs – from the early twenty-first century. So many people, all in one place, shouting and hollering at the players on the field. It wasn't just the sport that was mesmerising; it was the entire event. So many people, completely oblivious to the future, in which their oxygen consumption would be controlled and gauged.

Jake arrived at Cray's shack and rapped on the door. As he waited, he regretted being there. But it was too late. A dog barked in the distance, then a second started up.

The door opened.

'Jake?' It was Cray, wrapping an old dressing gown around himself. 'What are you doing here?'

'Who is it?' a woman shouted from inside.

'No one. Go back to sleep.' Cray closed the door. He stepped down onto the ground and motioned with his head for Jake to follow.

'What you said earlier,' Jake said. 'About the Blue Oxygen...'

'Yeah? What about it?'

'I know where we can get some.' Jake regretted saying it. But now it was too late.

'You do?' Cray leaned in eagerly. 'Where?'

'But if I do this,' Jake said, 'it has to be without the Engineer. I don't trust him.'

Cray looked around, as if there might be people listening. 'But if we come back into the village with Blue Oxygen, there will be questions. You know no one sells Blue Oxygen without the Engineer knowing about it and getting his cut.'

'That's the thing,' Jake said. 'We're not going to sell it.'

Cray frowned, confused. 'Then what are we going to do with it?'

'Give it away. To Bailey ... to whoever needs it. We can keep some. Give it to people when their letters arrive.'

Cray shook his head, backing away. 'There's no way the lads are going to risk raiding to bring back a load of Blue Oxygen just to give it away.'

'Then we'll go with just those who want to do it.'

Cray paused, scanning the park. Another dog barked. Cray's breath plumed out into a cloud. 'I don't know.'

'My brother-in-law will soon be out of O. And there are people in the village getting the letters every day. Why should *they* have it all?' Jake waved towards the city. 'Let's even things up.'

Cray stared at the ground between his slippered feet.

Jake lowered his voice. 'You should have seen how many canisters this guy was delivering. Just to one apartment.' He raised a finger. 'We can bring it all back. To help those in the villages.'

'And you can get us in and out?' Cray asked.

'No problem. I can show you where it is, take it without them knowing, and be back here before sunrise. I have the code to get into the tower.'

'You want to go tonight?' Cray asked, surprised.

He checked his watch. It was approaching midnight. 'I have to. Bailey doesn't have long left.'

Cray nodded eagerly.

'Are you in?' Jake asked.

Cray scanned the park and inhaled deeply. Then finally he smiled. 'Sure. Let's do it.'

Jake gave Cray a stern look. 'But you can't let the Engineer hear about this. It's just us.'

'Just us,' Cray said, nodding. 'Don't worry.'

'Good. Meet me at Ash Hills in thirty minutes.'

Cray went back inside his shack, throwing off his dressing gown at the same time.

Jake headed for the tram stop, fighting the urge to run. Maybe, by this time tomorrow, he would have enough Blue Oxygen to run the length of the village.

# CHAPTER 14

## ASTRID

THIS WAS HER CHANCE. Astrid had seen many times how her father's drinking led to him being out of it for a long time.

She checked on her mother, resting an ear against her door. She was a sound sleeper, so Astrid didn't fear her waking. Her father hardly slept at all – without alcohol. After drinking, as was apparent now, he would pass out until she or her mother shook him awake. It was as though he saved up all his sleep for these prolonged stretches.

The only way she was going to get enough Blue Oxygen, and get out of the tower without the security system raising the alarm, was to deactivate the alarm using the laptop. She knelt in front of it, checking on her father, and found the security platform. Typing quickly and as silently as she could, she unlocked the Blue Oxygen storage room, then deactivated the lock on the front door that led out into the city. After that, it was down to her to make it out of the city and into the villages, then to Moscov City.

She threw her rucksack onto her shoulder and tiptoed towards the door, then out into the corridor leading to the stairs. The Blue Oxygen was stored on the third floor. She checked she still had her grandmother's ring tucked securely inside her bra. She had little she wanted to take with her, but the ring was important.

Her footsteps echoed through the stairwell, even though she tried to tiptoe. She went over her plan. She would take the Blue Oxygen and leave the city. Her quota of oxygen was almost untouched, so she planned to use the Blue as money. She had no credits herself, but the Blue would be worth a lot. People in the villages, she guessed, would give her gold for it, which would then help her reach Moscov.

She'd unlocked the door to the Blue Oxygen storage using the computer, and the keypad beside it illuminated with a green light. She pushed the door and it yielded. The room was cool and smelled different to the rest of the building – sweet, like bubble gum.

She shrugged off her rucksack and opened the zip. Along the left wall of the room were the steel cupboards that housed the canisters. She had watched them be fired up the pipe from the ground floor earlier. They were then shunted along conveyor belts and attached to the air conditioning that fed the building. The first silver door was stiff, but finally she opened it, revealing a row of canisters. These were far down the conveyor and would not be missed. But she needed smaller measures of it. A canister of Blue Oxygen would be worth a fortune in the villages, but it would not be divisible. If she was going to find passage to Moscov City, she would need tubes of Blue Oxygen, like those her father used when he was outside the apartment. The men and women in the villages, she had heard, could be cruel and vicious. Fear washed over her, and she considered returning to her bedroom.

No. It was now or never.

She strode over to the other side of the room and opened several steel cupboards, some low and some high. There was so much Blue – more than they could use themselves. Again, it reminded her how fortunate she was. But she hated it too. It was too arbitrary. She had done nothing to deserve this oxygen. And neither, she figured, had her father. Not really. Why did they have all this Blue Oxygen? Anger and embarrassment made her snatch at the small tubes standing in rows inside the cupboard. She dropped them into her rucksack.

When she closed the cupboard, guilt surged through her. What about her mother? She'd be leaving her alone with her father. Maybe he would blame her for what Astrid had done. She shook off the idea. There was nothing she could do about that. She had to leave, and that was all there was to it.

Standing in the centre of the room, she turned on the spot. It would be the last time she saw this place – the last time she would see so much Blue Oxygen in one place. But what was the point in living two lives, even three, maybe four, if you didn't fill them with relative freedom? She was a prisoner and always would be, unless she did something about it. Leaving meant sacrificing years of life. But what kind of life would it be? There was no way she would get out of marrying Tom, so her only option was to leave. She would have to depend on her quota, like most other people. If she could make it through the villages to the next city, she would be free.

She left the room and headed downstairs. This was it. She was actually doing it. She was taking her life into her own hands.

## CHAPTER 15

JAKE

JAKE ATTACHED the magnetic disruptor to the control panel next to the pipe and the grate covering it.

'Through there?' Cray asked, hands on his hips. 'You're kidding, right?'

'It's the only safe way I know of. It's not on their radar.'

Cray shook his head and glanced around at the other three men.

'He's not serious,' Godfrey said. He was tall and gangly with long white hair that made him look like a wizard. He looked down at his grey suit. 'I'm not dressed for this.'

'I told you it was going to be a messy job,' Cray said.

Godfrey shook his head. 'I didn't think you meant messy as in dirty. I thought you meant it would be tricky.'

Cray let out a loud sigh. 'I'd have said tricky, wouldn't I, if it was tricky, not messy?'

'It's not that bad,' Jake said. 'Not once the water level drops and the pipe empties. We have a couple of minutes to crawl to the other end before it fills up and washes us back through.'

'This is bullshit,' Stan said. 'Can you even get us the

Blue Oxygen?' Stan was a well-built guy with long black hair tied up on his head in a clumsy-looking knot.

'Scared it'll mess up your hair, sweetheart?' Max said, the last of Cray's mates. Max, a wiry, quick-moving guy, jumped onto Stan's back and rubbed his head, trying to unfasten his hair. The two of them wrestled each other to the ground.

'Let's go,' Cray said, pulling them apart. 'Bickering won't get the job done.'

The three other men and Cray followed Jake towards the pipe, wading through the dirty water.

'Shit, Jake,' Cray said. 'What the hell is this? It's not enough that we have to watch them take all the Blue Oxygen for themselves, but we have to wade through their filth too?'

'It's the only way in,' Jake said, holding his breath.

Cray shook his head.

Water gushed from the pipe in a sweeping arc.

'How much longer do we have to wait?' Cray asked.

Jake checked his watch. 'It's nearly time.'

The water spilling from the pipe slowed down until finally only a lazy trickle fell from it.

'Let's go.' Jake led the way. He jumped up to hang from the pipe. Cray gave him a helping hand, pushing him up and into the pipe. The familiar stench hit Jake anew, and he remembered to breathe through his mouth. He shuffled through the narrow space on hands and knees, listening to the others behind him climbing into the pipe and following him, all the time complaining.

A memory of the woman on the other side of the wall came back to him. She'd been watching him, figuring out his dilemma. Would he leave or would he go for the Blue Oxygen? Maybe she wanted him to leave so she wouldn't have to take any action; she wouldn't have to call out and tell her father he was there. Jake had seen indecision in her expression. Maybe he'd see her again. Did he want to? In a way. But he didn't want her to have to deal with Cray or his buddies.

They made it out of the pipe and into the cover of the wooded area, following the same route Jake had taken a few hours earlier. The marks he'd made on the walls as a guide were still there.

'Is that it?' Cray asked.

Jake stared at the apartment tower and nodded. 'That's the one. We have to get in without them noticing.'

'That's what Godfrey's here to do.' Cray turned to Godfrey, then back to Jake. 'What's the code?'

'What about the alarm?' Jake asked.

'Godfrey will sort it.' Cray rested a hand on Jake's shoulder. Jake thought back to the woman's father entering the code.

'Two, two, four, seven,' Jake said.

'Don't forget to keep your hoods on at all times,' Cray said. 'We don't want the face recognition security taking shots of our bad sides do we?'

Cray motioned for Godfrey to open the front door. 'And don't forget: no names either.'

Jake didn't know, given how his crew had fooled around on the other side of the wall, how ready and prepared they would be. Godfrey, stooping, ran towards the apartment tower steps, bounded up three at a time, then pushed his back up against the wall next to the glass doors. He reached into his backpack, took out a metal box and held it against the wall. He hesitated.

'What's wrong?' Jake whispered.

Cray squinted, looking confused.

'What is it?' Jake asked again.

'Something's wrong,' Cray said.

Godfrey ran back towards them and huddled beside Cray, breathless.

'Can you get in?' Cray asked. 'Turn off the alarm?'

'That's the thing,' Godfrey said, catching his breath. 'Someone has already deactivated the alarm.' He shrugged. 'The door's open.'

Cray glanced over at the tower and frowned. 'Open? Why?'

'No idea,' Godfrey said.

'So we can walk straight in?' Cray asked.

Godfrey nodded. 'Yeah.'

'Something doesn't feel right,' Jake said. 'I don't like this.'

Cray was biting the inside of his cheek. Then he turned quickly to Stan. 'You go. Check it out.'

Stan jogged past Jake and across the street, then jumped up the steps. He turned the handle, opened it and was inside.

Jake waited for Cray to speak, but he just stared, squinting at the opened glass doors. Jake was about to say something when Stan appeared at the doors and beckoned them over.

Cray ran towards the steps. Jake followed. He was the last inside. Godfrey and Stan were already creeping up the stairs, their footsteps barely audible.

From above came the creak of a door opening, then the clunk of it shutting. The five of them stopped on the stairs, staring upwards. Godfrey, at the front, held up a hand, telling them to freeze.

The shuffle of steps echoed through the stairwell.

## *CHAPTER 16*

ASTRID

Astrid tiptoed down the stairs. She'd done it. The weight of the Blue Oxygen in her rucksack reminded her of what she had done. She had so much of it. Yet, if she wasn't careful, it wouldn't last long. If anyone in the villages found her with it, they would do everything they could to take it from her. Her feet were a blur as she descended the stairs, taking the steps three at a time. Now she had closed the door, the chances of her mother or father hearing her were remote. The bannister was warm to the touch, but slippery. She slowed to a halt. Something made her want to turn back. Why? There was nothing there for her. Her room, the apartment, the entire tower belonged to her father. It was no good pretending otherwise. And if he wanted her to marry Tom, there was nothing she could do to stop it from happening. She took another step down, then continued at speed.

Close to the doors at the bottom of the stairwell, she paused and looked back up the stairs. This was it. There was no going back once she was outside. She sniffed the air; a musty, damp smell wafted over her.

She took one more step down, then was knocked sideways.

'What—'

Before she could say anything else, a large hand covered her mouth and someone grabbed her from behind. She kicked out, over and over, but someone else had hold of her legs. She tried to bite the hand, but whoever was holding her was too strong. There was no escape.

'Stay quiet and we won't hurt you,' a hooded figure said in a deep voice. He was short with tufts of white hair curling beneath his hood. He came closer. 'Are you going to stay quiet?'

She nodded, still with the man's hand covering her mouth. His hand was clammy, and she wanted nothing more than for him to let go of her.

'Okay,' the man holding her said. 'But make one sound and it's over.'

She nodded again then felt the man's hand release. She could breathe again, and did so frantically.

'Take the bag,' the man said to one of the others.

'No,' Astrid snapped. 'You can't take it. I need it.' She wasn't sure why she said it; there was nothing she could do to stop them.

The man holding her pushed her forward, then snatched at her rucksack. She fought back then glanced behind at the man, who was well-built. If he wanted to, he could have her on the ground in an instant. She let him take the bag. These men were from the villages, she was certain. Everything she knew about them filled her with fear.

'Who are you?' the white-haired man asked.

'None of your business,' she snapped. 'Take the bag and go.'

The third man looked jittery. 'We should leave,' he said, his voice panicked.

The white-haired man ignored him. 'What's in the bag?'

Astrid glanced over her shoulder. The well-built man held two of the Blue Oxygen tubes in the air. 'Blue,' he said gleefully.

'Let's take it and go,' the third guy said, edging towards the doorway.

'Where did you get this?' the well-built man asked Astrid, his breath warm on the back of her neck. 'Did you steal it?'

'It's mine,' she snapped. 'Why would I steal my own Blue Oxygen?'

'Is this your apartment?' the white-haired man asked.

Astrid straightened her jumper. 'Of course.' Maybe this would keep her alive.

'Then where are you taking it?' the well-built man asked.

'It's none of your business,' she said. 'Now, are you going to leave? You can take it with you.'

'Let's go,' the third man said.

The white-haired man looked up the stairwell towards the other two men, who were waiting.

'What now?' the well-built man asked, placing the tubes back in Astrid's rucksack then zipping it up. 'We have a lot here.'

The white-haired man continued up the stairwell.

'Come on,' the third man said. 'We have plenty. Let's take it and leave.'

The white-haired man came closer to Astrid.

She held her breath. There was something unsettling about the way he tilted his head and looked down at her.

'Where did you get this?' he asked. 'There's more of it, isn't there?'

'Hey,' the third man said. 'It's not worth the risk. We've been lucky. She's handed us a haul without having to do a thing.'

But the white-haired man didn't budge. 'Show me where you got this.'

Astrid rolled her hands into fists. 'Take the rucksack. I'm not showing you anything. Damn villagers!'

The well-built man gripped her arm and pulled her close so she could hardly breathe.

'Leave her alone,' the third man said, coming towards her.

'Stop!' the white-haired man said, turning on the third guy. 'If you want to leave, then go.' He handed him the rucksack full of Blue Oxygen. 'Take it. It's yours. Payment. But I'm going after the canisters you said were in here.'

Then Astrid realised who the third man was. He was the one who had been there earlier, dressed in black, hiding in the bushes.

'It's you,' she said. 'You were here earlier.'

The man holding the rucksack shook his head, then stopped.

The well-built man pulled her towards the stairs. 'You're going to show us to the Blue Oxygen, or I'm going to make sure you never need it yourself again.'

'Take what you have,' she said. 'You'll never get out of here with the rest of it.'

'You've turned off the alarm,' the white-haired man said as though just realising. 'So you can get out of here yourself. Taking a load of Daddy's oxygen with you.'

She had no idea how he'd worked it out. 'You don't know what you're talking about,' she said.

The well-built man was virtually carrying her up the stairs.

'The only way you're getting out of this,' she heard the white-haired man say, 'is by showing us the rest of it.'

## CHAPTER 17

JAKE

Jake unzipped the rucksack, his hands shaking. There was enough Blue Oxygen inside to keep Bailey alive for a year, giving Jake time to find more.

Stan held the woman and was forcing her up the stairs.

'Make a decision,' Cray said to Jake. 'You can leave, but don't expect a share of what we find.'

Jake didn't care about the rest of the Blue; he had enough in the rucksack. But he didn't trust Stan or Cray with the woman. He wasn't sure why he cared, but he did. He pulled at Cray's arm. 'What are you going to do with her?'

Cray wrinkled his brow. 'What does it matter? She's one of them, isn't she?'

'You can't hurt her. They'll come for you. Come for all of us.'

'They wouldn't dare come into the villages,' Cray said, pulling his arm out of Jake's grip. 'They think we're scum. Take your rucksack and get out of here if you're scared. You've brought us this far.' He pointed at the rucksack. 'We're even.'

Whatever they were going to do to the woman, it was his fault. It was crazy, but he felt as though he'd betrayed her. Earlier, she'd had the chance to tell someone he was there, but she hadn't. She'd let him leave.

He turned to the door out of the tower. But he couldn't do it. Dropping the rucksack by the door, he followed Cray and the others up the stairs. He had to make sure they didn't hurt her. He'd never forgive himself.

With one hand around the woman's waist and the other over her mouth, Stan half carried, half dragged her up the stairs.

'Tell us which way to go,' Cray said to her. 'Point.'

The woman had given up fighting. She looked exhausted, one minute on the verge of lashing out, the next, giving up and crying. She pointed to a doorway. Ahead, Max checked the door then motioned for them to follow him through it. Jake was the last to enter.

It was cool inside the room. Lined up against the walls were the cabinets that housed the canisters of Blue Oxygen. Jake had heard of these oxygen operating rooms but had never actually seen one. The cabinets were all silver, made from what looked like stainless steel. All five men were speechless when Cray opened a cabinet to reveal rows of canisters. Each one of them contained months of Blue Oxygen. Cray staggered backwards, his hand covering his mouth.

'Nice,' Godfrey said. 'Very nice.'

Max laughed, headed for another cabinet, ripped the door open and grabbed a canister.

'Wait,' the woman said.

Max froze.

'What is it?' Cray asked.

The woman fought against Stan.

'Let her go,' Cray said, walking towards her.

Stan pushed her away and the woman stumbled, almost falling. She steadied herself and turned to scowl at Stan. 'There's a readout on my father's computer. It will show that canisters have been taken. When it reaches a certain level, it will sound an alarm to notify him. He will know something is wrong because we have only recently had a delivery.'

Cray stared at her suspiciously. 'I don't believe you.'

'She's telling the truth,' Jake said.

Everyone turned to face him.

'How the hell do you know?' Max asked.

Jake swallowed hard, then pointed to one of the terminals on the wall. 'Look. You can see for yourself. There's the gauge.' He didn't know why, but he wanted to help her – maybe because this would somehow make them even?

Cray rushed over to the screen and squinted at it. 'So what do we do?'

Jake looked more closely at the rows of canisters in one cabinet. He faced the woman. 'How many can we take before it notifies your father?'

She stared at him. 'Half,' she said finally.

'No way,' Godfrey said. 'We're not leaving half of this behind.'

'But how are we going to carry it all?' Max asked.

It was true. There were over one hundred canisters. They couldn't possibly carry all of them.

Godfrey took one canister and pulled it from the cabinet. 'If I have to make ten journeys, I will. Back and forth, until I've taken the lot.'

'What about the alarm?' Max asked.

'I'll find her father and see that he can't do a thing about it,' Stan said.

'No!' the woman said, panic in her eyes, reaching for him.

Stan slapped her.

Jake didn't think, just found himself running at Stan. He ploughed into him, knocking them both to the ground. He got in the first punch, banging the back of Stan's head against the floor. But before he could get up he felt a boot dig into his ribs, sending him crashing onto his side.

'Stop!' Cray barked. 'Fuck!' He was pointing at Jake's hood, which lay on the ground next to Stan's.

Stan coughed, holding the back of his head. 'This isn't good.'

Jake looked up at one of the video holes in the ceiling. There was no escaping now. The security system would have captured his face.

## *CHAPTER 18*

### ASTRID

It was the man she'd seen earlier, ready to steal the Oxygen. Astrid was sure of it. He was lying on his side, holding his stomach. His hood had come off, revealing his face to the cameras in the ceiling. His friend's hood had come off too. This was bad for them – and for her.

Astrid's face burned with the slap the large man had given her. She held her face, a bolt of pain spasming across her jaw.

'Fuck!' the man with white hair snapped, kicking one of the hoods across the ground. 'Now they're going to know who you are. Face recognition.'

Astrid got to her knees, then tried to get to her feet. But before she could manage that, the white-haired man placed a hand on her shoulder. 'Stay there,' he barked.

She flinched at his touch, then froze.

'Maybe it's turned off,' one of the other hooded men said, pointing to the ceiling. 'Like the alarm.'

The white-haired man held his head in his hands. 'No.' He sighed noisily. 'The face recognition software is always running. It won't notify anyone because the alarm is off, but the moment we leave here and someone realises what's happened, they're going to check the records.'

'We'll be long gone by then,' the other hooded man said.

'It won't make a difference,' the white-haired man said. 'They'll turn off their oxygen. And then they'll come looking for the rest of us.'

The hooded man looked down at the ground. 'God damn!'

'Exactly,' the well-built man said, brushing down his clothes.

The white-haired man punched him in the chest. 'This is all your fault. Why don't you just keep your big mouth shut?'

The man pouted, then extended a finger towards the man Astrid had recognised, who lay curled up on the floor. 'It was him. He came at me.'

The white-haired man strode around the room, now and then glancing up at the cameras in the ceiling.

'Just leave,' Astrid said. 'Leave now and I'll make sure no one sees the records.'

The men stared at her. For a moment, she thought they were going to go for it.

'Bullshit,' the white-haired man said. 'I don't trust you. No. We need to work something out.'

'Should we take the canisters down the stairs?' one of the other men asked.

The white-haired guy stroked his chin, then strode over to two more of the silver cabinets and yanked the doors open. 'Yes. Make a start. I need to think.'

The tall man and the shorter hooded man started to haul the canisters out of the cabinets, stacking them in rows on the other side of the door next to the stairs.

'Don't take it,' Astrid said. Already she was thinking

about how she would be blamed for what was happening. It was she who had turned off the alarm system and who had led the gang to the oxygen. There were thousands of credits' worth of Blue Oxygen that she would never get back. Her father would do much worse than disown her.

The white-haired man turned on her. 'I suggest you stay quiet. Listen carefully if you want to stay alive.'

The well-built man sneered at her. Astrid wanted the cameras to recognise him so that her father could find him and turn off his oxygen.

'We should take her with us,' the large man said, flexing his shoulders as if ready to pick her up again.

Astrid shuffled away until she was sitting up against the wall. The man she recognised was getting to his feet. He coughed, still clutching his stomach. 'We can't take her with us.'

'You can shut up too!' the white-haired man said. 'I'll have to get you out of this mess as well.'

'Taking her with us will only make it ten times worse.'

The white-haired man sneered. 'Ten times worse than having your oxygen cut off? How do you work that out?'

'We can take her,' the well-built man said. 'Then work out what to do after. Take the oxygen and the girl.'

'Let me think,' the white-haired man said.

'I'm not leaving,' Astrid said. Then she gave them all a pleading look. 'Go. Take the oxygen. Just leave me here. I promise, I will delete the records.'

Again, it looked as though the white-haired man was considering it.

'She's right,' the man she'd recognised said. 'The best we can hope for is that she does what she says.'

'We can't trust her,' the white-haired man said.

'You can,' Astrid said. 'You can trust me.'

The other two hooded men had taken nearly half of the oxygen. They stood in the middle of the room, breathless.

'Should we keep going?' the tall one asked.

The white-haired man strolled over to Astrid and stood over her. 'Were you telling the truth? About the alarm going off when the oxygen goes to fifty per cent?'

'Yes,' she said. 'Leave the rest of it. Please.'

The white-haired man leaned over her, his eyes bright through the small holes in his hood. Astrid stared back at him, desperate for him to believe her.

The white-haired man turned to the others. 'Find her mother and father and keep them quiet.'

'No!' Astrid shouted.

'Tell them that if they make a sound or try to call for help, we're going to kill their girl.'

Astrid scrambled to her feet and ran for the white-haired man, but one of the others stopped her and tugged her away from him.

'Wait,' she gasped. 'I was lying. There's no alarm. Take the Blue. Just leave my parents alone. Please.'

'I figured as much,' the white-haired man said. With a jerk of his head, he told the other two hooded men to continue taking the canisters.

Astrid was pushed to the ground. She wasn't going to get out of this mess alive.

# CHAPTER 19

## JAKE

GODFREY, Max and Stan took the last of the canisters to the ground floor. Jake figured it was best to help them get the canisters out so they could all leave. He didn't want to go without them. Not now. Not just because he didn't know what Cray would do to the woman, but because if he left, he'd have no one to help him get out of the mess he was in now his image had been captured.

'What now?' Jake asked Cray.

'We get the hell out of here,' Cray said.

That was what Jake wanted to hear. He turned to leave.

Then the other men returned from the ground floor.

'What about her?' Stan asked. 'The moment we leave, she'll tell the world about us.'

Cray took two small steps towards the woman. 'What do you think?' he asked her.

The woman sat against the wall, arms around her knees. 'I told you – I won't say a thing. Leave, and I'll make sure no one sees their faces.' She glanced at Jake then Stan.

'No way,' Stan said. 'We can't trust her. We should take her with us.'

Cray folded his arms.

Jake didn't want to disagree again. He hoped Cray saw how dangerous that would be. They were raiders, but if they took the woman, they'd be kidnappers too.

'You have my word,' the woman said, getting to her feet.

Cray sniffed loudly, then rubbed his face with both hands. 'Why couldn't you keep your hoods on?'

'We have to get out of here,' Godfrey said, holding open the door. 'Her folks could come up here at any time.'

'We need more time,' Cray said. 'To work out what to do.' He turned quickly, then spoke to Stan in a low voice. 'Let's take her with us.'

'No!' the woman shouted, backing away from Stan.

Jake hated the idea of them taking her. Now he was involved with something ten times worse than stealing Blue Oxygen. But Cray was right. They needed time to think. And they might need leverage if they were going to get out of this. The chance that the cameras had identified them was high. Maybe there was a way to use the woman to ensure they would be safe. How, he didn't know exactly.

Stan grabbed the woman's arm and dragged her to the doorway and down the stairs.

'How are we going to carry all the oxygen as well as take her with us?' Jake asked.

'She'll be an extra pair of hands,' Cray said, turning to the woman. 'Either you help us carry the canisters out of here, or we kill you. Your choice.'

Jake felt sick. He didn't think Cray was capable of murder. As for Stan ... he wasn't so sure.

Stan half carried, half pushed the woman through the door. Jake followed, all the time trying to work out how the raid could have gone so wrong.

Outside the tower, in the darkness, Godfrey and Max

were already roping together the canisters, each around three pounds in weight, long and slender, and looping them over their shoulders.

'You need to lead the way,' Godfrey said to Jake. 'Grab some canisters.'

Jake glanced at the woman, wanting to tell her he'd do everything he could to help her when he had the chance. He used the rope to tie up the canisters, the way Godfrey had, then hauled them up onto his shoulders. They were heavy and made him stoop.

'It'll take us ten times longer to get out of here carrying these things,' Max grumbled as he descended the steps outside, the canisters clanging.

Jake glanced over his shoulder. Stan, with the woman, was the last out of the building. Stan carried almost twice as many canisters as the others. The woman carried what remained: two over each shoulder.

They had actually done it. So much Blue Oxygen. Even though Jake knew he could still be in big trouble, the thought that he might have actually saved Bailey gave him some relief. One of these canisters would keep Bailey going for months.

He led the way through the dark streets, passing several towers, until he recognised the stretch of wall up ahead. They were going to make it! If only he'd kept his hood on, he'd have gotten away with it. Maybe there was still a chance... But with his luck? No way.

He was the first to reach the pipe. Luckily, the pipe had already emptied. He lifted the canisters one at a time and pushed them into the pipe, then Godfrey boosted him up. He tied the canisters together and pulled them through. The others did the same. By the time he reached the other end of the pipe and dropped the canisters into the pool beneath, the others were close behind.

They'd done it. They'd actually raided enough Blue Oxygen to keep people in the village who needed it going for a long time.

# *CHAPTER 20*

## ASTRID

Astrid followed the white-haired man they called Cray. Now they were outside the city and back in the villages, she guessed there was no need for them to hide their names or their faces. That didn't bode well for her. They clearly didn't foresee a time when she might drop them in it. She needed to think fast and to take any opportunity she could to escape.

She'd never been out of the city, but everything she saw now confirmed what she had been told. The villages, unlike the city, were dirty, ill planned and haphazard. When she recalled her home and the city, the colour that came to mind was white. But here, everything was shades of brown. Untidy shacks lined the dirt tracks and rutted paths.

The man she had seen earlier, who was now trying to make eye contact, was called Jake. He was making jerky movements with his head, telling her to come closer. She checked on the others. They were breathless, having carried the canisters so far, but they were also laughing and joking about what they had done.

'My name's Jake,' the man said. 'What's yours?'

'This is your fault,' she whispered harshly. 'You led them to my apartment, didn't you?'

'I never meant for this to happen. I only wanted to take the oxygen.'

'Oh, that's okay then.'

'You don't understand,' he said, before checking on the others to see they hadn't noticed the two of them were talking.

'I understand alright,' she snapped. 'I could have told my father you were there. But I didn't say a word.'

He went to speak, then hesitated. Finally he said, 'Why *didn't* you say anything?'

It was her turn to hesitate. Why hadn't she told her father she'd seen a strange man who was clearly from the villages? She didn't understand it herself.

'That doesn't matter. The point is, you knew what I was doing for you, yet you brought these animals with you anyway. Everything I've heard about villagers is true.'

Jake bowed his head. He trudged on, the canisters draped over his shoulders. The four canisters he carried were getting heavier all the time.

'I shouldn't have done that,' he whispered. 'I'm sorry.'

'Your apology won't do me much good. How do I get out of this now? Even if I get back alive, my father will never forgive me for what I've done.'

'This wasn't your fault,' he said.

'You're not the brightest spark, are you? You saw I was leaving. He will know I was trying to leave. After everything he's done for me ... given me. You think he's going to accept my apology and be done with it?'

'We kidnapped you,' he said, frowning. 'You can tell him that.'

'I handed the oxygen over to you by turning off the alarm and unlocking the doors. He's not stupid.'

'We'd have got past the door and alarm. You being there only sped things up.'

'You know how to make a girl feel better, huh?'

'I won't let them hurt you,' he said.

The way he said it made her think he really meant it. She waited for a sign that meant she could believe him. But that wasn't the only problem.

'What can you do to help me?' she scoffed. 'That big guy back there took you apart pretty quick.'

Jake looked at Stan. 'Just leave it to me,' he said. 'It's my fault you're in this mess. I'm going to put it right.'

'Don't do me any favours,' she said. 'You've done enough already.'

She saw he was about to speak again when Cray turned around. 'We need to find somewhere to stash this lot,' he said to Jake.

'I need to get back to my brother-in-law,' Jake said. 'Give him the oxygen before it's too late.'

So that's why Jake needed the oxygen. She'd seen copies of the letter people received when their oxygen was about to run out. She hated the idea of the letter. Her mother and father had always told her how fortunate she was not to have to worry about ever receiving one. None of them would ever get the letter. Her father would ensure they never used up their quota. And yet here she was, using her given oxygen. She was just the same as everyone else in the villages. She felt lost for a moment, as though she'd swum out to sea and no longer knew where land was. Her chest burned with each inhalation.

'There'll be time for that,' Cray said to Jake. 'You'll have more Blue Oxygen than you know what to do with.'

'What about the face recognition software?' Jake asked.'

'Leave that to me,' Cray said. 'I'll see to it. I have a plan.'

Jake glanced at Astrid. She thought he looked sincere, as though he would keep his promise to help her.

'Where are we going?' Jake asked.

He seemed apprehensive. It was pretty clear that Jake was different to the others. And it was also clear that he didn't trust any of them.

'Last City,' Cray said. He indicated a vast mountain of ash up ahead.

Last City wasn't a city at all; it was the last outpost belonging to those who lived in the villages. It was rumoured that any unauthorised deals made between people from the city and those in the villages were done there.

'No way,' Jake said. 'The Engineer will be there.'

*The Engineer?* Astrid recalled Bartholomew talking about him. She'd read his messages to her father.

Cray smiled a strange smile. Astrid didn't like the look of it at all.

'You promised to keep the Engineer out of this,' Jake said.

Cray stopped and faced Jake, who also stopped. 'That was before you showed your face to every camera and face recognition algorithm in the city. Remember? He can help us.'

Astrid watched as Jake swallowed hard. There was a strange, scared look in his eyes.

## *CHAPTER 21*

### JAKE

TAKING the tram with all the Blue Oxygen they had on them was out of the question. Jake stayed close to the woman. 'Please,' he whispered again. 'Tell me your name.'

She ignored him. As he was about to ask again, she told him.

'Astrid.'

'We're going to Last City,' he said.

'I heard.' She gave him a stern expression.

'It's filled with crooks and losers. Be careful.' It was a stupid thing to say, considering he'd got her into this mess. But he wanted to gain her trust. He was drawn to her. Maybe he felt guilty that she was there. Or maybe it was just because she was pretty. Very pretty. Even after everything that had happened, he couldn't stop looking at her. It wasn't just her appearance. She was strong ... defiant ... smart. Maybe it was all those things together.

They had walked for close to an hour. The canisters wrapped around his shoulders and clanging against his back were getting heavier. His quota was being eaten up with each passing second. But there was so much oxygen in the canisters that the effort it was taking to carry them was negligible in comparison. There was enough Blue Oxygen for Bailey and his sister and his niece. But then he thought about the Engineer. It wouldn't be easy for Jake to take what he wanted. And if the Engineer was prepared to help with the face recognition, no doubt it would cost Jake.

Cray turned to face them all. 'Not far now, gentlemen. We've made the raid of a lifetime. Of a generation!'

Jake didn't look at Astrid. He could sense her distaste for both Cray and him.

They skirted the last of the Ash Hills and followed a worn dirt track towards the Last City. Smoke rose above the silhouetted shacks up ahead. The Engineer would be there. Why should they hand over any of the Blue to him? He was a crook, and everyone knew it. But no one was stupid enough to refuse him.

Dark, shadowy figures huddled together in the distance, waiting to greet them. Even Cray walked slower, warily. It had to be the Engineer.

'I'm not giving all this Blue away,' Jake said. 'I don't care who he is.' Even as he said it, he knew there would be little he could do if the Engineer demanded all of it. After all, without the Engineer's help, the police would hunt him down once the images were taken from the security system.

Cray said nothing.

Godfrey and Max walked closer to one another, as if for comfort. Only Stan continued as he had before the group came into view. It wasn't because he was brave, Jake thought, more that he was ignorant.

Jake imagined himself running. Just dropping the canisters and heading in the opposite direction. Everything he'd ever heard about the Engineer told him to get out of there.

But his feet continued to carry him in the same direction – towards the group of men.

Cray must have planned this all along. The Engineer would have been in on the raid from the beginning, and Jake had walked straight into it. He'd shown Cray and the others where the Blue Oxygen was, only for them to return it to the Engineer. And for what, exactly? Jake's forehead knitted in thought. There was no way he was leaving without the Blue Oxygen. He didn't care who the Engineer was, or what reputation he had.

Who was he kidding? He wouldn't get far. He was already exhausted. And there was Astrid. It was his fault she was in this mess. He couldn't leave her with Cray and the others. And he definitely couldn't leave her with the Engineer.

The shadowy figures took on shape and form. Now he made out the colour of their clothes and hair; even their faces emerged from the darkness. He'd never seen the Engineer in the flesh. He'd seen pictures, but that was all.

One man stood out front, separate from the others. It was him. The Engineer. Had to be.

'You made it, my friend,' the Engineer called out, walking towards them.

Jake continued, but had no idea why he wasn't walking in the opposite direction.

'I told you it wouldn't be a problem,' Cray said, throwing his canisters at the Engineer's feet.

Jake stared at Cray. This had been his plan all along. Jake felt like a fool.

Close up, the Engineer was much taller than Jake had imagined. He was also much broader around the middle – so much so, the buttons on his long gold jacket strained across his stomach. He ran a hand around the narrow rim that surrounded his silver hat. With a beaming smile, the Engineer welcomed Cray into his arms and embraced him.

'You are a good boy, Cray. A very good boy.'

The Engineer held on to Cray for what felt to Jake like an uncomfortably long time.

'It's all here,' Cray said, taking two steps away from the Engineer, pointing to the canisters he'd dropped and to some of those Jake and the others carried. 'Every last canister.'

'Remarkable,' the Engineer said. 'You said you could get it, and you didn't lie. Did you?' He smiled even wider, taking the time to pretend to clap, stopping short of his hands touching.

Cray held up one canister and offered it to the Engineer. But the Engineer didn't take it. For a moment, Cray looked confused. Then one of the man mountains behind the Engineer moved forward and took the canister in one hand, as though it was a toy. The man presented it to the Engineer, who examined it, squinting.

'Show me, Cray,' the Engineer said with a serious expression. 'You take a hit.'

Cray didn't hesitate. He held the canister in both hands, pushed the nozzle against his lips, pressed the button and inhaled deeply.

'Remarkable,' the Engineer said. 'I am very pleased with you, Cray.'

The other men walked around the Engineer and collected the canisters. One man reached for the rucksack Jake had over his shoulder. Jake tightened his grip on the straps, knowing it was hopeless. He was so close. To have so much Blue Oxygen in his hands, only to see it taken away, was too cruel. When one of the Engineer's men reached out a second time for Jake's rucksack, he had no choice but to shrug it off his shoulders and hand it over.

In less than twenty seconds, every canister and tube of Blue Oxygen was gone and was in the Engineer's possession.

'I am going to make sure you are well rewarded,' the Engineer said to Cray, resting his hands on Cray's shoulders. You have done an admirable job and I will not forget it.'

Even Cray looked disappointed when the Engineer's men began to haul the Blue away. Jake took three steps forward. Before he knew what he was doing, he was talking. 'I need some of that Blue Oxygen.'

There was a painful silence as the Engineer met Jake's eyes. No one moved, but all eyes were on Jake.

'Excuse me?' the Engineer asked, his stare icy. 'And who are you?'

Cray stood between Jake and the Engineer. 'Ignore him. His brother-in-law received his letter. He's upset, that's all.'

Jake pushed past Cray. 'We risked our lives getting that Blue Oxygen. At least let me take the rucksack and the tubes.'

The Engineer placed his hands on his hips, adding more strain to the already hard-working jacket buttons, and ambled towards Jake, his head tilted as if in fascination. One of his men arrived by his side.

'It's okay, James,' the Engineer said to the man, and continued strolling towards Jake. 'Let me talk to our new friend.'

At the sound of the Engineer's voice, which dripped with a strange sweetness, Jake's legs went weak.

'He means no harm,' Cray said to the Engineer.

The Engineer raised a hand and eyeballed Cray sternly.

Jake swallowed and told his feet to stay where they were, even though he wanted to take several steps backwards.

The Engineer stood directly in front of Jake, far too close. Suddenly, the Engineer offered his hand.

'We haven't met.'

Jake glanced down at the Engineer's hand, then reached out to shake it. The Engineer gripped Jake's hand tightly, then slowly pumped it up and down. 'People call me the Engineer.'

'Jake.'

The Engineer nodded and smiled. 'Pleased to meet you.'

After holding his hand for what felt like forever, the Engineer let go. 'How do you know Cray?'

Jake glanced at Cray, whose worried expression concerned him.

'I've known him for a long time,' Jake said. 'We went to school together.'

'Is that so?' the Engineer asked. 'And why does Cray have you on his team, I wonder? What skills do you contribute?'

His questions seemed strange, but Jake remained calm and played along. 'I found the oxygen. I helped him get into the city without being detected.' He had made an effort to ensure he'd had no dealings with the Engineer over the years. Now he'd met the man, he figured he'd been right to do so.

The Engineer raised his eyebrows in interest. 'And you say your brother-in-law has received his letter?'

'Yes. He doesn't have long.'

The Engineer took two, then three steps backwards.

'That is regrettable. I don't enjoy hearing of people receiving their letter.'

'Which is why I have to take the Blue to him,' Jake said, pointing to the rucksack on the ground.

The Engineer stroked his chin and nodded faintly, as though he was considering giving Jake what he needed. But then he turned to Astrid. 'And who is this?' he asked Cray.

Cray shifted his weight from one foot to the other. He scratched the back of his head. 'A bit of a complication.'

'I don't like complications,' the Engineer said, edging closer to Astrid, who frowned with what appeared to be a combination of hatred and fear.

'What kind of complication? I've told you before, Cray – it is important that you stick to the plan. Deviations from the plan cause problems that I cannot foresee. And you know how much I hate unforeseen circumstances.'

'I'm sorry,' Cray said, bowing his head.

The Engineer glanced at Jake with dark eyes. Jake feared he wouldn't get out of there with a head on his shoulders, never mind with the Blue.

# CHAPTER 22

## ASTRID

Astrid took a step closer to the Engineer. This was the man who had been messaging her father. There was something unsettling about him, maybe generated by the fear the men were showing.

'Their images have been recorded on the security system in my tower,' she said, interrupting Cray, who she could see was about to tell the Engineer the same thing.

All eyes were on her. She tried her hardest not to look frightened.

The Engineer raised his chin, looking down at her. He took a deep breath. It reminded her of how she was using her quota of oxygen. She held her breath.

'Is this the ... complication ... you mentioned, Cray?' the Engineer asked, his voice quiet but purposeful. He turned his head slowly towards Cray.

'Yes,' Cray said.

The Engineer strolled backwards and forwards, staring at each of the downcast faces. Only Jake met his eyes.

'Who?' the Engineer asked. 'Whose faces have been recorded?'

Cray moved quickly. 'It was a mistake. I'm—'

'Who?' the Engineer asked again, standing in front of Jake.

'Me,' Jake said.

'And Stan,' Cray said, pointing to the man who had manhandled Astrid out of her home.

The Engineer was motionless.

'I'm sorry,' Cray said, wringing his hands. 'We need your help.'

'My help?' the Engineer asked, and finally turned away from Jake.

This wasn't good. There was already tension, but now it was suffocating.

'How can I help?' the Engineer asked loudly.

Cray jumped. 'The cameras ... in the tower ... I thought ... we figured you might—'

'Complications,' the Engineer said, raising a hand to Cray. 'How many times have I told you? If you are going to work for me, I demand no complications.' He reached into the pocket of his gold jacket and took out what appeared to be a pair of gloves. 'I want simplicity.'

'I brought all this Blue Oxygen back for you,' Cray said with desperation.

The Engineer took his time putting on his gloves. 'This is going to cost you.'

Cray looked relieved, then disheartened. 'How much?' he asked.

'For the two of them?' the Engineer asked, intertwining his fingers. 'I'll see what I can do. You can leave the Blue Oxygen with me. I'll decide how much to give back to you once I've corrected your ... complication.'

Cray closed his eyes as though in pain, clearly coming to terms with losing the oxygen.

'You can't do that!' Stan said, striding towards the Engineer.

'Stop!' Cray said, reaching out to stop Stan.

It happened quickly. Two of the Engineer's men had guns in their hands, and were pointing them at Stan, who stopped and raised his hands.

'Come on,' Stan pleaded. 'There's enough Blue Oxygen to last a hundred lifetimes. Give us our cut.'

The Engineer gave a minute nod.

Two guns fired.

Stan tumbled backwards and then lay on the ground, dead.

'What the fuck?' Cray shouted. 'Why did you do that?'

Now there were even more guns aimed at Cray.

'No, no...' Cray said, raising his hands and bowing. 'It's all good. You don't have to do that. It's all yours. All yours...'

Astrid was panicking, turning one way, then the other. She backed away and felt someone behind her. It was Jake.

'Don't move,' he said. 'We'll get out of this. Running will get you killed.'

She held her breath. She wanted to believe him, but she didn't know why, if it was so easy for the Engineer to kill Stan, she, or any of the rest of them were still alive.

'Did I not make it clear?' the Engineer asked. 'I will take the Blue Oxygen and pay you when I see fit. Is that clear?'

'Yes,' Cray said. 'Of course.'

She noted how Jake's body sagged. He was losing the oxygen, too.

'What about the face recognition?' Cray asked. 'If the security has recorded Stan's and Jake's faces, it could lead them to me – to us.'

The Engineer flexed his shoulders and tilted his head one way, then the other. 'I said I will deal with it.' He turned to Jake. 'You shouldn't have let the security system see your face.'

It was an obvious thing to say. Astrid waited for Jake to tell him so. But he remained silent. He knew better.

'What about the woman?' Cray asked.

They were talking about Astrid as though she were an object to be sold or bartered for.

'You were right to bring her here,' the Engineer said. 'It will give us leverage.'

'Leverage?' Cray asked.

The Engineer ignored him and took several steps towards Astrid.

She wanted to run. Her legs told her over and over to run ... that this would be her only chance.

'It's going to be okay,' Jake whispered.

How the hell could he know that?

'I'll take her with me,' the Engineer said, motioning for two of his men to take her.

'Wait,' Astrid pleaded. 'No. I won't tell anyone. I promise.' She fought against the two men, but it was no good. She thought about telling him who she was ... who her father was. But she didn't know their connection, so that could simply put her in even more danger. If that was even possible.

'Let me take her,' Jake said.

The Engineer stopped and lowered his gaze. 'You have already caused enough trouble, young man.' The Engineer was clearly trying to control his temper. 'Because of you, and that huge idiot...' – he gestured at Stan's body without looking – 'I am going to have to perform a miracle to protect Cray and his buddies. Not to mention you.' He cleared his throat and continued in a low grumble. 'So excuse me if I am a little impatient and trying really hard not to put a bullet in your fucking head. I've been told I have anger issues. And Jake ... I am really trying to be a better person. You know? I am trying.' He placed a hand on Jake's shoulder. 'Do we understand one another?'

Astrid had given up fighting the two men. She wanted Jake to do something that would get her out of this mess. But Jake only nodded.

'No!' Astrid shouted as they dragged her away.

# CHAPTER 23

## JAKE

'What were you thinking?' Jake asked Cray. 'You told me it was just us. The Blue was supposed to be for the villagers. But the Engineer was in on it from the very beginning, wasn't he?'

Jake walked through Last City towards the track to West Gate.

'There was no way we could have kept it,' Cray said, following him. 'You know that. That much Blue doesn't go unnoticed. At least this way, we're in with the Engineer. He knows what we can do.'

'What about Bailey?' Jake asked. 'I don't have time to get more oxygen.'

The sun was coming up. Jake had been awake for what felt like a week. He stopped and faced Cray.

'I was looking out for you, Jake. You know that.'

'Bullshit! You were looking out for yourself. The way you always do.' Jake turned to walk away, but Cray reached his shoulder and pulled him back.

'You saw what happened to Stan,' Cray said. 'It was you

and Stan who got us into this mess. Remember? We had to strike a deal to get us out of the shit.'

Jake sighed and shook off Cray's hand. He didn't want to admit it, but Cray was right. Why had he let his hood come off?

'He'd have taken the lot anyway,' Jake said. 'He only needed an excuse.'

'Maybe,' Cray said. 'But we're alive. We can get more. Work together and get more Blue.'

'Leave me alone,' Jake said.

'You hate them as much as I do,' Cray shouted after him. 'The elite. Taking what they want and not giving a thought to any of us. They have more than their fair share of oxygen. While they're over there, sucking in Blue Oxygen, we're over here, dying. Like your brother-in-law.'

'I could have saved him,' Jake said, turning on Cray, his fists clenched. 'If I'd have done what I should have and gone myself, I'd be taking back enough Blue to keep him alive.'

'You'd never have done it without me, and you know it. That much Blue Oxygen...'

'I didn't need all of it,' Jake said. His anger was ready to be set free. He gripped Cray's collar and pushed him backwards. Godfrey reached over and tried to push Jake away, but he had a good hold of Cray.

'You should have told me!' Jake shouted.

'It's okay, Godfrey,' Cray said. 'Let him go.'

'My sister,' Jake said, spitting his words. 'And her kid. They're going to lose Bailey. They were counting on me.'

Cray smiled wryly but didn't fight back.

Jake let go of Cray's collar. It was no use.

Then a fist came out of nowhere and sent Jake hurtling backwards. His back slammed against the ground. His face burned where he had been hit. Though his vision was blurred, he could make out Max standing over him.

'Trust me,' Cray said, looking down at him too. 'You don't want to cross the Engineer. Or me.'

Jake was winded. He couldn't breathe. He wiped the blood from his face with the back of his hand.

'I'll be in touch,' Cray said, straightening his shirt and jacket.

From the ground, Jake watched Cray and the others walk away. He rolled onto his front and tried to push himself up, but dizziness came over him and he fell again. Their footsteps drifted away into the distance until only his own laboured breathing remained. Tiny amounts of air crept into his lungs. All the oxygen in those canisters, handed over, with nothing to show for what he'd done. And an innocent woman was in danger. Because of him.

He stared up at the dark morning sky. He needed to go home and see his sister and Bailey. It would soon be time. It was a terrible thought. That Bailey would count his last breaths. What would that feel like? He couldn't imagine.

Jake had been there when his niece was born. Grace and Bailey had given up so much to have her. Everyone took their first breath of air, expelling the liquid from their lungs after being in the womb, replacing it with that first breath. It was impossible to imagine.

Rain fell, striking his face, making him blink. It was cold.

Now, thinking about Bailey and his final breaths, he wondered how the last breath was connected to the first one. A lifetime of breathing in and out, always trying to fill the lungs. But it was never enough. When you expelled one breath, you were always looking to do it again. Over and over. That was automatic.

By the time he made it back home, the sky was dark blue. The stars were disappearing and the clouds were taking shape. Rain fell lazily, washing the dirt across the ground, forming rivulets that flowed beneath and around the shacks.

His sister's shack was right there. He didn't want to call in, knowing what would be happening. He should have been returning with the answers, with the Blue Oxygen. But he was empty-handed. He had been so close to pulling it off.

The door to his sister's shack opened. Grace stood in the doorway, beckoning him.

Jake couldn't move. He could tell that she knew Bailey had received his letter. She went back inside, leaving the door open. Then Jess appeared, wearing a long pink dressing gown. She was so tiny. Always had been, from the day she was born. But she was strong too. She leaned out of the doorway to look up at the rain. Then she jumped onto the wet ground.

'No,' Jake said. 'It's raining.'

She ignored his reprimand and ran towards him, her slippered feet splashing in puddles. When she reached him, she jumped into his arms. She held him tightly. Although he returned her hug, he knew there was nothing more serious or vital than a child's embrace. He couldn't compete.

'What are you doing outside?' he asked her. 'You'll be soaked through.'

'It's Daddy,' she said. 'He's not well.'

'I know, princess.' He kissed her on both cheeks and carried her to the shack, putting her down when he reached the doorway. He stepped into the shack and took off his shoes.

Jess ran through the shack over to the settee next to the

fire. Bailey lay on the settee with Grace lying beside him, her head on his chest.

Jake crept through the shack, ashamed that he had failed, and arrived beside them. 'I tried, Bailey. I really tried.'

'Hey, kid,' he said, smiling.

'Where have you been?' Grace asked seriously, in the tone only she ever used with him. She sat up, a hand resting on Bailey's leg.

'I wanted to get more Blue Oxygen. I nearly did it too.'

Bailey shook his head and reached over to mock-punch Jake on the thigh. 'I told you not to. It's okay.'

Jake didn't understand Bailey. Maybe he never had.

'It's not okay,' Jake said.

Jess, on the floor playing with her toy dolls, looked up at him, wide-eyed.

'Don't,' Grace said. 'We're not angry. We're dealing with it our way.'

Jake tried smiling at Jess to reassure her, but it was the hardest smile he'd ever had to pretend.

Bailey got up and motioned for Jake to go with him. Jake followed him to the kitchen. Bailey took two bottles of beer from the fridge and handed one to Jake. They headed out onto the porch and stared out at the rain.

'Where did you go?' Bailey asked.

Jake took a long swig of beer. 'The city. I had it. I had so much Blue. It was in my hands.' He held out his free hand and imagined a canister hanging from it.

'Don't get mixed up in all that, Jake.'

'It didn't work out,' he said.

Bailey gripped his arm. 'I mean it, kid. Don't get drawn into all that shit.' Bailey never swore, and Jake was taken aback. 'Your sister is going to need you. And so is Jess. You're no good to them if you're locked up, or dead.'

'Bailey, don't worry.'

Bailey's eyes were a dark blue. It was nearly time.

'Don't tell me not to worry. I see the state of your face, the limp, your bruised knuckles. I don't want you bringing any of that here. To your sister. To my daughter. Do you hear?'

Jake stood up straight. 'I promise. I won't let anything happen to them.'

'That doesn't mean getting your hands on Blue Oxygen. I've made my peace with my quota, and so has your sister. It's the way it is. You have to make your peace with it, too. Promise you'll leave it alone. That you'll stop raiding.'

Reluctantly, Jake nodded.

'Promise me,' Bailey said.

Jake didn't want to promise, but Bailey was down to hours, maybe even minutes.

'Jake? Promise me.'

'I promise. Okay. I promise.'

'No good will come of you chasing that stuff. It might hold off the inevitable for a time, but not forever. Do you hear? Live your life.'

'I hear you.'

Bailey put a hand out into the rain. 'Why do I get the feeling you're not listening to a word I say?'

'I just wanted you around a little longer,' Jake said, his head bowed. 'I tried. But I couldn't hang on to it.'

'Why don't you hear me when I tell you it's okay? I wouldn't have used it even if you'd brought it here.'

'Liar.'

Bailey smiled. 'Well, maybe for long enough to see my

next birthday. Your sister always looks after me on my birthday.' He nudged Jake's shoulder and laughed.

'That's my sister!'

Bailey's laughter died down. 'Stop chasing that stuff and live a little. Get yourself a woman.'

Jake stared at the puddle just outside the porch and recalled Astrid. Where was she, and what was the Engineer going to do with her? Why hadn't he done more to save her?

Bailey began to cough. His oxygen had run out. He reached for his throat and fell to his knees.

'No!' Jake said.

Jake moved past Bailey, ready to call out for Grace, but Bailey took his arm. 'No ... no. Don't. I don't want ... them to see me like this.' He coughed again.

'Not like this, Bailey. You can't do it. Not like this.'

But Bailey's eyes were fixed on Jake's, filled with intent and desperation. There was no way Jake could refuse.

Jake lowered Bailey to the wooden planks of the porch and held him. Bailey was suffocating, convulsing in his arms. Jake wanted to cry out for help, but he didn't want to let Bailey down.

'Bailey?' Grace called from inside.

Jake waited for Bailey's eyes to open one more time. But they remained closed.

## *CHAPTER 24*

ASTRID

Astrid peered through the window. It was bolted shut. Outside, the sky was black. So much had happened in a short time. She was being punished for trying to leave and take the Blue Oxygen with her. How had it all gone so wrong?

The door opened and Astrid spun around. Two men entered. One of them was the Engineer.

'Who are you?' the Engineer asked.

Astrid backed away towards the wall. Thinking of the messages she'd seen, and how easily he'd ordered the death of a man who had done little other than disagree with him, she feared the worst.

The Engineer scratched his chin. 'I have my doubts about you. There's something you're not telling me.'

'What do you mean?' Astrid knew what he was looking for. He wanted to know who she was. She didn't want to tell him the wrong thing.

The Engineer exhaled noisily and rolled his eyes. 'Come on, tell me who you are. Before I decide what's going to happen to you.'

Her mind raced with possible answers. 'Astrid,' she said.

'I know that.' The Engineer dragged a chair towards him, spun it around and sat on it the wrong way round. He rested his chin on the back of the chair.

'I told you,' the man with the Engineer said. He was bald, with the tattoo of what looked like a phoenix on the top of his head, the tail working its way down his neck and beneath his collar. 'I know who she is.'

Astrid did all she could to remain calm and not give anything away.

The Engineer stared accusingly.

'She's Solomon's daughter,' the bald man said.

God damn. They knew who she was. She didn't know if this was good or bad.

'Is that true?' the Engineer asked. 'Are you Gordon Solomon's daughter?'

She hesitated. But there was no point lying. 'Yes.'

The bald man smiled and slapped his leg. 'I told you!'

The Engineer glanced over his shoulder. The bald man's smile disappeared as he collected himself, crossing his arms and clearing his throat.

Slowly, the Engineer turned back to Astrid. 'You're Astrid Solomon?'

She nodded.

The Engineer sighed and got to his feet, arranging the chair so it was tucked beneath the table. 'Well, that changes things.'

Astrid wanted to ask whether the change was good or bad for her, but stayed quiet.

'I know your father,' the Engineer said.

She stared at him, unsure whether to tell him she knew that already. Maybe it would give her some control if he knew she was on to what he was doing to the people in the villages. But then, it might also give him the excuse he needed to keep her quiet for good.

'He runs a company that sells Blue Oxygen, doesn't he?'

She met his eyes and nodded faintly.

The Engineer laughed sarcastically and shook his head. 'Daddy is a good, honest businessman, isn't he?'

'What are you accusing him of?' she asked, her anger a surprise.

The Engineer raised his hands. 'Hey. I'm not accusing him. I was simply telling you what people think of him, that's all.'

Astrid was ready to challenge him, but she didn't want to know what this man clearly knew about her father. She hated the thought of giving in to him.

The Engineer gave her a despondent look. 'We're going to have to take you home. I guess that's okay with you?'

She looked from the Engineer to the bald man, then back again. 'Why?' The question surprised her, and judging by their faces, surprised them too.

'Why?' the Engineer asked. 'Because when people in the city hear that I have Solomon's daughter and they tell your father, he's not going to be too happy.'

'What do *you* care?' she asked.

'Do you want to go home or not?' The Engineer raised an eyebrow suspiciously.

'I want you to let me go.'

'But not to go home?' The Engineer took a step closer.

'That's none of your business.'

The Engineer sniffed. 'Well, it sort of is. You're not going anywhere unless it's with me, handing you over to Solomon. I want your father to know I looked after you and returned you in one piece.'

'Are you scared of him?'

The Bald man laughed to himself.

The Engineer's shoulders tightened and he stood up straight, glancing behind at the bald man. 'Something funny?'

The bald man shook his head and took two steps backwards.

The Engineer took his time to return his attention to Astrid. 'What makes you think I'm scared of your father?'

'Well, if you're not scared, then let me go. Who cares what my father wants?'

For the first time since she met the Engineer, she felt in control. But the feeling didn't last. He strode towards her, stopping only when he was so close she could smell his musty cologne. She turned away.

'Don't test me, girl.' He snarled. His breath gave off the sour smell of tobacco.

She couldn't back away any further, and had to wait for him to step away. Finally, he did.

'You'll stay here until I figure out what to do with you,' he said, his voice returning to the light tone he had used when he entered the room.

The bald man sniffed and offered her what she thought was a sympathetic smile.

She would have to go back to her father and explain everything. The thought scared her. She would have to tell him all about wanting to leave. And once he knew she had tried to do that, he would make sure she never succeeded in the future. The Engineer and the bald man left the room, shutting the door firmly. She told herself to be thankful that being a Solomon had protected her. She tried, but thankful was the last thing she was feeling.

## *CHAPTER 25*

### JAKE

Jake stayed with Grace and Jess until they came to take Bailey away. Then his sister wanted to be alone. Which suited him. He loved his sister, but he found it hard to tell her so. He couldn't talk to her, even after something like that. At one point, they had been silent for close to an hour as she nursed the cuts and grazes on Jake's face and his bruised ribs. Jess slept on the settee. The young girl never stopped amazing him. Maybe it was an uncle–niece thing, but he had always seen her as special. She seemed older than her years. As though she – and Jake gave no time to such thoughts usually – had an old soul. It made him shiver to think about it. But it was true too, somehow.

He left when the sun had been up for an hour or two. Although 'sun up' wasn't a useful way to describe what the sun did in the villages. It never seemed to shine fully on the villages or those who lived there.

Bailey had been right about him. What he had was never enough, and that was all he thought about. Why did those in the city have so much, and he and those in the village have nothing – not even the air they breathed? Only a child could fully, truly recognise unfairness for what it was. And for most of his childhood years, Jake had felt it. Deeply. As far as fairness went, and his ability to recognise it or its opposite, he had never grown up.

What was the Engineer going to do with Astrid?

It was a stupid thing to do: show Cray and the others where the Blue was. He'd been desperate. But that was no excuse.

He should have been out there trying to find her. If he did nothing else, at least he would have put that right. As much as he could, anyway. But there was no way he'd get her away from the Engineer.

When he was about to leave for the tram, something made him pause. A gentle knocking drew his attention to a door, opening and closing. It was O'Leary's place. He told himself to leave then and there, but he couldn't. Something was wrong, and he couldn't ignore it.

He checked one last time on his sister's shack before walking up to O'Leary's door and knocking on it. He didn't expect anyone to answer, but he did it anyway. Nudging the door open a little, he called out.

'O'Leary?'

No answer. He pushed through the door as quietly as possible.

'Anyone here?' he asked, louder this time.

Still no response. He crept through the living room, over to where he imagined he'd find the bedroom. A cold draught blew through the shack, stopping him from turning the handle and entering. He shivered, then plucked up the courage.

The room was empty. The bed sheets were ruffled, but

he got the impression that O'Leary and his wife had not been there for some time. The place felt unused.

He remembered what O'Leary had said about someone coming for him.

Jake stepped backwards and shut the door.

He left O'Leary's shack, jogging at first, then running for the tram. He needed to be alone. There was nothing he could do for O'Leary now – and there was nothing he could do for Bailey either.

The tram was empty. He sat and looked out of the window as the tram rolled through the villages, its wheels rattling and screeching along the wet tracks. The tram, he had often thought, said everything about life in the villages. Village after village, thousands upon thousands of shacks lined up, housing those who were waiting for their letters, informing them that their quota was up. The tracks dictated the direction in which the people could travel; there was no alternative.

He travelled the tram for close to an hour, going over everything that had happened, ending with O'Leary and his wife going missing. Then he recalled how Bailey had struggled at the end. The thought made Jake hold his breath. Like everyone, as a child, Jake had been taught the breathing rituals aimed at slowing the heart rate. It only worked for so long. What had always troubled Jake was that while he was sitting around preserving oxygen, he wondered what the point was. It was all so pointless, which made him want more oxygen, which made him head off and raid the city. But the amount of oxygen he expelled in getting into the city was far more than he gained in the odd tube of Blue Oxygen he bagged. Yet somehow that didn't matter to him. Using Blue Oxygen gave him a sense of freedom he could not get any other way.

Without thinking, Jake got off at West Gate and meandered through the market, ending up at the tunnel leading to Gambit's garden. He wandered through, not expecting Gambit to be there. But he was perched on a low wall, his legs crossed and his eyes closed.

'So, you're back?' Gambit asked, opening one eye. After a brief pause, he opened his other eye, unfolded his legs and stood. 'And I see you didn't heed my warning.'

Jake touched his face and his cut lip, then shrugged.

Gambit folded his arms. 'What happened?'

'I made it into the city. I bagged a huge haul of Blue Oxygen. We brought it back.'

Gambit nodded in a way that made Jake think he knew the story did not have a happy ending.

'The Engineer took it,' Jake said.

Gambit nodded. 'There isn't a tube of Blue Oxygen in the villages that he doesn't know about. You should have known that. You think there are dealers in the villagers who aren't in his pocket?'

'I wanted it for ... Bailey.'

'He is dead?'

For the first time since Bailey had died, Jake wanted to cry. But he didn't. Crying required too much oxygen.

'Sit with me,' Gambit said.

'That's not me,' Jake said. 'I can't sit still.'

'You can. And you should. It gives you perspective.'

Jake glanced over his shoulder.

'What?' Gambit asked, an eyebrow raised. 'Are you going to travel the tram all day?'

Jake shook his head, then shrugged. 'I guess so. Maybe for today.'

'Don't be a stranger,' Gambit said. He strolled over to the bench beneath a tree with red leaves, and sat cross-legged. 'We have coding to do.'

Jake thought about following him. Instead, he headed out of the garden and through the tunnel, out into the market, and waited for the tram on the corner. When it arrived, he jumped on board, unsure where he was going. He wanted to forget, to not think about Bailey, about his sister, about Astrid.

He got off the tram before the next stop. Up ahead was a bar he used to go to with Bailey – way before Jess was born. No one looked his way as he strode through the bar. Those inside were wrapped up in their own lives and their own stories. Of course they were. Why would anyone care about what had happened to him? And that was okay.

'Beer,' he said to the barmaid.

The barmaid turned away and dug a bottle out of the bin of ice behind the bar.

Jake hovered his wrist over the bar before slamming it down. The payment registered on the screen embedded in the bar and the barmaid pushed the bottle towards him. The digital penny was another form of control, and he hated using it. But there was no alternative.

He gave the barmaid a weak smile and set about downing the bottle. It took less than ten seconds to finish it.

'Another,' he said. 'Please.'

The barmaid raised an eyebrow and went through the same routine.

'Keep them coming,' Jake said.

'Sure thing,' the barmaid said.

She had long pink hair and lipstick to match. She wore a short black skirt and a tiny red vest that showed off her midriff and a shiny pink navel ring.

'One for yourself,' he said. 'What's your name?'

'You can call me anything you want as long as you keep buying the drinks.'

Jake hated the villages. But not as much as he hated the city.

## *CHAPTER 26*

ASTRID

SHE TRIED several times to push open the window, but it was no good. She had experienced some relief when the Engineer told her he would free her, but this was soon replaced with fear of seeing her father again. Once she was back in the city, there was no way she would get out again. Her only chance was to stay in the villages and find a way to Moscov City later.

The door clanged as someone on the other side unlocked it. It opened inwards. The Engineer entered, followed by his bald friend.

'I've made arrangements,' the Engineer said.

He waited for her to respond.

'Don't you want to thank me?' he asked.

'Thank you?' She scanned the room: the closed window and then the door. 'You locked me up. Why would I thank you?'

The Engineer pursed his lips. 'Fair enough.' He sauntered into the room, pushing his hands into his pockets.

She hated how he could control the mood or tone in a room.

'I've spoken to your father. He's a little unhappy with you. But he's willing to forgive.'

Astrid feared that her father had spurned her for good and had left her at the mercy of the Engineer.

'He's seen the footage of you in his Blue storage room. He says that you were leaving when those men entered. Is that true?'

'It has nothing to do with you.'

The Engineer laughed, then collected himself. 'You wanted to come here, didn't you? To the villages. Why the hell would you want to do that?'

The contempt on his face made her turn away. But he moved so he was in her line of sight.

'You have all the Blue Oxygen you could want in your home. Why would you give it all up to come here?'

'It's not mine,' she said.

'Of course it is. Your father is very successful.'

'It's his. It's not mine. I don't want to be under his control simply because he can afford to buy unlimited oxygen.'

The Engineer pointed at her, his expression serious. 'You're spoiled. That's it, isn't it? You're spoiled.'

She turned away, reminded of what her father had said to her.

'It's okay,' he said, as though he meant it. 'You don't know any different. But if you spend any more time in the villages than you need to, I think you might learn to. Which isn't good for anyone. Never mind a young, rich, spoiled girl like yourself.'

'I'm not a girl,' she said, immediately regretting it.

'Yes, you are.' The Engineer stretched, then folded his arms. 'Your father has footage of the two men who were stupid enough to let their hoods come off.'

Astrid turned to face him. For reasons she didn't understand, she felt sorry for Jake. It made no sense.

'You killed one of them,' she said.

'Yes.' The Engineer unfolded his arms and shrugged. 'I did. But he was asking for it.'

'What are you going to do to the other man?'

'Jake?' The Engineer asked. 'That's not up to me. That's for your father to decide. He's a little annoyed.'

'What's he going to do?'

'I guess we'll find out. But I think he's intent on sending a message to the people in the villages.'

'What's that supposed to mean?'

The Engineer winked and then turned to leave the room.

'Wait,' she said. 'When are you taking me back?'

The Engineer didn't answer. The bald man waited for him to go through the doorway and then shut the door and locked it.

## CHAPTER 27

### JAKE

Drunk, Jake stumbled through the village, now and then colliding with one of Bailey's cars, each one a skeleton of what it once was.

Staggering by his sister's shack, he sensed something was different. Maybe it was just knowing on some level that Bailey wasn't there. Maybe it was all the drink he'd consumed. Inside, he imagined, were Grace and Jess. He walked up to the door and knocked. There was no answer. The horrible thought they had been taken, like O'Leary, made his head swirl and his stomach flip with nausea. He was a fool to have drunk so much. He pushed against the door and it opened.

'Grace? Jess?'

There was no answer. The shack was cold, no fire burning. He stepped inside. Grace was sitting on the floor, her head bowed. Jake's relief was replaced by fear again. He didn't know what was wrong or what to do. He wished he hadn't had so much to drink, so he could understand what was happening.

'What is it?' he asked. It didn't sound like his own voice. He turned, expecting someone else to be there. Maybe it was someone else who had spoken.

Grace shook her head, not looking up at him.

'Grace?'

'You've been drinking,' she said coldly.

'Tell me what's wrong,' he said.

'I don't understand.' She reached down and grabbing two pieces of paper from the floor.

Jake took a step backwards. He didn't want to believe it. Not after Bailey. His sister couldn't have her letter already. She was younger than Bailey. She couldn't have used up her quota. It was impossible.

'It can't be right,' she said, finally looking up at Jake. She was ready to cry, her expression filled with disbelief and confusion. 'Jess too ... she's just a kid. It can't be right.'

Jess? That was impossible. Suddenly Jake was sober. His legs were heavy, unable to move or take his weight. He staggered backwards and collided with the table. He leaned against it, wanting everything to make sense again.

Grace scrunched up the pieces of paper and threw them at Jake. They struck his leg and fell to the ground. He stared at them before bending over to pick them up.

One name on each. One belonging to Grace and one belonging to Jess. It was impossible. There was no way Jess would have used even a billion litres, never mind ten billion.

'It's wrong,' he muttered. 'It has to be a mistake.'

Grace peered up at him, her eyes glassy. 'I don't understand, Jake.'

'I'm going to sort it,' he said. 'It has to be a mistake. Both of you.'

'Have you checked your place?' she asked.

He stared at her, working out what she meant. What if he had one too? Maybe this wasn't a mistake.

'I'll be right back.' He ran out of the shack then to his own. He fumbled with his keys, steadied himself, and finally managed to keep his hand still enough to put the key in the lock and open it. The letter was on the floor, its clean white envelope face-up, his name written in black. It was a relief. He wasn't expecting to feel that way. But it was a relief because his sister and Jess weren't alone. And neither was he. He picked up the letter and opened it. He'd seen versions of the letter so many times before. Everyone knew what they looked like. And everyone knew the wording. He would be down to his last thousand litres of oxygen.

He headed back to his sister's shack. She was waiting for him. He handed her the unopened letter. There was no need for either of them to read it, but his sister did, all the same. The little colour that remained in her face disappeared completely.

'Where's Jess?' he asked. 'Does she know?'

'Of course not,' Grace said. 'She'll be here soon.'

'I'm going to fix this,' he said.

She lowered the letter to her side and glared at him. 'What did you do?'

Jake's chest tightened. He couldn't look at her. She was right. This was his fault. It had to be.

'I wanted to get the Blue Oxygen for Bailey,' he said.

Her eyes filled with anger. She wasn't crying any longer. She pointed at him. 'Bailey told you not to do anything. Remember? He told you!'

'Grace. I don't know what happened. But I'm going to fix it.'

'Goddamn it, Jake! My baby girl! Bailey and I sacrificed everything to have her. Not once did we regret doing it. Not one day went by that we didn't thank each other for doing it. We never asked you for anything.'

Jake's mind raced, searching for an explanation. How did this happen? 'It's wrong. It has to be.'

'Get out!' Grace shouted, pushing him towards the door.

He wanted to make her understand. If everything could just go back to the way it was two days before. But that could never happen.

It had to be the security cameras that had identified his face. The Engineer hadn't done what he said he would do. The footage was out there.

'Grace, please. I can put this right.'

'Get out!' she screamed at him. 'You've always been the same. You think you can do what you want. Even when we asked you to leave us alone, you had to mess things up again. Get out!'

There was nothing he could say. He left and walked to his shack. Stumbling through the door, he ripped up the floorboards in the bathroom and grabbed his gun, which he had hidden underneath. He marched through the village towards the tram stop. Conscious of the oxygen he was using, he held his breath, not wanting to waste any of it. He needed more time and more oxygen. It was up to him to fix it. The tram turned the corner and headed towards him. It stopped with a loud clank. Jake jumped on board.

'You look like you've seen a ghost,' the conductor said. 'Are you okay, buddy?'

Jake ignored him and found a seat towards the rear of the carriage. He leaned forward, burying his head in his hands. Gambit's advice filled his head: breathe slowly, don't let your emotions win. More than ever, he needed to control his intake of oxygen. If he was going to help his sister and Jess, he needed to hold on to every breath.

There was no way he could go straight to the Engineer. He'd likely kill him before he spoke a word. The only person he could think of who might know what had happened was Cray. What he couldn't understand was, why had Grace and Jess been affected too? Why had their oxygen been deleted too?

Maybe it was a mistake. A simple error. But he'd never heard of anything like that happening. There was a first time for everything. But he couldn't believe that, no matter how much he wanted to.

He slowed his breathing, closed his eyes and focused on the rise and fall of his chest.

Cray must know something.

The tram took an age to reach Cray's park. Cray's shack was up ahead. Jake reached into his coat pocket and gripped his gun. Cray had set him up. Jake was making one bad decision after the next, and it was impossible to stop what was happening.

Two dogs jumped against the chain-link fence, barking. In an instinctive move, Jake pointed the gun at one of them. The dogs ignored his threat and continued to bark. Jake thrust the gun back into his pocket and pushed his back up against the shack next to Cray's. He panted, and his heart beat furiously. He told himself to calm down, but it was no good.

Someone hollered at the dogs to be quiet, which worked: they ran off towards a shack on the other side of the chain-link fence.

There were no lights on in Cray's shack. The thought that there might be no one there filled Jake with dread. What would he do then? Where would he go to find out what was happening? He had to move now. Under the cover of darkness, he ran around the back of Cray's shack and found an open window. He raised his head to look through it. There was a TV playing inside.

Making sure his gun was hidden securely in his coat pocket, he jumped and pulled himself up through the window, falling into a bedroom. The TV was loud, only just drowning out the dull sound of voices.

Crouching by the door, he waited, listening. It was Cray and his wife, Geraldine, arguing. Jake took out his gun and, in one quick movement, pulled open the door and raced through the hall, arriving in the living room. Cray was watching TV, his feet up on a footstool.

'Don't move!' Jake shouted, his gun sweeping the room. 'Stay there!'

Geraldine screamed and Cray pushed himself off the chair, getting to his feet.

Jake fired the gun, smashing the TV screen.

'Wait! Wait!' Cray shouted, holding out his hands in a calming gesture.

Geraldine screamed words Jake didn't understand. He strode towards Cray. 'I said, don't move!'

'Jake!' Cray said, panicked. 'What the hell are you doing?'

'What did you do?' Jake asked. Anger replaced any fear he might have had. 'Tell me what you did! It's Jess. She's just a kid. What did you do?'

'I don't know what you're talking about,' Cray said.

'Don't bullshit me! I know it has something to do with you and what happened in the city. Tell me what you did.'

Cray shook his head. 'I'm telling you, Jake. I'm being honest with you, mate.'

Jake swung the gun around and pointed it at Geraldine, who fell to her knees and covered her head.

'No!' Cray said. 'Don't hurt her!'

'Either you tell me what the hell is happening, or I put a hole in her head. Then I do the same to you.'

'Jake. I swear to you ... I don't know what you're talking about.'

For a moment Jake believed him. Maybe Cray didn't know.

'Tell him, Cray!' Geraldine shouted. 'Just tell him!'

Jake edged closer to Geraldine and thrust the gun towards her.

'Okay, okay,' Cray said. 'Just put the gun down. Please, Jake. Put it down.'

Slowly, Jake lowered the gun. 'I don't have much time. Tell me everything. And do it quickly.' For a moment, he had been sure he was going to pull the trigger. He could taste metal.

'We fucked up, Jake,' Cray said, holding out his hands, palms upwards, as though offering him the reason.

'You mean the security cameras?' Jake asked.

'That woman we brought back ... her father is Gordon Solomon.'

'Who the hell is that?' The name meant something to him – a vague memory sparked in the back of his mind.

Cray brushed back his hair. 'He's one of the biggest manufacturers and sellers of Blue Oxygen. He has ties to the governor – Cameron Carlisle. They're in it together. As soon as Solomon found out his daughter was missing, he checked the security and informed Carlisle.'

'But the Engineer said he could get rid of the evidence.'

'That's the thing,' Cray said. 'When he found out who he was dealing with, he had to make a deal. Not even the

Engineer could get around that one. He's in with Carlisle. There's no way the Engineer would do anything to risk his relationship with Solomon.'

Jake's head was spinning. 'What do you mean? What has Solomon got to do with the Engineer?'

'He turns a blind eye to all the Blue Oxygen the Engineer gets his hands on. In return, the Engineer does his dirty work and finds more Oxygen.'

'Finds?' Jake asked. 'You mean, he kills people?'

Cray threw his hands into the air. 'Come on, Jake. You know as well as I do there's all kinds of shit we don't know anything about. Who knows what deals they have going on between them?'

'I don't get it,' Jake said. 'What has this got to do with my sister? With my niece?'

Cray glanced at Geraldine, who was looking warily at Jake.

'Cray?' Jake snapped. 'Tell me.'

'The Engineer had to appease Carlisle,' Cray said. 'I didn't know about it. Not until it was too late. Not that there was anything I could have done.'

'About what?'

'The Engineer gave you up. And your family.'

'Gave us up? I don't understand.'

'I'm sorry. But Solomon was pissed off. He wants payback. And this is his revenge.'

'But ... he can't do that,' Jake said. 'He has to take it back.'

Cray shrugged.

'What about Astrid?' Jake asked.

'Who?'

'That's her name.'

'The Engineer is going to hand her over. He doesn't have a choice.'

Jake stared at the floor. 'I don't believe it. I can't let him do this.'

Cray turned away from Jake. 'I'm sorry. I tried to help. But the moment the security cameras got a look at your face, there was no way out of it.'

'So it's Carlisle who has stopped their oxygen? My sister and niece?'

Cray gave him a sympathetic shrug. 'At Solomon's request, I guess. The Engineer has had to hand over most of the Blue Oxygen and the woman. He's pretty pissed off with me.'

'They can't do that!' Jake walked back and forth, making Cray and Geraldine cower.

'I don't know what to say,' Cray muttered. 'Please, Jake, put the gun away. I hate this, too.'

'You don't give a damn!' Jake aimed his gun at him.

'Don't!' Geraldine shouted.

Jake spun around quickly and pushed the gun back into his pocket. What was he going to do? He needed to think. He leaned against a wall for support and bent forward – ready to pass out or throw up, he wasn't sure which.

'How much oxygen do you have left?' Cray asked.

'I don't know. Less than a thousand litres.'

'I can get tubes,' Cray said. 'Keep you going.'

'It won't do any good,' Jake said. 'I need to fix this. For my sister and niece.'

'How?' Cray asked. 'It's done. They will have programmed the oxygen blockchain.'

Jake thumped the wall with the side of his fist. 'Then someone is going to have to code another lot of oxygen. My sister ... my niece ... they've done nothing wrong. They don't deserve this. I won't let it happen.' He leaned against the wall and closed his eyes. The thumping in his temples was deafening.

'Where is he?' Jake asked Cray after a pause.

'Who?'

'The Engineer. Where is he?'

'You won't find him,' Cray said. 'It's done. They're taking the woman back. Along with the Blue.'

'She's not going anywhere until Solomon puts this right. I don't care about my oxygen. But there's no way I'm letting them take Grace's or Jess's.'

'It's suicide,' Cray said. 'You won't get anywhere near her.'

Jake got close enough to Cray to smell the alcohol on his breath. 'Let me deal with that. Tell me where the Engineer is.'

Cray hesitated. 'West Gate,' he said finally.

Jake gripped Cray's shirt. 'Where in West Gate?'

'The Engineer will kill me and Geraldine if he finds out I told you.'

'It's either that or you die now,' Jake said. 'This is my family we're talking about. I'd do anything for them.'

Cray rubbed his head with both hands.

'Tell him,' Geraldine said.

'Okay, okay,' Cray said. 'The handover is happening at the edge of West Gate, at the south entrance. He'll be there with Astrid and the Blue.'

A surge of relief flooded Jake's body. At least he stood a chance, no matter how slim it was. He strode through the shack to the front door, jerked it open, and left.

He needed a plan. But every time he visualised himself getting close to the Engineer or Astrid, it ended badly. There was an army between him and them. And even if he could take Astrid ... what then? What should he do after that? It was too much to think through. He would go to West Gate and work out what to do when he was there. He was a dead man, anyway. But this was no longer about his own oxygen, his own life. It was about his sister's and niece's.

# CHAPTER 28

## ASTRID

Outside, the morning air was cool and damp. Astrid followed the bald man with the phoenix tattoo running down the back of his bald head.

'Where are you taking me?' she asked.

'Does it matter?' he asked without turning around. 'I figure you don't get a say either way.'

She jogged to catch up with him. 'Then tell me.'

He sniffed, then spat on the dusty ground. 'West Gate. South entrance to the city.'

Even though she knew they were taking her back to the city, hearing him say so made her clench her fists. He was right too – it didn't matter what she wanted. That had never mattered.

'I can get you Blue,' she whispered. 'Help me get out of this and I'll get more Blue than you can ever inhale.'

He laughed sarcastically. 'You sure are a privileged madam, huh? Used to getting her own way, is that it?'

'Which is it?' she snapped. 'Either I don't have a say in what happens or I get my own way. You can't have it both ways.'

The bald man gave her a serious look. 'You got me. You're clever. But still ... all the Blue in the world ain't gonna do me no good if I'm in the ground.'

'I can fix it so they'll never find you. The city and the villages are not the be-all and end-all. There's a whole world out there.' She pointed to the dawn horizon.

He continued marching towards a large wooden shed. She racked her brains, trying to work out how to convince him. As soon as she was back in the city, she'd be trapped. She'd have no way out ever again. She told herself she wasn't going back there. Whatever it took.

'You don't want the Engineer telling you what to do forever. Do you?'

'I work for him,' he said. 'That's all.'

'You're scared of him. And he tells you what to do.'

'It's not like that,' he said.

'It looked that way to me.'

He stopped and turned on her. 'You need to keep your mouth shut. You hear?'

She waited.

With a quick snarl, he turned away and headed across the ash.

She followed. 'What do you want to do?' she asked, ignoring his threat.

He strode across the ground, not reacting to her.

'There's a big world out there. You don't want to be stuck here in the villages, being the Engineer's lap dog.'

He stopped, but this time, he didn't face her. Even so, his anger and annoyance was there in his tight, hunched shoulders.

'Doesn't matter where you or I go,' he said. 'The government controls the oxygen on the blockchain. A few seconds tapping away on their keyboards and I'd be down to my last thousand. No thanks.'

'What's your name?' she asked.

He walked onwards. 'Give it up, will you? You're not getting out of this, no matter how clever you think you are.' He hesitated. 'Look, I don't have any reason to hurt you. To tell you the truth, I couldn't give a damn what happens to you. Besides, the moment you get back into the city, you'll get a telling-off and then Daddy will put you back in your tower with as much Blue you can snort. It really isn't the end of the world for the likes of you.'

He stopped. She hated the look he gave her. Like she was undeserving ... as though she'd asked for her life. But she hadn't. What did he know about any of it?

'It's no good looking at me like that,' he said, raising an eyebrow. He set off again. 'Let's go.'

She stood her ground. 'What if there was no blockchain and you could go anywhere. Where would you go?'

The bald man stopped and raised his hands into the air. 'Can we stop with the questioning? Hurry up. I can carry you if you'd like. I'm getting you to the south entrance and that's all there is to it.'

Reluctantly, she followed him, walking as slowly as she could without angering him further.

'Where's the Engineer?' she asked. 'Is he going to be there?'

He sniffed and spat again as he lumbered towards the shed. 'He'll be there.'

'He's afraid of my father, isn't he? And Carlisle?'

'Afraid?' he shook his head. 'It's not a matter of being scared. It's about being smart. Not doing nothing stupid.'

'Are *you* afraid of them?'

'You talk way too much. You know that?'

'And you spit too much.'

He spat again.

They continued in silence. Astrid took in the horizon, which was turning lighter blue with shades of purple. She hadn't managed to stay out of the city for more than a night. Thinking back to Jake and the others, she cursed her luck. What were the chances of them turning up only minutes after she'd switched off the security, ready to escape? What had she done to deserve that sort of bad luck?

'Bear,' the guy said, stopping at the entrance to the shed.

'What?' she asked.

'My name. That's what they call me. And if I could go anywhere, it would be the Barren Sea.'

She felt a glimmer of hope. Maybe she could convince him to help her. Many things raced through her mind, but all she could do was nod at him.

He opened the shed doors. She peered inside and saw a car. She had never seen one like that before. No one actually drove petrol cars any more – the fuel was way too scarce.

'How did you get that?' she asked, walking inside. She'd seen images and videos of them. This one looked brand-new, its blue paint reflecting the little light coming in through the open doors.

'It's the Engineer's. He has a few of them.' He held her arm and pushed her towards the passenger side.

'I can do it,' she said, snatching away her arm and opening the car door.

'Get in,' he said.

'I get the idea.' She fell into the seat and Bear slammed the door shut. She watched him walk around the front of the car and get in the driver's side. He took a key from his pocket and pushed it into the slot, causing the dash to light up. A second later the car's engine growled, and they rumbled out through the shed doors.

She watched him operate the lever beside his left thigh, then place both hands on the steering wheel, directing the car across the same dirt track they'd walked along. He was operating the pedals with both feet. She watched him, wanting to know how it was done.

'It's not too late,' she said. 'We can leave. I'll get Blue Oxygen for you. As much as you want. I don't want to go back to the city.'

He ignored her.

'Please,' she said.

'It's too late.' He moved the lever again and the car sped up, the engine growling even more loudly.

She glanced at the door beside her.

'It's locked,' he said. 'You're not getting out that way.'

She tried pressing the button to open the window, but it didn't work. Now she was in the car, any chance of escape was disappearing fast. It was over. She'd soon be back in the city and would never leave it again.

## CHAPTER 29

### JAKE

JAKE MUST HAVE BEEN DOWN to his last few hundred litres of oxygen. He wanted to be unaware of the air he breathed, but that was impossible. He'd always been aware – everyone was.

The tram rattled as it changed track and headed for West Gate and the south entrance to the city. It stopped short of the gate, but it was the best he could do. He'd have to find a way of getting closer without being seen. Easier said than done. Particularly now it was morning. The area leading to the south entrance was in the open. The Engineer would see him coming. Without thinking, Jake reached into his coat pocket for his gun. Not that it would do him much good if he couldn't get close to the Engineer. His stomach twisted.

'Last stop,' said an electronic voice from the speaker above his seat.

He pulled himself up using the bar that ran across the back of the seat in front of him. His legs were stiff. He stumbled to the open tram doors, willing himself to jump out onto the dirt track. A swirl of dust surrounded him as the tram started up and headed back the way it had come.

'Go,' he told himself. 'Go.'

He strode across the ground. He would do whatever it took to take Astrid from the Engineer. Using her was the only way out of the mess he was in.

He was close enough to the city to see individual windows reflecting the grey clouds hovering above the villages behind him and the towers in front. He pulled his coat hood over his head. The wall to his left, leading up to the south entrance, was the only cover he would find, so he picked up his pace and followed the wall. Columns held up a tattered awning running alongside the wall that he used for cover. The solid concrete wall emitted – or reflected – a warmth that reminded him of his sister's shack, which in turn reminded him of Bailey and Jess. No matter how hard he tried to do the right thing, he always seemed to make things worse. How was that possible?

He followed the wall as it arced to the left. To his right were open fields of ash. A haze of ash spiralled upwards from the ground, carried by the growing breeze. He tasted it, felt it coating his face.

Movement ahead made him stop. People walking beside a car. The car's engine was running, grey smoke spurting from its exhaust. He'd seen cars outside his sister's shack, but Bailey had only used those for parts. He hadn't seen one actually functioning for some time. It was a shiny blood-red. It had to be the Engineer. Flattening himself against the brick, his hand in his pocket holding the gun, he shuffled along the wall. There were several people surrounding the car, but he couldn't make out who they were. He continued to creep alongside the wall, using the shade of the awning as cover. As he got closer to the south entrance, the wall led out into the field of ash, allowing him to get closer. Unable to see them, he jogged for nearly a minute until the wall curved back towards the south entrance. The car came back into view, followed by the figures. He could make them out now. There was the Engineer, standing next to the car. Close to the south entrance were three men dressed in black suits. They worked for Carlisle. He'd seen the type before. It would be their job to make the exchange and take Astrid back into the city.

A deep rumbling made Jake spin around and duck. It was another car. This one was blue and was moving fast. The car's wheels kicked up plumes of smoke as the car careened across the ash, as though ready to take off. The three men in black suits took guns from their holsters. Jake watched as the Engineer raised his hands, placating them. The blue car slowed as it approached the Engineer and the red car, circling both and coming to a stop.

Simultaneously, one man got out of the red car and one out of the blue car. They sauntered to the back of the blue car. One of them opened the boot. They reached inside and began to pull out bags. It had to be the Blue Oxygen they had taken from Astrid's tower. Jake clenched his fists, remembering why he'd stolen that oxygen in the first place. But Bailey was gone.

The two men carried the bags over to the three men in suits, and threw them down. Then the Engineer pushed Astrid towards the men.

Jake took the gun from his coat pocket. His only chance of saving his sister and niece was to take Astrid and make her father listen to him. What else could he do? He was going to run out of oxygen soon, anyway. He gripped the gun, his hands and legs trembling.

'Do something,' he told himself. 'Do something!'

Two of the men in suits collected the bags and turned to go back through the south entrance. The third man reached for Astrid. She refused to take his hand.

Without realising it, Jake was running. It made no sense; why would he run *towards* these men, who had guns and who would kill him on sight? But he was running all the same. He lifted his gun, aimed it at the Engineer and fired.

# *CHAPTER 30*

## ASTRID

GUNFIRE EXPLODED over Astrid's head. She fell to the ground, crawled towards the car Bear had driven, and got into the driver's seat. The Engineer and Bear were running for cover behind the blue car. Gunshots came from across the ash next to the south entrance. She kept her head down, now and then popping up to see who it could be. Bear rummaged inside the boot of the blue car and pulled out a rifle.

'Shit! Shit!' Astrid checked the key was still inside the slot, then fumbled for the button that would start the car's engine. She went over what Bear had done. 'Where is it?' She tried several buttons until finally the car barked into life.

'Hey!' Bear shouted. 'Don't you dare!'

A bullet ricocheted off the bonnet. She ducked then raised her head again, wanting to see who it was and work out which way she should drive.

She pushed and pulled the lever to her left, with no idea what she was doing. The car jolted forward, making her grip the steering wheel. She pushed her foot against one pedal and the car lurched forward. Instinctively, she slammed her foot on another pedal. It made the car shunt forward and skid to a stop.

She checked over her shoulder and saw Bear running towards her. Another bullet ricocheted off the car and she ducked, slamming her foot down on the first pedal. The car hurtled forward. A dust cloud rose behind her. Bear was running after her, then he stopped and shielded his eyes with both arms.

The car was going faster. She'd never driven before, but she told herself that all she needed to do was keep her foot on the pedal and keep the car aimed in one direction – away from the city. It was difficult to focus on anything in front, as bullets smacked into the rear of the car. The back window smashed.

'No!' She tugged the steering wheel to the left, making the car skid sideways and lose control. The car was doing what it wanted, without her input. It came to a stop and the engine cut out. She fumbled again for the button that would bring the engine back to life. Clouds of ash submerged the car, making it impossible to see out of the windows.

'Come on!' she snapped, pressing every button she could find. One button made the car sputter and choke, but wouldn't bring it back to life. She thumped the steering wheel in frustration. For all she knew, Bear would be there in seconds.

'Hurry!' someone shouted. 'Get us out of here.'

The passenger door swung open and someone got in. It was a man, covered in ash so only his eyes shone through. She recognised the eyes. It was Jake.

'Go!' Jake shouted.

'How did you...?'

'Get out of here!' Jake said again, pressing buttons at

random on the dashboard. The car growled. More bullets pinged against the car.

Astrid slammed her foot on the pedal. The car's wheels spun in the ash before finding purchase. The car shot forward. She held on to the steering wheel and pushed her foot down on the pedal as hard as she could, all the time screaming in time with the car's engine. She glanced over at Jake, who had turned to aim his gun through the smashed rear window.

'They're following,' he said.

'Who?' she asked, squinting in the rear-view mirror. She leaned closer to the mirror until there it was – the blue car, bursting through ash, moving faster than her car.

'Faster!' Jake shouted.

'I'm going as fast as it will let me.' She couldn't imagine going any faster. She was barely holding on to the steering wheel as it was.

'They're catching up,' Jake said, sitting forward, reading the buttons on the dashboard.

Astrid looked over her left shoulder. The blue car was about to draw level.

'I'm going to try something,' Jake said. 'Hold on to the steering wheel.'

'What the hell do you think I'm doing?' Astrid shouted.

Jake wiped the dust from the dashboard then rested a finger on a button. 'Ready?'

Astrid gripped the steering wheel even harder, her knuckles white. 'For what?' she asked. 'What does that button do?'

'Bailey told me all about them. It's a turbo. It pushes more fuel and air into the engine. Brace yourself.'

Jake glanced across at the blue car, which was nearly level with them. Astrid followed his gaze. The Engineer was in the back seat. He was holding a gun, ready to shoot.

'Now!' Jake said, and pressed the button.

The car responded immediately, the rear dropping and the front rising. A loud bang followed by a violent roar shook the car.

'What the hell?' she shouted. Her hands shook, until she felt she couldn't hold the steering wheel any longer. Jake reached across and held the steering wheel with one hand, his other reaching across her, aiming his gun through the window at the blue car.

Just as Astrid thought the car would slow down, it seemed to pick up even more speed. 'I can't hold it!' she screamed. 'It's too fast!'

'A little more,' Jake said. 'Just a bit further.'

The ash cleared, revealing the villages in the distance. 'We're going to run out of ash,' she said, taking her foot off the accelerator. The car didn't respond.

Jake pressed the button on the dashboard again. The car engine responded, easing back.

'Head for the villages,' he said, pointing in the distance.

There was no sign of the blue car.

## *CHAPTER 31*

JAKE

'Pull over,' Jake said. But Astrid wasn't listening. She was still panicked, looking over her shoulder, driving erratically. Jake had directed her through several streets, and was pretty sure they'd lost the other car.

'Pull over!' Jake shouted.

Astrid jerked the car to the right, her eyes wide, staring at him.

'It's okay,' he said. 'They're not following. We lost them.' He placed a hand on her arm, motioning for her to release her fierce grip on the steering wheel.

'What's going on? Why were you shooting at the south entrance?' she asked, stopping the car.

'I need your help,' he said.

She frowned. 'What?'

'Please,' he said. 'I'm sorry. I should never have done it. It was wrong. But—'

'It was wrong?' she asked, sitting up straight then opening the door.

'Wait,' he said, reaching to stop her getting out of the car and pointing the gun at her. 'I'm sorry. But I need your help.'

'What the hell?' She closed the door and leaned away from him.

He scanned all around, worried there might be people watching. But there was no one there. He lowered the gun.

'What do you want from me?' she pleaded, her eyes on the gun sitting on his lap.

He reached over and tried to touch her arm again, but she flinched and pulled away. He rubbed his forehead and exhaled. 'Look. I don't want to hurt you...'

'It's too late,' she said. 'This is all your fault.'

'No!' he snapped. 'I tried to stop them from taking you.'

'It was you who brought them to my home. Just leave me alone.' She reached for the door.

'Stop,' he said. 'They'll find you. If you go on your own, they will find you before the hour is out.'

'What makes you think I don't want them to find me?'

He shook his head. 'I saw what you did. You risked everything to leave your home. Why did you do that?'

She went to speak, but hesitated.

'I'm guessing you don't want to go back to the city. You were trying to leave when we found you, weren't you? Where were you going?'

'Why should I tell you anything?' she said.

'I'm not going to hurt you. But I need your help. And I can help you. I can stop them from finding you.'

She stared straight ahead.

'You want to leave the city,' he said. 'I know the villages. I know people who can help.'

'I don't trust you. I don't trust any of you.'

'Any of who?' he asked. 'You mean us ... villagers?'

She lowered her gaze.

'You think you're different, don't you?' he said. 'You think villagers are like animals?'

'You've done little to convince me otherwise.' She hesitated, then quickly reached for the door handle.

'Wait,' he said.

'You said you won't hurt me. So what are you going to do to stop me leaving?' She opened the door.

'Goddamn!' he said. 'Just wait. We can help each other. When we have what we want, we can each go our own way. I promise. You'll never make it on your own. Trust me.'

She stopped, the door left open.

'Trust you?' she asked. 'Why would I do that?'

'You don't have a choice,' he said. 'We have to be quick. They'll track us down and take you back to the city.'

Groaning, she slammed the door. 'What do you want from me?'

'You have to help me speak to Carlisle.'

She laughed. 'Carlisle? You're kidding, right? What makes you think I can get you anywhere close to him?'

'He's the only one who can reinstate oxygen. I have to find him.'

She looked suspiciously at him. 'Reinstate? Are you out?'

'It's not me. It's my sister and my niece. Carlisle has deleted their quota.'

She frowned deeply. 'Because of what you did?'

'Yes. It's your father. He did this. He saw my face on the security cameras and got Carlisle to delete mine, my sister's, and my niece's oxygen.'

Astrid bowed her head. 'I'm sorry. For your sister and your niece. But I can't do anything to help you.'

'You can,' he said. 'I don't care about my oxygen. But my

sister and my niece have done nothing wrong. I can't let this happen to them because of something I did.'

She looked at him with what he saw as genuine sympathy. 'Once they have amended the oxygen blockchain, they can't change it back. You know that.'

'There has to be a way. To add more oxygen for them.'

'It's not that simple,' she said. 'There's a fixed amount. They can't create it out of nothing. Their oxygen will have been distributed elsewhere. Into Blue Oxygen.'

Jake rubbed the back of his neck and closed his eyes. 'I have to do something. If you can get me to Carlisle, I can make him see reason.'

Astrid brushed hair away from her eyes with a trembling hand.

'Please,' he said. 'I promise I will keep you safe. You want to leave the city. I can't say I understand why ... but I can make it happen.'

'I'm not going back to the city,' she said.

'It will only be for a short time. I just need your help to find him. Leave the rest to me.'

She stared at the steering wheel. 'You can help me reach Moscov City?'

'Yes,' he said. 'Of course. Once you've helped me, I can help you.'

She waited, then nodded slowly. 'You drive.'

He watched her get out of the car and walk around the front. He moved across to the driver's seat and started the engine. Astrid opened the passenger door and got in.

'Thank you,' he said.

She shook her head. 'Don't thank me yet.'

## *CHAPTER 32*

### ASTRID

THEY FOLLOWED THE TRAM TRACKS, heading for somewhere Jake had told her was called West Gate.

'We should leave the car on the outskirts,' he said. 'We can't be seen in it.'

'How long before the Engineer finds us?' she asked.

Jake checked the rear-view mirror, as if he might already be behind them. 'I'm not sure. He'll have already let those who would benefit from getting hold of us know.' He turned the steering wheel and hit the brakes. 'We need to keep a low profile.'

'Where are we?' she asked.

'My sister's place.' Jake drove the car into a tight spot then got out and covered the car in a polythene tarpaulin. He picked up a rock and hid the key beneath it.

Astrid longed to be as far away from the city as possible. But it was still there in the distance, looming over her.

'This way,' Jake said, jogging towards an untidy shack.

Astrid hesitated. Jake hopped up onto the porch and opened the door to the shack. He turned to Astrid. 'Come on. We need to be quick.'

Astrid sighed, folded her arms and walked over to the shack and up the steps. She followed Jake inside.

There was no mistaking the woman inside: she was Jake's sister. The similarity was obvious. His sister even had Jake's cold, stern, dark eyes.

Astrid nodded at her before looking around the shack.

'You're from the city?' Jake's sister asked.

Jake stood between them. 'Astrid, this is my sister, Grace. Grace, this is Astrid.'

Grace stood with arms folded.

'Where's Jess?' Jake asked his sister.

'She doesn't know what's happening. If that's what you're asking,' Grace snarled at Jake.

'I'm going to fix it,' Jake said. 'I promise.'

Grace seemed to give in, and beckoned Astrid towards her. 'Come inside. Sit down.'

'I'm fine,' Astrid said. 'Thank you.'

Jake rushed into a room next to the kitchen area.

'What are you looking for?' Grace asked. She looked confused as the sound of Jake moving things echoed through the wall. His sister followed Jake into the other room but stopped as he walked back through the door.

Grace gasped when she saw what he was carrying. 'What the hell are they doing here?'

Astrid leaned to the side to see two guns in Jake's hands.

'They're Bailey's,' Jake said. 'He said if I ever needed them, to take them.'

'Why are they in my home?' Grace asked, trying to take them from Jake.

'I need them,' he said.

'You're going to get yourself killed.' Grace tried to wrestle them from Jake, who lifted a hand, motioning for her to stop. He spoke in a gentle voice that Astrid had not heard before.

'You know I'm going to die anyway.' He pushed the guns into his coat pockets then reached for Grace's hand.

She nodded, biting her lip.

'I'm sorry, Grace. But I promise I'm going to fix it. I'm going to make sure you and Jess have all the oxygen you need.'

'I don't care about me,' Grace said. 'But get Jess's back. I couldn't bear it if she...' Tears filled her eyes.

Jake reached out to hold her. This time Grace gave in and let him. Astrid looked away. Jake kissed Grace on the top of her head. He whispered something to her Astrid couldn't make out, then let go of his sister and hurried through the shack towards the door.

'Who are you, exactly?' Grace asked Astrid. 'What are you doing here?' Disapproval coloured her words.

'I want to leave the city for good. I don't approve of what my father has done,' Astrid said. 'Or those in control of the oxygen blockchain.'

'But no doubt you still have most of your quota?' Grace asked, her words barbed.

'Grace,' Jake said, turning back. 'Don't. She's going to help us.'

'It's not my fault,' Astrid said, and immediately regretted saying so. Even she recognised how childish it sounded.

Grace raised an eyebrow.

'I mean...' Astrid stuttered. 'I never asked to ... to be treated differently.'

'But you are,' Grace said. 'And so are many of your friends who live in the city.'

'They're not my friends,' Astrid said. She composed herself. 'I'm sorry.'

'You don't have to apologise,' Jake said.

Grace gave Jake a confused look. He took a step towards his sister. 'Astrid's going to help me speak to Carlisle.'

'You're crazy,' Grace said. 'You won't get anywhere near him. And even if you do, what makes you think he'll help us?'

'I'll make him,' Jake said. 'I'll do whatever it takes.'

His sister sighed heavily and shook her head.

'I'll be back soon,' Jake said. 'I promise.'

'Don't make promises you can't keep,' Grace said.

There was nothing left for Jake to say. His shoulders slumped, he turned and headed outside. Astrid followed him.

'Where now?' Astrid asked him.

'We find Carlisle,' he said.

# CHAPTER 33

## JAKE

THEY BOARDED the near empty tram and headed for the city.

'I don't like this,' she said. 'I want to stay out of the city, not go back there.'

'I know,' he said. 'We'll leave as soon as possible, I promise.'

Jake was sitting opposite Astrid, avoiding eye contact with the man beside him; he wasn't in the mood for talking to strangers.

'Do you know what you're going to do or say?' Astrid asked him.

'No,' he snapped. He noticed the man next to him lean away. 'I'm sorry, but you do understand why I have to do something, don't you? I'm not lying. My sister and my niece are going to run out of oxygen in a matter of hours.'

Astrid scratched her temple and leaned back in her seat.

'Look,' Jake said, leaning forward. 'I promise I'll help you once I've done this. All I want is for you to get me close to Carlisle. He's the only one who can help them.'

Astrid's body was rigid, her arms folded.

'By this time tomorrow,' he whispered, 'you could be out of the city for good.'

Astrid leaned towards him. 'I won't be able to get Carlisle to see us. Not without him telling my father. I'll never get back out.' Her eyes were wide, reminding him of the look she had given him when Cray and Stan were threatening to kill her.

'You're scared,' he said. 'I get it.'

'No. I'm not,' she said, crossing her legs.

Jake ran a hand through his hair. 'I won't leave you in the city. I promise.'

'You could be dead before nightfall. Where does that leave me?'

Jake recoiled at the thought.

The tram clattered along the tracks, rocking him back and forth. His own breathing caught his attention. She was right. He might not see another morning.

After a brief silence, Astrid spoke flatly. 'I shouldn't have said that.' Her eyes were softer, filled with sympathy. At first it was a consolation, but then he remembered his sister and Jess, and he was filled with resentment again towards people like Astrid – those who lived in the city – who gave no thought to the villagers.

'I don't need your sympathy,' he said. 'Just your help. Then I will help you and we're even. You can speak to Carlisle and get him to do something.'

She opened her mouth, but no words came out. She sat back and looked away from Jake.

It took another twenty minutes for them to reach the end of the line. Jake and Astrid were the last off the tram.

Inhaling the familiar dry stench of the ash fields, he headed off towards the city wall. He turned sideways now and then to check that Astrid was with him.

'Should you be using up your oxygen?' she asked.

'I don't have a choice,' he said.

'We could have used the car.'

'How many cars do you see around here?' Jake pointed off into the distance towards the villages. 'We'd have been spotted long before we got close to the city.'

Astrid faced the opposite direction, walking backwards. 'Do you think he'll come after us? The Engineer?'

'Yes,' Jake said. 'As soon as he works out where we are.'

When she turned back, he saw something in her expression. He wasn't sure what it was, but intuition told him she was hiding something.

'What?' he asked.

'Nothing,' she said, lowering her head.

He tried to control his breathing. Astrid was right – the walk to the city would use up much of his oxygen.

'What will your father do?' he asked, wanting to take his mind off his breathing.

'Do?' she asked, frowning.

'To find you. What will he be doing now?'

Astrid's jaw clenched, as if she was remembering something painful. 'I don't know.'

'Why would he do that to my sister and my niece?' he asked.

'We don't know he did it,' she said. 'You're only guessing.'

'Who else could have done it?'

She stopped dead. A cloud of ash billowed up around her feet.

'*Who?*' he snapped.

She muttered something he couldn't make out.

'What?' he asked.

'I don't know!' she said. 'But you assume it's my father.

And you were the one who kidnapped me – took me out of my home and put me in danger.'

'I stopped them from hurting you,' he said. 'Remember? I stopped them from killing you. Me!' He turned and walked away.

'You brought them to my home!' she shouted. 'It was your fault.'

He stopped but couldn't face her. She was right. He peered over his shoulder.

'I was ready to leave,' she said. 'I had it all planned, and then you turned up, ready to take what wasn't yours.'

'Not mine?' he said, spinning around and glaring at her. 'That oxygen does not belong to you or your goddamn father. That oxygen belongs to everyone. What makes you think it belongs to you?'

Astrid clenched her fists and pushed them down by her sides. 'You're a thief!'

Jake pinched his nose and stared at the ground, wanting to collect his thoughts. 'Yes,' he said. 'I'm a thief. I am.' He exhaled, his chest loosening.

A gentle breeze raced across the ground, lifting swirls of dust in the space between them.

'I never wanted to hurt you,' he said. 'When I took them to your home, I planned to take the Blue, and that was all. But I would never have let them hurt you.'

'Is that so?' she said, one eyebrow raised.

'Yes,' he said, trying to show how serious he was. 'I'm a thief. But that's where it stops.'

The breeze died down, and a quiet unlike any he could remember fell over the two of them.

She shook her head and walked past him towards the city.

## *CHAPTER 34*

ASTRID

Astrid waited behind Jake for him to unlock the grate at the far end of the pipe.

'There,' he said as the metal grate clanked and swung open. 'I'll help you down.'

'I can do it myself,' she said, turning around and letting her legs swing down. She lowered herself into the pool and gasped at the cold water.

Jake swam away from her, only his head above the water. Now it was light, they'd be easier to spot. She pushed off with her feet and swam behind Jake.

Climbing up the ramp into the undergrowth, she shivered.

'You need to show me the way to Carlisle's home,' Jake said.

At that moment she resented him. She was back in the city and was now wet and freezing cold.

'I need to find a change of clothes,' she said.

'We will,' Jake said, ducking down behind a row of bushes. 'But I need you to show me where he is.'

'I'll need a change of clothes to get inside.'

Jake frowned at her.

'Today is Carlisle's fundraiser,' she said. 'He's holding a masquerade ball. People will come to it from all over the city.'

'Why does he need more credits?' Jake asked.

'Who knows why rich people want more?' She shrugged. 'But they tend to be the ones who do.'

'Won't your father be there?' he asked, raising his head above the bushes.

'I think he'll be pretty occupied trying to find his wayward daughter.'

Jake looked confused for a second, then nodded. 'Will you get me inside?' he asked.

'I don't know. I will have to get in and find a way of sneaking you inside, too.'

'But how will you get in?' he asked. 'You can't just walk in. The moment they see you, they'll be on to your father.'

She shivered more violently. 'Since it's a masquerade, that will give me time to find his son.'

'His son?'

'His name is Tom. I know him. He will help me.'

Jake scratched his head. 'Maybe we should wait until after the party. When he's alone.'

Astrid stared at Jake's chest as though his quota was etched there. 'You don't have that much time. The ball will go on all day and night. If you want to see Carlisle, this is your only chance.'

'Where will we find clothes?' he asked.

'This way.' Astrid ran towards the first street on the other side of the park that separated the city from the wall and the pipeline.

It was early, so few people were outside. Only two cars passed them. Jogging helped to keep her warm, but her wet clothes were heavy. She checked on Jake. He was also breathing heavily, which wasn't good. Her back to a wall, she stretched and inhaled deeply.

'Are you okay?' she asked him.

'You mean, because of the oxygen?' he asked.

She said nothing, just waited for him to continue.

'If we can find some Blue,' he said, 'that would be useful.'

She remembered all the Blue stashed away in her home. She was also using her quota. It gave her a sensation of both fear and excitement ... as though she were both dying but more alive simultaneously.

'Follow me,' she said.

Lucy's place was on Cardinal Street, near her own tower. Astrid's mother and father were most likely at home, waiting for news about where she was. It was not her intention to hurt them or make them worry. But they had trapped her for so long, she had no choice but to leave.

Breathless, Astrid stopped and ducked behind a low concrete wall at the rear of one of the smaller towers on the street. 'My friend will help us,' she said.

Jake nodded, scanning all around.

Astrid grabbed a handful of small pebbles from beneath a row of plants that ran alongside the rear of the building. She threw pebbles, one at a time, against a window two storeys up. She missed several times before striking the glass window. A face appeared. It was Lucy. Astrid stood and waved. Lucy peered down, frowning, her hands in the air, asking what she was doing there. Astrid motioned for Lucy to come down to her, placing a finger to her lips. Lucy shook her head, confused. Astrid continued waving. Finally Lucy vanished from the window.

Astrid hid behind the low concrete wall next to Jake.

'Can we trust her?' Jake asked.

'Yes,' Astrid said without hesitation.

The click of a door made them both peer over the wall. Lucy appeared and gestured for them to go to her.

Astrid grabbed Jake's arm and pulled him with her.

'What are you doing here?' Lucy asked. 'Your mother and father have been looking everywhere for you.'

'I'll explain everything,' Astrid said, holding open the door.

Jake rushed inside, panting.

'Who's this?' Lucy asked before covering her mouth, her eyes wide in panic.

'It's okay,' Astrid said, holding Lucy's shoulders. 'He's with me. It's okay.'

Lucy, still with a hand covering her mouth, shook her head violently.

'Yes, he's from the villages,' Astrid said, reading her mind.

'What's going on?' Lucy asked. 'Astrid?'

Astrid was shivering. 'I'll explain everything, I promise. But I really need to get out of these clothes. Is there somewhere I can change?'

Lucy stared at Jake, who, Astrid thought, was trying to look as harmless as possible.

'Lucy?' Astrid said. 'Please. I need your help.'

As if waking from a dream, Lucy moved quickly. 'Yes. Follow me.'

Astrid glanced at Jake before following Lucy up the stairs.

## CHAPTER 35

### JAKE

Jake waited in the hall by the bedroom door as Astrid tried to calm her friend.

'Lucy,' Astrid said, stopping her from using a phone. 'Listen to me.'

'I'm telling your mother you're here,' Lucy said.

'You can't do that,' Astrid said, grabbing the phone from Lucy's hand.

'What's gotten into you?' Lucy asked, wide-eyed.

Astrid threw Lucy's phone onto the bed and faced her friend. 'Look, I need your help. You know how much I want to get out of the city. I'm going to do it. But I need your help.'

Lucy stared nervously at Jake. Astrid looked over her shoulder at him.

'Jake's going to help me reach Moscov City.'

'Why?' Lucy asked. 'I don't understand.' She gave Jake a disdainful look before leaning in closer to Astrid. 'He's ... a villager.'

'I can hear you,' Jake said.

Lucy was short, almost childlike, with her hair tied up in a ponytail with a white ribbon.

'Look at me,' Astrid said, placing a hand on Lucy's shoulder. 'I need clothes.' Astrid looked down at herself. 'I'm freezing.'

Lucy sighed and turned away to look through her drawers and wardrobe. She took out a pair of trousers and offered them to Astrid.

'No,' Astrid said with an embarrassed glance at Jake. 'I need a dress.'

'A dress?' Lucy frowned. 'Why? You never wear dresses.'

Astrid reached past Lucy into the wardrobe and pulled out a black dress. She laid the dress on the bed then went back to the wardrobe. 'I need shoes.'

'Astrid?' Lucy pleaded. 'Tell me what you're going to do. You're scaring me.'

'I'm going to see Tom Carlisle.'

'Tom?' Lucy asked. 'Why? You've just refused to marry him. Have you changed your mind?'

Astrid stood, holding a pair of black heels. She glanced at Jake, her face colouring.

Jake wondered who this Tom was, and why Astrid had turned him down.

'Of course not,' Astrid said. 'I need to speak to his father.'

'Cameron Carlisle? Why?'

Astrid removed her jacket and dropped it to the floor. Astrid and Lucy faced Jake and then froze. Jake stared at one, then the other, confused.

'Can you give me a moment?' Astrid asked, nodding towards the door.

Jake flinched, banging his hand against the open door. 'Yes. Of course. Sorry.' He stumbled out of the room, pulling the door almost fully closed behind him. He stood in the hallway staring up at the ceiling, thinking how foolish he was.

Astrid and Lucy were moving around inside the room, their voices muffled. A gentle breeze came from the slightly open door. He was about to close it but, as he could make out what the women were saying, he stopped.

'He's going to help me,' Astrid said. Her voice was muffled, and Jake guessed she was changing into the dress. 'I'm leaving the city for good. I can't stay here. I need some things from you. Do you have a rucksack?'

Then there was rustling and the banging of cupboards and drawers being opened and closed. He couldn't make out what they were saying.

He edged closer to the door in order to hear better.

'How can you trust him?' Lucy asked. 'You don't know him. He could hurt you.'

'No,' Astrid said. 'He tried to stop the other men from hurting me. He's not like that.'

Jake concentrated on their quiet voices.

'What does he want you to do?' Lucy asked her.

'He wants me to talk to Carlisle. He has no oxygen left. His sister and niece have been punished too. Carlisle has taken away their quotas.'

It was silent. Or were they just talking too quietly for him to hear? But then he could hear them again.

'There must be a reason,' Lucy said. 'What did he do?'

'He's a raider. He was at my house, raiding Blue Oxygen.'

Lucy gasped. 'What? He's a thief? Why are you helping him?'

'Like I told you, he's going to help me reach Moscov City. I can't carry on living here, Lucy. I can't.'

'Why would you want to leave here and use up your quota? I don't understand.'

'I know you don't,' Astrid said.

Jake understood, and he fought the urge to tell Astrid.

'Come in,' Astrid said.

It took a few seconds for Jake to realise she was talking to him. He pushed open the door and entered. The moment he saw Astrid, he froze. She was standing on the far side of the room, illuminated by the dull, smoky light coming through the window. She was a different woman, yet it was Astrid, in high heels and a black dress. He knew she was pretty, but seeing her now made her look more than pretty. Whatever he was feeling for Astrid, it was new, unlike any sensation he had experienced before. Everything was sinking and lifting, his stomach twisted, his vision swirling. And in the back of his mind was a warm, nostalgic feeling that reminded him of the sensation he felt when inhaling Blue Oxygen. He was alive and paying the price for it. He was living, and he was there with Astrid.

'What is it?' Astrid asked, her face worried. She looked embarrassed, and he hated that she felt that way because of him.

'Jake? What's wrong?'

'You're going to wear that?' he heard himself say.

Astrid's shoulders fell. 'It's all I can come up with. You were the one who dragged me through a pipe filled with dirty water, then took me for a swim in a stagnant pool. Remember?'

'Yes. I mean, I know. But—'

'We need to go,' Astrid said, striding towards the door. 'Do you have any Blue?' she asked Lucy.

Lucy shook her head. 'Sorry.' She glanced up at the ceiling. 'The storage room is locked.'

Astrid kissed Lucy's cheek and turned to leave.

'Wait,' Lucy said, and reached for the rucksack on the bed. She handed it to Astrid. 'Don't forget this.'

Astrid checked inside the rucksack. 'Are the earbuds and masks in here?'

'Yes,' Lucy said eagerly. 'Just like you asked.'

'Thank you.' Astrid headed for the door.

Jake watched Astrid leave the room and head for the stairs, wishing he could tell her what he was really thinking.

## CHAPTER 36

ASTRID

ASTRID POINTED to the street that led past a group of enormous towers.

'Carlisle's place is in the centre of those towers,' she said.

Jake had said nothing since leaving Lucy's apartment, and she thought he was acting even more strangely than usual.

She wasn't used to wearing such a tight dress – or any dress, in fact. She hated the way most young women dressed in the city – as though they were competing with each other to see who could wear the latest, hottest designs. What she'd give to wear her usual loose-fitting flannel trousers. The heels weren't helping either. She tiptoed as much as she could, sticking to the shadows of the towers.

'What am I going to say?' she asked.

'To who?' Jake asked.

She stopped. 'Are you okay? You're behaving really weird.'

'Yeah. I'm fine.' He looked down at himself, then at Astrid's dress. 'Feeling a little underdressed, that's all.'

Astrid blew out air, puffed her cheeks, and rolled her eyes. 'I'm doing this for you. If you're going to make fun, then—'

'No,' he said. 'I'm not making fun. You look...'

Astrid waited, but it soon became clear that he wasn't going to finish his sentence.

'What do I say?' she asked again, checking the way they needed to go. 'To Carlisle?'

Jake rubbed the back of his neck. 'Tell him the truth. That I helped kidnap you, but that it would be wrong to punish my sister and niece for what I did.'

'But why would he listen to me?'

'Make him listen.' A car drove by almost silently. 'Or help me get inside to talk to him myself.'

Astrid thought for a moment. 'I don't see how I could get you inside.'

Jake leaned closer to her. 'I have to try something.' He dropped his chin, and Astrid figured he was thinking about his oxygen quota. 'As long as my sister and niece are okay, that's all that matters.'

Astrid recalled his sister and how defiant she had been. Even in the face of what was happening, she had a hardness that Astrid both feared and admired.

She opened her rucksack to show him the earbuds Lucy had given her. 'We can stay in touch with these.' She offered one to Jake.

He took it.

'Put it in your ear,' she said, fixing hers.

'I didn't think I had to swallow it,' Jake said, sliding the bud into his ear.

'You really can be an arsehole, you know that?'

'Yes,' he said, tapping the bud to test it.

'There will be people arriving soon,' Astrid said. 'These parties begin at midday and end at midday.'

'The city...' Jake said, shaking his head.

Jake's contempt was obvious. She understood why.

Astrid led the way. Now and then, through gaps between the towers, she spotted the odd car drive past, heading for Carlisle's home.

Finally, they arrived in the central region of the city. It always surprised her, no matter how many times she visited. It was a space almost five kilometres square, an open space filled with trees and brightly coloured flowers.

'What is this place?' Jake asked, turning on the spot to take it all in.

'It's Carlisle's home.'

'I've never seen anything like it,' Jake said. 'But ... I don't see a home?'

Astrid pointed into the distance. The small gold box was hard to make out, hidden behind a row of tall trees.

'It's tiny,' Jake said.

Astrid peered down at her feet. 'Most of it is underground. Beneath us.'

Jake took two steps backwards and stared at his feet. 'Why?'

Astrid shrugged and gestured towards the towers in the distance. 'I guess when most people were trying to reach the clouds, Carlisle wanted to do the opposite. That's the way he is.' She took the mask from her rucksack and threw the empty bag by the wall.

'Will it work?' Jake asked.

Astrid stared at the graphite-coloured masquerade mask. It shimmered with pearlescent paint and reminded her of a cat. She held it to her face and looped the attachments over her ears.

Jake stared in that way that unsettled her.

'Wait here,' she said. 'If there's a way to get you inside, I'll let you know.' She tapped the bud in her ear.

Jake nodded.

She looked both ways. There were people walking among the flowers to her right. Where the road ended was a row of cars, from which guests were being dropped off. She tiptoed between the flowers. Men and women in suits and dresses, each wearing a mask, meandered across the open ground. They looked ridiculous. But everyone was headed for the golden box at the centre. There was no way any of the people there would suspect who she was. Why would they? People would have heard how Solomon's daughter had been kidnapped. They would never have believed the truth – that she wanted to leave the city.

Astrid avoided eye contact with anyone. She joined a queue to enter Carlisle's home, standing behind a man and woman who held hands.

'Good afternoon,' the man behind her said.

'Afternoon,' she said, without looking.

'Your dress is stunning,' a woman said.

'Thank you,' Astrid said, lowering her chin and looking away.

She followed the people in front into the gold cube. It was cool inside, with the scent of coconut wafting in from an open door to her right. She passed through the door and stood in the lift with around ten other people. The floor descended. She hadn't been in Carlisle's home for a year, but the memory of the lift had stayed with her. She kept her eyes on the floor, ignoring the walls rushing past her. The lift slowed and finally stopped. She was inside Carlisle's home. In every direction were people – more people than she had ever seen in one place.

Astrid meandered through the crowd, heading for the centre of the underground space. She kept her head down, not wanting anyone to recognise her behind the mask. She knew very few people who would be at this sort of fundraising event. All the same, she moved quickly, glancing up now and then, looking for Tom. The thought of using him to get to his father troubled her, but it was the only way she could get to speak with Carlisle.

'Can you hear me?' Jake asked.

She touched her earbud and answered in a whisper, 'Yes.'

'Can you see Carlisle?' he asked.

'He won't be out in the open,' she said.

'It's his party,' Jake said. 'Why wouldn't he be there?'

'People like Carlisle like to make an entrance. He'll take his time.'

'You have to find him,' Jake said, desperation in his voice.

'I told you,' she said. 'I'll try my best.'

Jake sighed through the earbud. 'Hurry.'

She didn't respond. What did he want from her? She was doing everything she could. And she was risking everything to do it.

She descended a flight of stairs into a lower tier of the vast room. She remembered the enormous space from the last time she had visited. But now the space opened up, reaching higher and higher, until it seemed to reach the sky. How was that possible? It wasn't real. The roof must have been covered in LED screens that painted an artificial sky. Now and then bumping into people, she stared straight up, unable to take her eyes off the vastness of such a construction. A dizziness came over her, as though she was not at the bottom of such a vast space but at the top, peering down.

'What can you see?' Jake asked.

'It's incredible. I've never seen anything like it. Above, on the ceiling, is what looks like a real sky.'

Then the image on the ceiling began to alter, the blues and flawless whites turning to oranges and reds. It was a sunset. There was an excited buzz of conversation, the sound amplified in the enclosed space. The image continued to darken until finally pricks of light emerged. The sky was turning to night.

Astrid shifted her attention from the ceiling and to looking for Tom. She walked one way, then turned and headed another. The longer she stayed there, the more likely it was that someone might try to talk to her, or maybe even recognise her. To her right were many people facing one direction. She pushed her way through the groups of people until she had reached the front. Ahead, behind a glass wall, was a family of lions. She had only ever seen lions on vidi-screens. But there they were, walking through a mock African landscape. The glass was so clear, so tall, that it was almost invisible. So many people talking, pointing in wonder, meant she was pretty much invisible herself. The male lion, bringing up the rear of four females and several cubs, stopped and turned towards her. Its mane was dark brown and black. It raised its head, sniffing the air, then licked its muzzle with a large pink tongue.

How was it possible to house a family of lions underground? There could only be a handful of lion prides left in the world. The male lion paced lazily towards the glass, making the people around her even more excited.

'What's happening?' Jake asked.

It made her jump. 'Lions.' There was silence for a moment, then she said, 'There are lions. Here. Underground.'

Jake was still silent.

'Can you believe that?' she whispered, edging closer to the glass and the oncoming lion.

'Knowing the city?' Jake said. 'Yes, I can.'

Astrid kept her eyes on the lion.

'Please hurry,' Jake said.

Astrid tore her gaze away from the lions and told herself to move. She walked beside the glass, keeping pace with the female lions on the other side. She reached the corner of the cage and followed the glass to the right. Ahead was a ramp that led to the left, away from the lions, and to what looked like a viewing platform overlooking the cage. She followed a silver path, apologising for pushing past people, each holding a flute of champagne. No one took any notice of Astrid, which meant she could raise her head and look for Tom. Loud laughter made her turn to face the viewing area at the top of the winding path. Two suited men peeled away from a small group and headed to the bar next to the glass wall. There he was: Tom, talking to three men. Even wearing a mask, she recognised his body and mannerisms. Astrid turned on the spot, wary that she might have been spotted. She told herself no one was looking for her.

She touched her earbud. 'I see Tom.'

'Hurry,' Jake said.

Astrid strode up the shallow incline towards the viewing platform. As she was working out how to approach him without giving away who she was, Tom bowed to the other men, fastened his suit jacket and left. He walked towards the bar. Astrid tapped his sleeve just as he was about to ask the barman for a drink.

He spun around, frowning deeply.

'It's me,' she said. 'Astrid.'

Tom stared at her, as if trying to look through her mask, then opened his eyes wide. 'Astrid?'

She pulled him away from the bar. 'I have to talk to you.'

# CHAPTER 37

## JAKE

MEANWHILE, on the outside, Jake searched the ground around the golden box, looking for another way inside. Listening to Astrid talking to Tom made him nervous. He heard an apprehension in her voice he'd not heard since Stan had her in his grip.

In the distance, on the other side of the clearing, was a couple walking towards the golden box. Jake ducked down, making sure he was hidden behind the building. As he crawled across the ground, his knee struck something hard, unlike the rest of the undergrowth. He paused, then started digging at the ground beneath him. It didn't take long to shift the weeds and dirt to reveal a metal door. The handle, a metal ring, was inset into the door, covered with dirt.

'Can you hear me?' he said, touching the bud in his ear. 'Astrid?'

There was no response – not even the background noise he'd heard since she entered the party.

He examined the edge of the trapdoor, using his fingers to make out its shape. Then, using all his strength, he pulled the metal ring until the door shuddered open. It was heavy, and he was forced to let it go again.

The bud in his ear buzzed and whistled, then he could hear Astrid again. She was talking to Tom.

## *CHAPTER 38*

ASTRID

'WHAT ARE YOU DOING HERE?' Tom asked her. 'I thought you were—'

Astrid pulled him away from the crowd towards the end of the bar and the glass separating them from the lions beneath. She checked there was no one nearby.

'I'm okay,' she said. 'As you can see.'

'But what are you doing here? Your father is looking everywhere for you. I have to tell him you're safe.' He turned to leave.

'No,' she said, pulling him back. 'Listen to me.'

He stopped, his brow furrowed. 'I don't understand.'

'I need your help,' she said.

'Your mother will be beside herself with worry.'

'Never mind that. I need to talk to your father.'

He shook his head slowly.

'I know this is crazy,' she said, trying to look as sympathetic as she could. 'But it's important.'

Tom breathed in deeply and straightened his jacket. 'You made it clear you weren't interested in us ... in me.'

'Yes,' she said. 'I know. And I'm sorry. I didn't want to hurt you. But I don't ... you know we're not in love.'

His shoulders dropped and his face darkened. She'd hurt him. He really had feelings for her. Genuine feelings. He took a step to the side and looked into the lions' cage.

Astrid followed his line of sight. The female lions were lying down, with the male standing behind them.

'Please,' she said. 'We've known each other a long time. Will you help me?'

He recovered his composure. 'Why do you want to see my father?' He pushed back the sides of his jacket and buried his hands in his trouser pockets.

She took a moment to work out how much to tell him. She knew what she wanted sounded foolish. No one in the city cared about the people in the villages.

'I don't have time to go into it,' she said. 'Will you help me?'

Tom took a hand from his pocket and stroked his chin. 'Will you reconsider?'

'Reconsider?' she asked, surprised. 'Us? You know it wouldn't be right.'

'Our families want this to happen.' He took a small step closer. 'Please reconsider.'

She wanted to tell him she was going to disappear, that she hated living in the city. But Tom wouldn't understand. There was no way she could tell him what she really thought.

'Give me some time to think,' she said. She hated lying to him, but she had no choice.

He smiled. 'Really?' Then his eyes narrowed with suspicion. 'How do I know you're not just saying that?'

She tensed her jaw, then reached over and ran a finger

down the lapel of his jacket. 'Like you said, our fathers will do everything they can to get us to marry. I don't want to go against my father. Just give me some time to think it through.'

His face coloured. He glanced down at her hand touching his jacket, then at her dress. His stare was heavy, and it made her want to run. But she held her breath and stayed as still as she could.

'You will think about it?' he asked. 'Reconsider?'

She tilted her head, looking up at him. 'You know you're a handsome man.' She let go of his jacket. 'It wouldn't be the worst thing.'

'The worst thing?' he asked, straightening his shoulders. 'That's hardly a resounding declaration of love.'

She took a step closer. 'I'm not going to pretend I think of you in that way, Tom. We've known each other for years. But if we try to get to know one another better, then...'

'Then what?' he asked, staring at her mouth.

'Help me,' she said. 'Please.'

She had him where she wanted him. She moved in closer. His Adam's apple moved up, then down.

'Will you talk to your father about us?' he asked.

She nodded.

'I don't know if my father will see us,' he said.

'Try. Please. For me.'

He waited, glancing over at the lions, then turned away and led the way past the bar and over to a narrow doorway guarded by two tall men. They nodded to Tom as he walked by.

'Through here,' he said. 'I will see if he has time to speak to us.'

'He sounds like a catch,' Jake said in Astrid's ear. She couldn't answer, but she hoped she wasn't blushing too much. She breathed in and out slowly, trying to compose herself.

At the end of the corridor was a dark room, lit with pale blue lights that hung from the ceiling like small planets. As her eyes grew accustomed to the dark, she made out a table at the far end of the room, underneath several bigger round blue lights.

'Is my father here?' Tom asked a woman who sat at the table.

There were four women, each dressed in dark blue dresses, their hair dark red, their faces made up with elaborate make-up that made them look almost identical. They each held a glass of champagne.

'He is not ready,' the woman said, placing her glass on the table. She stood and looked Astrid up and down.

'It won't take long,' Tom said.

It was strange, but Tom sounded afraid of them.

The woman strolled by Tom, towards Astrid. 'Your dress is wonderful,' she said. 'But it isn't yours.'

Astrid looked down at her dress. 'How did you know?'

'It's too small for you. Although the slight tightness around your waist and chest is doing you no harm.' She smiled.

Astrid blushed even harder.

'My father?' Tom said with more force.

The woman raised an eyebrow at Tom. She smiled. 'Here he is.' She winked.

'My boy!' someone said from the other side of the room.

It was Carlisle.

'Father.' Tom went to him. 'I have someone who would like to speak to you. It's urgent.'

'Is that so?' Carlisle was as tall and slender as Astrid had remembered. His black hair shone with wax. A dark red tie and red patent shoes punctuated his black suit. Even though short black hairs sprinkled his chin and upper lip, he appeared well-groomed.

'Can we speak alone?' Astrid asked, touching her mask, not wanting the women to recognise her.

Carlisle hesitated before raising a hand to wave the women away. Immediately, the four women stood and left, walking in single file out through a narrow door on the opposite side of the room.

'I hope I am not disturbing you,' Astrid said when the last one had closed the door.

Carlisle waited, glancing from Tom to Astrid and back again.

Astrid took off her mask.

Carlisle laid a hand on his chest. 'Well...'

'I believe that Astrid's father is looking for her,' Tom said.

'I dare say he is,' Carlisle said, his eyes narrowed in suspicion. 'Astrid Solomon?'

'Yes.' Astrid brushed her hair back behind her ears. 'I must speak with you. If I may.'

Cameron scratched his chin then folded his arms. 'I hear you turned down my son's proposal?'

Astrid bowed her head. 'Yes. But we have spoken.' She glanced across at Tom, who was nodding eagerly.

'You have?' Carlisle asked, unfolding his arms. 'And what have you agreed?'

'Can we talk about another issue?' Astrid said. 'Before I discuss Tom and me.'

Carlisle sighed deeply. Astrid was sure he suspected she was only telling Tom what he wanted to hear.

'What's so urgent?' Carlisle asked, checking his watch.

'I'm due to speak to my guests shortly.' He pointed to the door.

'Of course,' she said. 'I won't take up too much of your time.'

Carlisle straightened his shoulders and jacket.

'Are you aware of what happened to me?' she asked.

'You were kidnapped,' he said. 'And now you are here. Which I must confess, is rather baffling.'

'I believe my father spoke to you about who was involved in the kidnapping?'

'Yes. He was adamant about punishing those responsible. The security system identified the images of two men.'

'One of those men is already dead,' she said.

Carlisle opened his eyes wide. 'That's interesting. Not from lack of oxygen, I take it?'

'No,' she said. 'And the other man you have punished is the wrong man.'

Carlisle let out a sharp laugh. 'Is that right?' He looked to compose himself. 'Even though his image was right there on the security system? You think I'm wrong?'

'Not exactly,' she said. 'But the man you have punished was helping me – at least, he tried to help me. It was the other men who were intent on hurting me.'

'I don't have time for this,' Carlisle said, walking past her. 'If you'll excuse me.'

'Please,' she said. 'You have also punished Jake's sister and his niece. You have taken their oxygen too.'

Carlisle stopped and looked over his shoulder. 'Jake? So you know this man?'

'It is wrong to punish them,' she said, ignoring his question.

Carlisle faced her. 'Do you know how many people live in the villages, compared with those who live in the cities?'

Astrid glanced at Tom, unsure where Carlisle was going with his questioning.

Carlisle pushed his hands into his pocket. 'One thousand to one. At least. Have you any idea what would happen if we allowed people from the villages to get away with raiding the city?'

'I don't understand,' she said, again looking at Tom for help.

'You don't,' Carlisle said. 'Few people do. We must be ruthless. If we are not, then they will overrun us. You have unlimited Blue Oxygen, don't you?' His eyes were heavy with accusation.

A childish urge to deny his claim came and went. 'What has that got to do with anything?'

'You are not the same as they are,' he said.

'The same? Of course I am.'

'No, my girl.' Carlisle strolled towards her and touched beneath her chin, his eyes on her lips.

She pulled away.

'You will learn,' he said. 'I know many people who have thought the same as you. But you will learn.'

A surge of defiance made her stand tall. 'You have to give back their oxygen.'

Carlisle stepped backwards and smiled. 'If you'll excuse me. I must see to my guests.' He looked at Tom sternly. 'See your friend out.'

'Wait,' Astrid said.

Carlisle didn't stop.

'I will accept Tom's offer,' she said, and immediately regretted saying it. What was she thinking?

That made Carlisle pause. She couldn't look at Tom, but she could feel his eyes on her.

Carlisle faced her, another smile curling his lips. 'My

girl, Tom asking you was only a formality. You will marry my son. We have already decided that.'

She rolled her hands into fists. She wanted to tell him he was wrong, that he couldn't make her do anything. But the look in his eye made her doubt that she had a choice.

'No,' was all she could say.

Carlisle's smile faded. 'Your father owes me. And don't think for a second you have the freedom of choice. You have all the Blue Oxygen you will ever need. There's a price to pay for immortality, young lady. And you will pay your debt.'

'Father,' Tom said, his voice weak. 'Can't you help her friend?'

Carlisle strolled across the room towards Tom and, without a moment's hesitation, slapped him across the face.

Astrid covered her mouth, her eyes wide with shock.

Tom held his cheek.

Carlisle straightened his tie. 'You should not have brought her to see me. Just when I think you can't disappoint me any more...'

He strode out of the room. Astrid followed, but two men walked into the room and blocked her.

'Please come with us,' one man said.

Astrid tried to push her way between them, but it was no good. They grabbed her arms and pushed her back into the room.

# CHAPTER 39

## JAKE

Concentrating on the earbud, even though Jake couldn't hear exactly what was happening, it was clear Astrid was in trouble.

'Astrid?' he said. 'Can you hear me? What's happening?'

No response.

He gripped the handle of the trapdoor and pulled with all his strength. This time the door lifted, sending dirt falling into the space beneath. With one last effort, he pulled the door open, until it folded over and crashed onto the ground. It was dark inside the rectangular hole, a musty, damp smell rising out of it. He leaned in closer and made out concrete steps.

'Astrid?' he said again.

Still no response.

He took a deep breath and stepped down into the hole, wishing he'd brought a torch. He climbed down the steps, keeping his hands flat on the wall beside him. As the stairs spiralled downwards, the sliver of sky above vanished and he was in total darkness, with only his own breathing to keep him company. This had to be a way into Carlisle's home, but whether there was a door at the end of the dark staircase was a different matter.

He continued to climb further down. The air was heavier, more difficult to inhale. The temperature was rising too. There was no point using the earbud now – all he heard was static.

He was blind and had to rely on his other senses, the most important being his sense of touch. Maintaining contact with the wall gave him some comfort.

Finally, the steps came to an end. Instinctively he reached out and felt for a door, which he found. He searched for the handle and turned it, expecting it to be locked. It wasn't. He pushed the door open and squinted at the light, shading his eyes with a hand.

He was standing on a steel platform, high up. He squinted down at the ground. It was dry and barren, dotted with boulders. What the hell was this place? He was inside the building – he had to be – yet it looked as though he was outside. He squinted upwards. There was the artificial sky that Astrid had described.

There was some kind of glass wall circling the dry ground.

He inhaled deeply, his heart thumping. How much oxygen had he used up climbing the stairs? There couldn't be much of his quota left.

The metal platform led to another set of stairs. These were steel and appeared much flimsier. As he stepped onto the first step, the stairs shuddered. He held on to the railing. As he climbed down, he saw people on the other side of the glass.

He stepped off the last step onto the dry ground. What was this place? He couldn't hear what the people were saying, but they were pointing urgently, looking worried. He scanned the curved glass wall for a doorway or opening. But there was no obvious way out. Then a woman on the other side of the glass, her eyes wide with horror, caught his attention. Slowly, she raised a hand and pointed to something to his right.

'What?' he asked, even though she couldn't hear him.

She was looking at something over his shoulder. With a shudder, he remembered what Astrid said about lions. He turned then froze. A lion. No – two lions. He told his feet to move, but they refused to obey. He raised his hands, trying to look harmless. Both lions were still, until the larger one licked its muzzle. A low grunt made him turn to his right. Another lion. Male.

'Okay,' he said. 'Steady.' Finally, he was walking backwards. He reached into his coat pocket for his gun. Maybe he would have to kill them. Why would Carlisle have lions? The lions remained still, but their gaze was fixed upon him. One of the female lions raised its head and sniffed the air. This wasn't good. He tripped over what felt like a rock, and struggled to regain his balance. He risked looking down. What he had thought was a rock was a dead animal. The carcass was still fresh, the rib cage white, spattered with blood.

He pulled the gun from his pocket. As if it understood, the male lion padded towards him.

'Hey,' Jake said. 'Oh no, you don't.'

But the lion was not interested in listening. Nor did the lion understand guns.

Jake aimed the gun at the lion. It continued to stroll towards him. To his right, the two lionesses were coming closer. He spun around. He couldn't hear them, but the people on the other side were shouting and pointing. The male lion was reflected in the glass. Jake aimed the gun at the base of the glass and fired. The glass wall cracked and splintered, then the entire pane collapsed a second later. He checked over his shoulder. The lions were loping away, scared by the gunshot.

Sound rushed in from outside the glass cage. People were screaming and shouting, many of them running away from the smashed glass cage. Jake jumped over the broken glass and followed them, putting as much distance between himself and the lions as he could.

'What have you done?' one man asked, running in the opposite direction – towards the cage and the lions.

'Where's Astrid?' Jake shouted. He didn't know whether anyone would know who she was, or where she would be, but he began to ask other people. No one was listening. Jake had caused a panic, and people were more concerned about fleeing the lions than talking to him.

Several men, holding rifles, headed for the broken cage. Jake looked all around before heading up a ramp towards what appeared to be a bar. Where was Astrid?

# CHAPTER 40

## ASTRID

THE TWO MEN dragged Astrid out of the room.

'Let me go!' she shouted.

All around, people were screaming, running away from the central part of the building. Even the two men dragging her stopped and spun around, wondering what had caused the mayhem.

Astrid tugged her arm from the man's grip. He reached for her again but before he could grab her, he fell forward, skidding across the floor.

'Leave her alone!' a man shouted.

It was Tom, holding a gun, aimed at the second man, who had now raised both hands.

'Go!' Tom shouted to her.

The second man hesitated, before helping the first man up and running with everyone else towards the exit.

'What are you doing?' she asked Tom.

He lowered the gun. 'I hate him,' he said. 'I know you're not interested in marrying me. I understand that.'

She didn't know what to say. She hated herself for using him in that way.

'You should go,' he said.

'Astrid!' a new voice called out. She spun around to see Jake running towards her.

'What the hell is going on?' she asked him.

'I may have let the lions out of the cage,' Jake said, looking back the way he'd come.

Jake faced Tom and glanced at the gun by his side.

'It's okay,' Tom said. 'You can go.'

Astrid hugged Tom. 'I'm so sorry.'

When she let him go, Tom smiled gently and blushed. He reached into his coat pocket and handed her a piece of paper.

'What's this?' she asked.

'You need to speak with Saifedean Burhan.'

'You know where he is?' Astrid asked.

'I do. But he won't welcome you. As you know, he's a recluse. But if you want help with oxygen, he's the only one who can do anything about it. He lives in an abandoned library on the outskirts of the city.'

'Thank you,' Jake said. 'I don't know what to say.'

Tom gave him a stern look. 'Look after Astrid. That's all I ask.'

Astrid kissed Tom on the cheek, then reached for Jake's hand and led him to the exit.

# CHAPTER 41

## JAKE

Jake entered the library, Astrid close behind. The room was dark and musty, making him imagine hidden corners covered in damp and mould.

'Have you ever seen him?' he asked, making his way through a narrow corridor of book shelves. 'Would you know what he looks like?'

'Does it matter? He'll be the only man here.'

She was right, but he still wanted to be ready. He'd heard many things about Saifedean Burhan but had never seen an image of him. He was a recluse, and probably the least well-known famous person in the world.

Astrid was staring at him.

'What is it?' he asked.

'Your eyes,' she said. 'They're changing.'

He was scared, but the moment he began to feel sorry for himself, he thought about his sister and Jess, and knew he had to keep going.

Astrid pulled his arm, ushering him down another corridor of bookcases. 'This way.'

He followed her. The bookshelves rose to meet the ceiling, each one filled with books of all sizes and colours. Suddenly the claustrophobic bookshelves opened up onto a mezzanine with a high, arched timber roof. Astrid led the way to a balcony that overlooked more bookshelves that went on forever. She looked around for any sign of Saifedean Burhan.

'Where is he?' Jake asked.

On cue, they heard footsteps. A tall, well-built man ambled towards them. It had to be Saifedean Burhan. But he didn't look the way Jake had expected. He wore large sunglasses. A heavy cream woollen jumper and burgundy scarf gave him an easy-going demeanour. He was groomed, his dark hair parted. His temples were flecked with white, like his grey beard. He checked his silver watch then folded his arms. Jake imagined that whatever he was going to say would be intelligent. Some people, he thought, exuded intelligence.

'You are Astrid?' Saifedean asked.

'Yes,' she said.

'Tom told me to expect you.' He took another step closer and faced Jake without speaking.

Jake glanced at Astrid, but she was staring at Saifedean.

'My name is Jake,' he said.

'Yes,' Saifedean said, unfolding his arms and reaching into his trouser pocket. He took out a pipe. From his other pocket, he took out a silver lighter. 'Do you smoke?' he raised a pipe to his lips.

'No,' Jake said.

Astrid shook her head.

'It is a bad habit.' Saifedean sucked on the pipe, then puffed smoke into the air.

'Do you read, Astrid?' Saifedean asked.

Astrid took in the rows of bookshelves. 'I have had limited access to real books. But yes, I have read some.'

'I'm glad to hear it. Who's your favourite writer?'

'I don't...' Astrid looked confused.

'We don't have much time,' Jake said, taking a step towards Saifedean.

Saifedean stepped backwards warily and raised his pipe. 'Wait. Don't come any closer.'

'What's wrong?' Jake asked.

Saifedean took a moment then seemed to recover, taking deliberate breaths. 'I am not accustomed to company.' He took off his glasses, folded them, and pushed them into his pocket.

'We need your help,' Jake said.

One of Saifedean's eyes was green and the other brown. Jake couldn't remember seeing someone with two differently coloured eyes; there was something hypnotic about them.

'My help?' Saifedean asked. 'What could you possibly want from me?'

Astrid spoke in a soft, sympathetic tone. 'Jake's sister and niece have been punished. Their oxygen has been taken from them.'

Jake waited for Saifedean to speak, but all he did was stare at Astrid blankly.

'They did nothing wrong,' Jake said.

'That can't be right,' Saifedean said with a genuinely confused expression. 'People are punished for the wrongs they commit.'

Jake told himself to remain calm. This was his only chance to help Grace and Jess. 'It was my fault. They had nothing to do with what happened. They have been punished for something I did.'

Saifedean squinted at Jake. 'What did you do?'

Jake sighed. 'I took Blue Oxygen that did not belong to me.'

'It belonged to my family,' Astrid added.

Jake wanted her to look at him – to show him he was forgiven. But she stared straight ahead at Saifedean.

'Were you punished for this?' Saifedean Burhan asked Jake.

'Yes. But so were my sister and niece.'

'That's the way society works,' Saifedean said, shrugging. 'The family must answer to the wrongs of one of its members.'

'But it was wrong,' Jake said. 'It was me, not them.'

Saifedean peered back at him, as if he was inspecting a strange animal. 'I'm sorry. If the oxygen has been taken, there is nothing I can do. The oxygen blockchain works only one way. There is no changing what is now cryptographically stored.'

'There must be something you can do,' Astrid said.

'I don't understand,' Saifedean said. 'He took your Blue Oxygen and yet you want to help him?'

'Not just him,' she said. 'His family.'

Jake wanted to ask Astrid whether she wanted him to be punished.

'There's nothing I can do,' Saifedean said sternly. He took one long inhalation of his pipe and turned to face the way he'd come.

'Wait,' Jake said. 'I need your help. You can't ignore this.'

'Ignore it?' he asked, glancing over his shoulder. 'I only wish that I could.'

'Help us,' Astrid said. 'Please.'

Saifedean's shoulders rose and fell. Jake recognised both his reluctance and indecision.

'This can't be what you wanted,' Jake said. 'Is it? This was your creation. I don't believe this is what you wanted for it.'

Saifedean was clearly thinking it through.

'Very well,' Saifedean said. 'But I'm not sure what I can do to help you.'

# CHAPTER 42

## ASTRID

Saifedean placed his pipe on the table, then edged around it, finally backing into a low, cushioned chair. He crossed his legs. Now and then, his cool demeanour altered, as though he was scared. Or at least, wary.

'Tell us how it works,' Astrid said. 'The O blockchain and the Blue Oxygen.'

'Do you know how to code?' he asked Jake, seeming to ignore Astrid's question.

'A little,' Jake said. 'Why won't you answer her question?'

'Are you being modest?' Saifedean asked. 'Sometimes I find it hard to read someone's genuine meaning.'

'Can you help me? I have to help my sister and my niece. It is my fault they are in this situation. We've tried asking Carlisle, but he refused.'

'Can you give them back their oxygen?' Astrid asked, losing patience.

Saifedean uncrossed his legs and sat forward. He stared at the pipe on the table. 'I don't see how I can.'

'Do you still control the O blockchain?' Astrid asked. 'There has to be something you can do.'

Saifedean shook his head with what Astrid saw as disdain. 'I no longer have any influence over the coding of the O blockchain.'

'But you designed it,' Jake said. 'It's yours.'

'It was,' Saifedean said.

'People are going missing from the villages,' Jake said. 'What's happening to them? Where are they being taken?'

Astrid spoke in a flat, emotionless tone. 'They're being killed for their oxygen, aren't they?'

Saifedean didn't respond.

'Why is there even an O blockchain?' Jake asked. 'It's a form of control, isn't it?'

'We have stripped this planet of its energy,' Saifedean said. 'Because we increased human life expectancy considerably, the lack of resources became an existential threat. We had to do something ... *I* had to do something.'

Astrid edged closer.

Saifedean appeared to enter a kind of trance, his gaze fixed on a spot in the distance, on the other side of the room. 'It was a simple idea,' he continued. 'Not to execute, but the idea itself was simple ... elegant. We arrived at two numbers. The first was the optimal number of people that could live on the planet in order for each to live a good, worthwhile life.'

'An optimal number?' Astrid asked, her face twisting with disgust.

'With the help of general intelligence,' Saifedean said, 'along with human reasoning and the careful study of history, we arrived at a number.'

'What is it?' Jake asked.

'The optimal number of humans is 2.479 billion.'

Astrid couldn't understand how he could say something like that with so little emotion. 'How can you possibly know that?'

'We know,' he said, and shrugged as though this was obvious.

'What's the second number?' Jake asked.

Saifedean appeared confused, then nodded. 'The second number is the number of years an individual needs to have a good life.'

'You're crazy,' Astrid said.

'What is the number?' Jake asked.

'We settled on one hundred years,' Saifedean said. 'Our studies reached a number just short of this, but we thought it was the perfect number.' He was animated by what he was saying. 'Instead of giving people time, to make it fair, the blockchain was set up to issue oxygen.' He looked down at his own chest. 'When you are born, you are issued with your oxygen. The mathematics is straightforward. If we say there should be 2.4 billion people, each living one hundred years, then we arrive at 48 quintillion litres of oxygen per year. Instead of arriving at a set number of people on the planet, we reached the perfect amount of oxygen consumed each year. As it stands today, as there are over twice the amount of people than is optimal, the share of oxygen leads to people living around fifty years. Without the supplementation of Blue, of course.'

'This is crazy,' Jake said.

Astrid tried to work it out in her head. How could Saifedean be so calculated ... so cold about it all?

'That's why people have to pay for their children in oxygen?' she asked him.

'Yes,' Saifedean said. 'And because it costs people in

oxygen, many people do not have children. This brings down the overall population.'

'Except for those who are wealthy,' Jake said, his face twisting with disgust and anger. 'They can afford Blue Oxygen and not use their own quota.'

Saifedean bowed his head sheepishly.

'What is it?' Astrid asked him. 'What are you hiding?'

Jake edged closer, staring at Saifedean who had clenched his hands together.

'Tell us everything,' Jake said.

'It was not my decision. When I found out what Carlisle wanted to do, I wanted no part in it.'

'No part in what?' Astrid asked.

Slowly lifting his head, Saifedean gave her a pitiful expression.

'My father?' Astrid asked. 'He's involved too, isn't he?'

Saifedean nodded reluctantly. 'The only way they would allow me to leave was if I agreed to say nothing. Not that anyone would have believed me, anyway.'

Astrid wanted to throw up. Her stomach tightened. 'Tell us,' she said.

Saifedean stood. 'There is very little Blue Oxygen in comparison with the oxygen in the atmosphere. It is negligible.'

'That doesn't help those who can't afford it,' Jake snapped.

'Why have Blue at all?' Astrid asked. 'Where does it come from?'

'You know where it comes from,' Saifedean said.

'I want *you* to explain,' Astrid said.

'The oxygen that is not used up in issued quotas is recycled. Blue Oxygen is the oxygen left over. The O blockchain is amended and the leftover oxygen redistributed.'

Jake held his head in his hands. 'That's why people are going missing in the villages, isn't it? That's why Carlisle is taking my sister's and niece's oxygen. He's going to sell it.'

Astrid couldn't speak.

'This is wrong!' Jake said, striding across the room towards Saifedean as though ready to strike him. Saifedean didn't move. It surprised Astrid to see him stand up to Jake's aggression. Jake also looked surprised, and stopped short, his fists by his side, his chest heaving.

'I'm sorry,' Saifedean said. 'Truly I am. I did not want the oxygen blockchain to be used in this way. It is wrong.'

'But you didn't stop it?' Jake snapped.

Saifedean pursed his lips. 'There was nothing I could do.'

Astrid didn't know what to say. Maybe he was lying. But the more she thought about it, the more she realised he was telling the truth.

# CHAPTER 43

## JAKE

'THERE HAS to be something you can do,' Jake said again.

For the first time since they met, Jake saw anger in Saifedean's posture. 'What would you have me do?'

Jake scratched the side of his head. 'Tell me where I can get more Blue.'

Saifedean shook his head. 'I'm sorry. I have none.'

'You must have,' Astrid said.

'Why?' Saifedean's anger returned. 'I don't want anything to do with it. Why would I use it?'

Jake walked to the edge of the mezzanine and looked down at the bookshelves. Yesterday, he had been inhaling Blue Oxygen and running across Ash Fields. It felt like weeks ago. He went over the past couple of days in his head. He recalled Shuk and the two men who took the tubes of Blue Oxygen. Cray and his cronies. The Engineer. He'd watched Bailey suffocate and die. Gambit had promised he had never used Blue Oxygen. Then it struck him. He spun around.

'We have made connections,' he said to Saifedean.

'Across computers. I have a friend called Gambit. Along with many other coders.'

'I didn't think there were coders still out there,' Saifedean said.

Jake saw a glint in his eyes. It encouraged him. 'Our system is rudimentary, but with your help, and with better processors, we could bring down the oxygen blockchain. For good.'

Saifedean's enthusiasm vanished from his eyes.

'You can't compete with the O blockchain,' Astrid said. 'It would be impossible.'

'Why?' Jake asked.

'We would need more time,' Saifedean said. 'Besides, once they discovered I was helping you, they would delete my quota too.'

'But that wouldn't matter,' Jake said. 'Don't you see? Once we hack into the O blockchain, we can end its control.'

Saifedean shook his head. 'It would be impossible. There is hardware in each person, connected to the O blockchain. The best we could do would be to reset the overall amount of oxygen.'

'Then let's do that!' Jake said, raising his arms into the air.

'*Can* you do that?' Astrid asked Saifedean.

Saifedean stared at the floor. 'I'm not sure. It would take a lot of processing power.'

'We can get it,' Jake said. 'We can connect coders across the villages. Carlisle would never expect this sort of attack. No one knows about the network Gambit has created. When we take control of the O blockchain, it would be decentralised so that no one person or authority could control it. It would belong to everyone.' He saw that Saifedean was on the verge of agreeing.

'How many programmers are we talking about?' Saifedean asked.

Jake didn't know the exact number, but Gambit had spoken about the possibility of hundreds of other coders. 'Many.'

Saifedean nodded to himself. 'They destroyed the internet years ago. What you're talking about is a replacement.'

'Yes,' Jake said. 'We need it now more than ever. It's the only way to take back control of the blockchain and divide the oxygen fairly among the people. Without Blue oxygen. You can help us do that. The O blockchain was yours. You programmed it.'

'I'm not sure you understand the enormity of what you're proposing,' Saifedean said. 'Although it is not possible to reduce someone's oxygen to zero, as soon as they recognised our attack, which would be almost immediately, they could reduce my oxygen to one thousand litres. I wouldn't have time to program the new O blockchain.'

'We can do this,' Astrid said.

Relief filled Jake. He wanted to hug and kiss Astrid. She was on board, and he hadn't realised until that moment how much he needed her to be with him.

Saifedean was unmoved, puffing on his pipe.

'I know we're asking you to risk a lot,' Jake said. 'But this is your chance to put things right.'

Saifedean looked at both of them with what Jake began to see as his default expression of disinterest.

Astrid was looking to leave. 'If we're going to do this, we have to begin now.'

It struck Jake that Astrid would be in danger too. 'When

Carlisle realises you're helping us, he will delete your quota too, no matter who your father is.'

Astrid nodded. 'I know. Which is why we have to make sure this works.'

'There's a good chance it won't,' Saifedean said. 'In fact, I suspect the odds are very much against us.'

Jake hesitated. 'I don't have anything to lose,' he said to Astrid. 'It's different for you. You're risking everything.'

Astrid's stare was determined and Jake thought it beautiful.

'If we succeed,' Astrid said, 'we can help millions of people around the world. In one moment, the oxygen will be reset. We can rid the system of Blue Oxygen so it's fair for everyone.' She spoke directly to Saifedean. 'You can return your code to the way it was supposed to be used.'

'Until we work out how to delete the blockchain completely,' Jake said.

Saifedean stared at his pipe. 'I'm not sure that would be a good idea. The original problem with overpopulation and prolonged lives would be present yet again.'

'There's time to work all that out after we have taken control of the O blockchain,' Astrid said. 'Let's go.' She jogged back towards the narrow corridor of bookshelves.

Saifedean walked in the opposite direction across the mezzanine.

'Where are you going?' Jake asked him. 'We have to go to Gambit's place.'

'If we're going to do this, we're going to need processing power.' Saifedean looked back, his expression determined. 'And lots of it.'

## CHAPTER 44

ASTRID

THE AFTERNOON AIR was still and Astrid felt as though she was fighting through it. A heaviness had come over her. She followed Jake through the village streets, wondering whether he knew which way he should go. But he seemed confident.

She tried to make sense of it all, but things had happened without her having any say in any of it. The world around her had changed permanently. She would never see things in the same way again.

Her chest burned. She exercised at home, but that was inside, with access to Blue Oxygen. Walking through the villages, in the open air, weaving through streets she had never seen before, was more difficult. It was as though her body knew she was no longer taking in free oxygen, but was using up a finite store of it.

If Carlisle discovered she was helping Jake and Saifedean to take down the O blockchain, he would take away her oxygen. Jake had spoken about it, and she had acknowledged the possibility. But had she really understood? She told herself she did understand, but part of her knew it would be impossible to truly come to terms with the sacrifice until it was actually happening. A part of her hoped her father would not allow Carlisle to take the oxygen. But her father would be angry with her too. Maybe he would want to punish her.

'Is it much further?' she asked Jake.

Jake, who turned to look at Saifedean and her, pointed into the distance above the rooftops of the shacks they were walking between. 'Gambit's place is over there. Not far now.'

At first Astrid was relieved, but then she thought about how she would be taking part in something many people, including Carlisle, would consider an act of terrorism. The word rang in her ears. Even though she tried to convince herself that what she was doing was right, she couldn't help imagining what people in the city would say about her. They would see her as a traitor. Maybe that's what she would be. If she had more time to think about what she was doing, then maybe she could make the right choice. But there was no time.

She thought about asking Saifedean if what they were planning was the right thing to do, but stopped herself. The chance of him giving her a straight answer was remote. He would most likely only confuse her further.

All of her oxygen – gone in an instant. All but the last thousand litres. She recalled the blue of Jake's eyes, getting darker with every passing hour. Her eyes would also turn blue.

Over her shoulder, in the distance, was the hazy form of her home – the city. She had never been happy there. That was the overriding thought when she considered home. The thought of having to go back there and live a life as a prisoner made her clench her fists and quicken her steps. No –

she wasn't going to go back. If she had to risk losing her oxygen to reset the blockchain and to destroy the business her father had created, then so be it. She would not let her father or Carlisle, or whoever they had working for them, take advantage of innocent people.

'Will he help us?' she asked Jake.

'Who? Gambit?'

'Yes, your friend. Can he do what we need him to do?'

She wanted Jake to answer straight away, to convince her that this was going to work.

'I don't know,' he said.

That was not what she wanted to hear. But he was being honest.

They kept on walking through the narrow streets.

'Thank you,' he said to her.

'What for?' she asked him.

He gave her the sincerest look she could remember ever seeing. 'For helping me.'

'You promised to help me escape the city,' she said. 'That will be all the thanks I need.'

'I promise,' he said. 'Whatever it takes.'

# CHAPTER 45

## JAKE

Jake led the way through the back streets of the village. He had used these routes many times when he was younger, hiding from teachers or opposing gangs. It was in his nature to find the best way. As a raider, in the city, he kept to the shadows, moved swiftly and with purpose. It frustrated him when others, like Astrid or Saifedean, didn't follow his exact movements. They were clumsy without knowing it. But he did his best to direct them through the streets.

When he turned the last corner and arrived outside Gambit's house, Gambit was there, watching Jake approach with an expression of confusion.

'We need your help,' Jake said, opening the gate to Gambit's garden. He glanced over at Astrid, who was gazing up at Gambit's trees.

'You appear distressed,' Gambit said, talking to Jake, but looking at Astrid then Saifedean. 'What's wrong?'

There was so much to explain, Jake didn't know where to begin.

'This is Astrid,' Jake said, glancing at her. 'And this is Saifedean Burhan.'

Recognition illuminated Gambit's eyes. '*The* Saifedean Burhan?'

Saifedean was also taking in Gambit's garden and home. He didn't seem to hear Jake's introduction.

'He's agreed to help us,' Jake said.

Gambit walked slowly towards Saifedean and offered his hand. 'It is an honour.'

Saifedean's attention shifted from his surroundings to Gambit's hand. For what felt like ages, he stared at the outstretched hand. Finally he shook it.

'You are something of a mystery to many coders,' Gambit said. 'But your work is no mystery. Your coding is second to none.'

Saifedean tilted his head and frowned with an expression that made Jake think he was working on a math puzzle. 'Thank you,' he said finally.

Even though it was an acceptable response, the tone of his voice made the interaction far more uncomfortable than it needed to be.

'We need to get to work,' Jake said, wanting to end the uncomfortable meeting.

Gambit folded his arms and faced Jake. 'And what do you want from me?'

'The network we have been working on,' Jake said.

Gambit uncrossed his arms. 'Have you told them about that?' he asked.

Jake had promised to not tell anyone, but these were extraordinary circumstances. 'I'm sorry. But it gives us the chance to change everything.'

'What are you talking about?'

'With Saifedean's help, we're going to take back the O blockchain,' Astrid said.

Gambit let out a sharp laugh and looked at Jake, as if

expecting him to join in. But Jake remained stern-faced and silent.

'Are you serious?' Gambit asked.

'Yes. We can do it,' Jake said. 'With your help, and with the others on the network, we can take back control. No one knows the O blockchain better than Saifedean. If we have enough computing power, we can fork the blockchain and decentralise it. There will be no more central control. Those in power will no longer be able to take away anybody's oxygen.'

'We will begin again,' Astrid said. 'Everyone will be given the same oxygen, with no Blue Oxygen.'

Gambit shook his head in disbelief. 'There's no way we can break the computing power of the central government. Besides, as soon as they find out what we're doing, they would cut off our oxygen. We'd be down to a thousand litres. What then?'

Jake raised a clenched fist. 'If we succeed, then our oxygen will be renewed.'

'There's a bigger chance that we will fail,' Gambit said. 'And that will be the end of us.' He looked over at Astrid, then Saifedean. 'Are you both prepared to lose your oxygen?'

Astrid stepped forward. 'Yes, we are. We can do this. It's the right thing to do.'

Saifedean scratched his chin and shrugged. 'I must admit, I'm intrigued to see whether it can be done.'

'Intrigued?' Gambit said, giving out a nervous laugh. 'That's one way to put it.' He edged backwards and sat on the low wall outside his front door. He bowed his head, clearly thinking.

Jake sat beside him. 'We have talked about this for a long time. Now it's time to actually do it.'

'We talked about creating an internet like the one that was destroyed. This is different. This is on another level.'

'This is what all our work has been about,' Jake said. 'I know it is. There are other coders out there who, if they knew the opportunity we have, would be prepared to risk it all in an instant.'

'I wouldn't be so sure,' Gambit said.

'At least let's try,' Jake said. 'Let me ask them.'

Gambit sighed. 'How many coders would you need? The central computer is powerful. Forking the blockchain will require an immense amount of coding.'

Jake glanced over at Saifedean, who placed his bag on the floor.

'I have state-of-the-art processors,' Saifedean said.

Gambit opened the bag and looked inside. His eyes widened. 'Around one hundred,' he said. 'We would need around one hundred coders, all joined together on one network. But we have less than a third of that number.'

'There will be more coders out there willing to help,' Jake said. 'I know it.'

Gambit strolled over to one of his trees and looked up through the canopy of coppery leaves. 'I don't know how much oxygen I have left.'

Jake recognised Gambit's willingness to help. There was nothing more he needed to say.

'Let's do it,' Gambit said, striding towards his front door. 'Come with me.'

Jake hesitated. He had always wondered what Gambit's home was like. Now he had the chance to find out.

'Come on,' Astrid said, gripping his sleeve and dragging him up the steps to the front door.

# CHAPTER 46

## ASTRID

ASTRID CLOSED the lid on the last computer and fastened the screws. Her back ached from bending over. Her eyes, too. The thought that these computers, along with those on Gambit's network, could compete with the central computers in the city struck her as foolish. But at the same time, people in the city would never imagine the villagers would contemplate attacking them. Maybe it could work. She wanted to believe it was possible.

Gambit entered the room. 'I have contacted as many coders as I can. They're finding others.'

Saifedean, typing at one of the terminals, spun around on his chair. 'It is essential that nobody they contact tells anyone what we're doing.'

'Of course,' Gambit said with clear annoyance.

Saifedean didn't appear to register Gambit's annoyance. He continued. 'If Carlisle discovers I'm here, and that we're attempting to infiltrate the O blockchain, then—'

'I get it,' Gambit said. 'But either we find enough people to help us, or we don't stand a chance. Simple as that.'

Saifedean frowned, then his forehead smoothed out, as though he had argued with himself and had won.

Astrid collapsed onto the settee in the corner of the room. She was exhausted. The room was small, every inch filled with computers, processors, motherboards, power packs and other computer paraphernalia. If it wasn't for the impending doom of losing her oxygen, she would have taken her time to look through it all and learn. Back home, her father's computer had been given to him complete, functioning, ready to go. As far as she knew, computers worked by magic.

Jake came in and sat beside her.

'We're nearly ready,' he said.

'Do you really think this is possible?' she asked.

He rubbed his hands along his thighs. 'I hope so. Yes.'

But what did Jake know? He was a raider. He had brought those men to her home. And now she was prepared to risk her life to help him. How had that happened? But this was about more than helping Jake and his family. This was about her own freedom. If she didn't reset the O blockchain, eventually her father would find her and take her back to the city. And who knew what he would do to her?

'I hope you're right,' she said.

He bowed his head. 'You should get some rest. It's going to take another hour or so before we're ready.'

His eyes were dark blue, close to black. Jake didn't have long left. There was a real chance that he would run out of oxygen before they had taken over the O blockchain, and she knew it would be on his mind too.

'I'm not sure I can sleep,' she said.

Jake laid his head on the cushion and closed his eyes. 'I love to run,' he said.

'Run?' she asked. 'I didn't think people in the villages ran.' She regretted saying it. Her words sounded foolish to her own ears.

'They don't. But I did. I would raid oxygen and use it to run.' He opened his eyes. 'Does that sound stupid?'

She wondered what she should say. 'Yes,' she said eventually.

His smile was sad. 'I wish I could go back and save it all up. Give it to my sister and my niece. All that oxygen, wasted.'

'You risked your life to get oxygen so you could run?' she asked. 'Why did you need Blue Oxygen to do that?'

'Like I said, it sounds stupid. But running, using the oxygen I had stolen, felt good. It's difficult to explain. I don't think I fully understand it myself. I guess it has something to do with always having to be careful with oxygen. You know?'

She didn't know.

'Of course you don't,' he said.

'I didn't choose my parents, or my life,' she reminded him.

'That's not what I meant,' he said. 'I'm not judging you. I was trying to explain, that's all.'

She closed her eyes. Now she felt as though she might sleep for a short while.

'I think I do understand why you did it,' she said. 'In a way.'

Jake didn't respond, and she didn't open her eyes. But she felt him next to her, the rhythm of his breathing matching her own.

She imagined Jake running, his legs and arms pumping furiously. She listened to her own breathing: in and out ... in and out...

## CHAPTER 47

### JAKE

Jake watched Astrid sleeping. Her breathing had slowed and her eyes flickered beneath her eyelids. Maybe she was dreaming. Her life had been so different to his, and it made him wonder whether her dreams were different too. She'd lived her entire life without the danger of her oxygen running out. There was no dagger hanging over her head like there was for him or his family. Yet, she wasn't happy. In fact, she seemed sadder than anyone he knew. Jake had always longed for a limitless supply of oxygen. He hated that he couldn't do the things he wanted to do because of his quota. Even so, he remembered being happy. He thought back to his childhood with his sister, who had always looked out for him. He couldn't have been the easiest child to look after, yet he'd been happy.

Astrid's head shifted and she sighed deeply. He reached for the blanket beside him and draped it over her legs.

'We're getting there,' Gambit said, entering the room.

Jake placed a finger to his lips.

'Sorry,' Gambit said, and motioned for Jake to follow him out of the room.

'How many do we have?' Jake asked, following him.

'Around fifty,' he said.

'That's not enough.'

Gambit was clearly disappointed. 'I didn't think we'd get this many,' he said.

'We're going to need twice that amount,' Saifedean said, working at a terminal on the far side of the room.

Gambit sat at his terminal and spoke to Saifedean. 'If you have fifty coders hidden away somewhere, now is the time to save the day.'

Saifedean didn't respond, his fingers tapping the keyboard at speed.

Jake watched the code on Gambit's monitor. 'Have you asked the coders to find others?'

'Of course,' Gambit said. 'But it will take time.'

Jake wanted to tell Gambit that they didn't have time but it would have been pointless. Gambit knew that as well as anyone.

'We have to begin as soon as we can,' Saifedean said, his fingers still a blur on the keyboard. 'It will take time to fork the O blockchain.'

Jake glanced over to his own terminal, its cursor blinking in the top left corner, then back to Saifedean. 'If we begin now, without the computing power to back us up, they will know it's you and they will delete your quota.'

Saifedean didn't look away from his monitor. 'Carlisle will have sent any number of people to look for you. He will find you – and us – soon enough. If we wait much longer, we won't have another chance.'

Gambit stopped typing and sat back in his chair. 'He's right.'

Saifedean's fingers paused on the keyboard. 'There it is.'

Jake walked over to Saifedean's monitor. There was

nothing surprising or special about the code – but it was the code that dictated life and death for each human on the planet.

'That's the O blockchain?' Jake asked.

'In all its glory,' Saifedean said. He sighed. 'I regret creating it.'

Neither Jake or Gambit responded. Jake wished it hadn't been created too. Although it was impossible to know what might have happened otherwise. So many people, capable of living for hundreds of years and of having more children, would have put a great strain on the planet and its resources.

Saifedean interlaced his fingers and cracked them. 'Once I begin infiltrating the code, they will suspect that it's me. I'm the only one who could have got this far into the blockchain. They will come looking for me and will find that I am missing. That's when they will delete my quota.'

'We need more computing power,' Gambit said. 'Once Saifedean has forked the O blockchain, it must be sent to each and every node on the network. Otherwise they will simply take it back. We need more time.' He stared at Jake and caught his breath.

'It's my eyes, isn't it?' Jake said. 'They're turning a deeper blue?'

Gambit nodded. 'Do you have any Blue Oxygen? You'll need it if you're going to make it. Taking over the blockchain is going to take time.'

'I don't matter,' he said. 'What matters is that we help my sister and niece. That we end the control Carlisle has over the O blockchain.'

'I get it,' Gambit said. 'But there's a chance that you, your sister and niece aren't going to stay alive long enough for us to do this.'

Gambit was right. Jake needed Blue Oxygen. But where would he get some now? He had no money, and there were people looking for him. People like Cray.

'Go,' Gambit said. 'Help your sister and niece. You need to buy yourself and them more time. I will find more coders.'

Saifedean nodded. 'And I will begin coding the O blockchain.'

The moment Saifedean began to hack the code, they would have a limited time. Not only would Saifedean's oxygen be deleted, leaving him only one thousand litres, but they would know what Jake and Saifedean were up to. There was also the possibility that Carlisle would delete Astrid's oxygen.

'I'm coming with you,' a voice from behind him said.

Jake spun around. It was Astrid.

'It's too dangerous,' he said. 'If they find us, they'll take you back to the city. You should stay here.'

Astrid shook her head. 'If you run out of oxygen, you're going to need my help. Your sister and niece will have more oxygen than you, but they will run out soon too.'

She was right, but he hated the thought of putting Astrid in danger again.

'Let's go,' Astrid said, walking towards the door.

'Go,' Gambit told Jake.

It startled Jake, who found himself walking towards the door. Not for the first time, he felt as though he wasn't in control of anything. But following Astrid out of the room, filled him with purpose.

# CHAPTER 48

## ASTRID

Astrid pulled a hood over her head and Jake did the same. She walked with her head bowed, avoiding eye contact with anyone they passed.

'Where do we get Blue?' Astrid asked.

'I know someone,' Jake said, leading the way. 'But I don't know if he'll be happy to see me, never mind hand over Blue.'

'That doesn't sound promising.'

They arrived at a tram stop just as the tram turned the corner. It screeched to a stop in front of them.

'How far is it?' she asked, following Jake onto the tram.

'Twenty minutes.' He sat and turned away from the two men sitting on the opposite side of the tram.

Astrid sat beside him. She couldn't help glancing at the two men. Neither of them looked back at her, but there was something in their demeanour that told her to keep her distance.

The tram made its way through the villages, now and then stopping to let passengers on and off. She'd heard of the trams in the villages, and had often fantasised about travelling them. They had always seemed to represent freedom – taking her from one distant place to the next. But now she was on one, the freedom she imagined she would feel wasn't there. Instead, she felt trapped inside the narrow metal box. The thought that the tram could only go in two directions, restrained by its metal tracks, made her anxious. They were headed in one direction; none of the passengers had any choice.

When it was time, Jake tapped her arm and nodded towards the tram door.

She stood and, with one hand on the rail above, stumbled towards the door, ready for the tram to stop. Jake was behind her, his head bowed, his face shrouded by the hood.

The two men they had sat opposite remained seated, which gave her some relief.

The tram stopped and the door opened with a loud hiss of air. Astrid stepped off the tram onto the dusty ground. Jake followed, and the tram almost immediately set off.

She followed Jake towards a beaten-up row of shacks, behind which the city skyline was visible. Part of her missed the city, but she told herself that was foolish.

Two women on a street corner watched them. Their eyes were cold and stark, almost calculating. Astrid hated the way they looked at her, but she couldn't look away.

'Keep your eyes down,' Jake said. 'We don't want any trouble.'

Astrid didn't want trouble either, so she did as he said.

Across the street, outside what appeared to be a bar, was a huddle of men dressed in matching black T-shirts, each in a brown hat. One of the men was sitting on the kerb, his hands behind him, propping him up. He watched her closely. Again, Astrid found it difficult to look away, even though she knew this would have been the better option.

'Nearly there,' Jake said, turning into a narrow alleyway.

They arrived outside a beaten-up door. The hinge at the top of the door was broken, leaving the door hanging precariously.

Jake waited outside.

'What is it?' she asked.

He took something from his pocket. Holding it in both hands, he offered it to her. She was about to take it when she saw it was a gun.

'I can't,' she said, taking away her hand.

'You won't have to use it,' he said. 'It's just in case.'

'I won't need it if I'm not going to use it.'

Jake looked along the street, then back to Astrid. 'Please. Take it. I don't know how this is going to go.'

Astrid stared at the gun, then grabbed it and pushed it into her pocket. She wanted to get off the street before the men she had seen outside the bar came after them.

Jake sighed, then walked over to the beaten-up door and edged sideways into the building. Astrid followed. The room was dark, with red and blue square lamps hanging on walls and from the ceiling. It took a moment for her eyes to adjust, then she made out a counter at the other end of the room. There was no one else there. Music played – possibly in the room she could now make out, behind the counter.

Jake was clearly nervous, turning his head from side to side as he walked towards the counter.

'What is this place?' Astrid whispered.

'This is pretty much the only place you can buy computer parts. And the only place you can buy Blue.'

Someone appeared behind the counter. He was short and well-built, his long brown hair matted.

'Well, well, well,' the man said in a husky voice. 'If it isn't Jake the thief.'

This was not the welcome Astrid had hoped for.

'Hey, Shuk,' Jake said, raising his hands. 'You know I had nothing to do with what happened.'

Shuk wiped his mouth with the back of his hand, then tapped the side of his head, which was bandaged. 'All I remember is you showing up. Then I was out of it.'

'It was your friends.' Jake gestured to the table beside the counter. 'Playing chess. Remember?'

Shuk folded his arms and nodded. 'Yeah. Well, I haven't seen either of them since. I figured all three of you were in on it.'

Jake took a step closer. 'No. You got it all wrong. I stopped them from hurting you any more. And I kept the Blue for you. They were ready to take it.'

'I was down one tube,' Shuk said, eyeing Jake suspiciously. 'Remember?'

'Yeah, they took one.' Jake inhaled deeply, 'I need your help.' He walked towards the counter.

Shuk reached for something beneath the counter and then moved back, raising a shotgun and pointing it at Jake.

Jake stopped and pointed to his face. 'My eyes,' he said. 'Look.'

Warily, with the shotgun still aimed at Jake, Shuk came closer. 'They're blue.'

'I know,' Jake said. 'That's why I'm here. I know you have some Blue.'

Shuk appeared almost sympathetic. He lowered his shotgun. 'How long do you have?' he asked.

'Not long. But they've deleted my sister's quota. My niece too.'

'What the fuck did you do?' Shuk asked. 'You must have messed up royally, kid.'

'Do you have any?' Astrid snapped.

Shuk and Jake stared at her.

'You're not from around here,' Shuk said, his eyes narrowing.

'She's Gordon Solomon's daughter,' Jake said.

'My name's Astrid.'

'Holy shit!' Shuk said to Jake, letting out a surprised laugh. 'You really know how to get yourself into trouble, huh?'

'How much Blue do you have?' Jake asked.

Shuk slid the shotgun back where he'd taken it from. 'You don't have enough gold,' he said.

'Give me time,' Jake said. 'And I'll pay you double what it's worth.'

'Don't kid yourself,' Shuk said. 'You'll never get that kind of gold.'

Astrid took the ring from inside her bra. 'How much is this worth?' she asked.

Shuk came closer and peered at her ring. He smiled. 'Now we're talking.'

# CHAPTER 49

## JAKE

JAKE PUSHED the two tubes of Blue into his pocket.

'Do you think that's really all he has?' Astrid asked.

Jake didn't know. 'It will have to do,' he said. 'Thank you. You didn't have to do that.'

'It's only a ring,' she said, pushing her hand into her coat pocket.

He didn't know how to make her see how grateful he was. Saying thank you wasn't enough. Especially after everything he had done to her.

'We should find your sister,' she said.

They boarded the tram and again did everything they could to hide their faces. Jake kept checking that the tubes of Blue were safe in his pocket.

The tram trundled through the village then took a right towards his estate. He had travelled this route thousands of times. Day in, day out, taking the tram from one village to the next, never wanting to use up his oxygen by walking. He hated the trams. The sounds, their smell, the way they shunted you back and forth. Always the same, no matter which one he took. Over and over...

It was only a matter of time before someone spotted him. The Engineer and Cray would be looking everywhere for him. But the more time that passed without being found, the more Jake began to think he was free to go where he wanted. These were his villages. But that was a dangerous thought. The moment he stopped being careful would be the moment they found him. And then it would be over. For himself and for his sister and niece. He couldn't let that happen.

As the tram approached his estate, he spotted Bailey's mountain of cars. The thought that his sister wouldn't be there troubled him. But where would she go? Running away would only use up oxygen, and she wouldn't do that.

He hopped off the tram and led the way towards his sister's shack, checking on the car he had hidden before knocking on the door. There was no answer. Jake opened the door.

'Grace?' he said. 'Jess?' He stepped inside.

Then something struck him from behind, sending him crashing to the ground. Astrid fell beside him.

A boot struck Jake in the ribs, winding him. He rolled onto his side. Through blurred vision, he made out the figure of a white-haired man. It was Cray.

# CHAPTER 50

## ASTRID

No. It was Cray and his mates.

Astrid rolled onto her side and held the back of her head where she had been hit.

'Listen,' Jake said, trying to get to his feet. Someone kicked him a second time. He lay on the ground, an arm raised to his attacker.

'You really fucked up this time,' Cray said. 'Coming to my home and threatening my woman. That was really not cool.' Cray kicked Jake again.

'Where's Grace?' Jake asked, gasping. 'And Jess?'

Astrid got to her knees and crawled over to the wall, where she sat. She touched the back of her head and stared at the blood on her hand.

Cray stooped beside Jake and gripped his chin so he could stare into his eyes. 'Your eyes. You're nearly out.'

'Where are they?' Jake shouted.

'Now, now,' Cray said. 'You need to save your breath.' He let go.

Two of the other men laughed.

Jake moved so he was leaning against the wall opposite Astrid.

Cray turned his attention to Astrid. 'You're Solomon's daughter. You were supposed to go back to Daddy.'

Astrid's upper lip curled in a snarl. 'I'm not going back.'

'You're used to getting what you want, aren't you?'

She hated the look he gave her, like he was above her ... better than she was.

One of the men reached down to Jake to take his coat and the gun, as well as the two tubes of Blue. Jake tried to stop him, but he winced with pain and had no choice but to give in to them. Seeing the man with the gun made Astrid remember the one in her pocket. Why hadn't they searched her? She guessed they didn't see her as a threat.

'Two tubes of Blue,' the man said to Cray, holding them up.

'An extra bonus,' Cray said, smiling.

A shuffling, followed by a bang, came from the only other room in the shack.

'Jake!' someone shouted.

'Grace?' Jake shouted back. 'I'm here.'

Cray motioned for one of the men to go to Grace.

Jake tried to stand. 'Leave her alone!' he shouted.

One of Cray's men pushed him down, threatening him with a clenched fist. The back of Jake's head smacked against the wall.

From the next room came the sound of struggling, along with Grace shouting, then Jess crying.

'Leave them alone!' Jake said. 'If you hurt them, I'll make you pay!'

Cray knelt down and punched Jake. Jake fell to the floor once again, and stayed there. Astrid worried that he was out of it completely. But after a few seconds Jake spat blood across the floor, groggily lifted his head and shuffled upright again.

'The easy way out of this,' Cray said, 'is for you to do as I say. Let's face it, you're not going to make it.' He smiled. 'Your eyes – they're almost black. It's your time, kid.' Cray rubbed the fist he'd used to strike Jake with his other hand. 'But your sister and niece have a little more time. They can spend their last few hours in some sort of comfort. Or they can spend it suffering.'

'Why?' Jake asked. 'Why are you doing this?'

'I get a whole lot of Blue,' he said. 'As simple as that. And all I have to do is hand you over to the Engineer.'

'Take me,' Jake said. 'Leave Grace and Jess here, with the Blue Oxygen.'

Cray stared at him, his brow furrowed. 'What good would a tube each do them?'

'What do you care?' Jake said. 'All you need is me.'

Cray appeared to think it through. He reached over to the other man to take the tubes from him, and held them in one hand. 'No. I think I'll leave your sister and niece here, but take the Blue with me. I can have a pop on the way. You know how good Blue feels.'

'Please,' Jake said. 'Leave it with them. We've known each other a long time.' Jake's desperation was obvious. 'Give them a little more time.'

Astrid watched, longing for Cray to agree. If Grace and Jess each had one of the tubes, they might have a chance of making it. They just had to hang on long enough for Saifedean and Gambit to fork the O blockchain.

Cray walked towards the other room and looked in on Grace and Jess. He then walked back into the room and crouched next to Jake. 'I don't think so. It would only give them false hope. That would be cruel. We know what you and Gambit are doing.'

'I don't know what you're talking about,' Jake said.

Astrid saw how hard he was trying to not give anything away.

Cray smiled, then motioned for one of the other men to take Jake outside. 'Saifedean too. The Engineer didn't expect it – have to admit. You caught us out there. But the Engineer is on his way. We're going to stop Gambit and Saifedean meddling.'

'You sound crazy,' Jake said.

'I do, huh? There was no way all those coders Gambit reached out to were going to keep it to themselves. There were enough of them ready to give you up for a little Blue.'

Two men wrestled Jake out of the shack. A third man reached for Astrid's arm, pulled her to standing, then marched her outside too.

'What are you going to do to me?' she asked him.

'The Engineer wants to hand you over to your father.'

Jake was trying to fight off the two men, but he didn't stand a chance.

Grace and Jess appeared at the door, being held back by a fourth man.

'Jake!' Grace shouted.

Jake tried to go to her, but the two men struck him again, sending him sprawling to the ground.

In the distance, at the other end of the estate, came the sound of a car. It had to be the Engineer.

It was over.

No. Astrid wouldn't let it end this way. She reached into her pocket and pulled out the gun.

## CHAPTER 51

JAKE

Jake wrenched himself away from Max and Godfrey and headed back towards the shack for Grace and Jess.

'Don't do anything stupid,' Cray said, facing Astrid.

Astrid thrust her gun at him. 'Don't move! *That* would be stupid.'

'You're not going to use that,' Cray said, taking a step towards her.

'I said don't move.' Astrid jabbed the gun towards him.

A bolt of pain shot through his chest. He was pretty sure one or more of his ribs were broken. He pushed past a man he didn't recognise. 'Grace! Jess – let's go.'

'Jake – your eyes,' Grace said in horror, reaching out to him.

'Never mind that. Let's get out of here,' he said.

'We'll be out of oxygen soon,' she said.

She had given up. Jake hated the thought. He pushed past her and reached for Jess's hand, but she didn't want to go with him.

'Jess, please, we have to leave.'

Jess's eyes were wet with tears, her shoulders hunched. She was scared.

Then Jake remembered the tubes of Blue Cray had taken from him. He went back outside, stumbling down the steps of the porch.

'Where is it?' he shouted at Cray, who was staring at Astrid and her gun. 'The Blue?' He tugged at Cray's coat pockets, found the tubes, and turned back to Grace. 'I have Blue. We can get more. But I need you to come with me, now.'

Grace took Jess's hand and helped her out of the shack and down the steps.

'You're not going to get far,' Cray said. 'Look.'

Jake couldn't see anything, but the sound of the car engine was growing louder. 'Hurry!' Jake said, guiding Grace and Jess towards the car he had hidden on the other side of the shack.

Astrid walked backwards after them, her gun aimed at Cray the entire time. Jake was amazed at how controlled she was, how fearless.

'Over there,' Jake whispered to Grace, pointing to the car, which was covered with polythene. He knelt down, moved the brick he'd used to hide the key, and gave the key to her. 'Uncover it and get in the back.'

'What are you going to do?' Grace asked.

'I'm coming,' he said, pushing her away, urging her to go to the car. 'I'll help Astrid.'

Reluctantly, Grace, holding Jess's hand, jogged towards the hidden car.

Cray folded his arms and smiled. 'You're not going to last much longer, Jakey.'

Jake ignored him and stood beside Astrid. 'Are you ready?' he asked her.

She nodded, still walking backwards, her steps slow and measured.

Cray turned away towards the sound of the Engineer's car. He uncrossed his arms and looked at Astrid. 'From the moment we met, you have been nothing but trouble. Well, we're going to put all that right. We're going to stop Gambit and Saifedean.'

For the first time, Cray seemed frustrated, even scared. The Engineer would not be happy with him.

Jake and Astrid had backed away far enough that they could make a run for it.

'The Engineer's close,' Jake said.

Astrid didn't take her eyes off Cray, but whispered to Jake. 'You get in and start the car. Then I'll jump in.'

Jake didn't want to leave her. He glanced back towards the car. The door was open and Grace and Jess were in the back seat.

'Let me take the gun,' he said. 'You drive.'

'No,' she snapped. 'Go. Hurry!'

Her aggression made him jump. He ran to the car, dived into the driver's seat, and took the key from Grace. He fumbled before finally finding the slot. The ignition button clicked when he pressed it and the car roared into life. He shifted the gear stick into gear. The car shot forward towards Astrid. He slammed on the brakes, making the car skid.

'Get in!' he shouted.

Astrid took a final step backwards and bumped into the car. With her gaze – and the gun – on Cray, she reached behind to open the door. Jake leaned over and pushed the door open for her. In one quick movement Astrid fell into the passenger seat and slammed the door. Jake hit the accelerator.

Astrid's face was different – was pale.

'Are you okay?' Jake asked, one eye on the dirt track, the other on Astrid.

'Just drive,' she said. 'I've never used a gun before. The thought of using it...'

He placed a hand on her shoulder. 'It's going to be okay.' As soon as he said those words, he recognised how stupid they sounded.

He reached into his pocket and handed the two tubes of Blue to Grace. 'You need to use these.'

'No,' Grace said. 'You'll need it before me.'

'Just take it!' Jake snapped. He took a moment, telling himself to stay calm. 'Please, Grace. You have to. We have a plan. We're going to reset the O blockchain so everyone's quota is reset.'

'You're not making any sense,' Grace said.

Frustrated, Jake closed his eyes briefly. 'Just trust me. I got you into this mess and I'm going to get you out of it. I need you to take the Blue and use it when the time comes.'

Grace sank back into her seat, the two tubes held loosely. Astrid looked through the rear window.

'Do you see them?' he asked.

'No,' she said, opening her window. 'But I hear their car.'

Jake floored the accelerator.

## CHAPTER 52

ASTRID

Astrid stared at the gun in her hand. She had never held one before, never mind used one. Things had taken a crazy turn. She dropped the gun to the floor at her feet.

'Can you see them yet?' Jake asked.

'Why are they chasing you?' Grace asked.

Jake shook his head. 'It's a long story. All we have to do is keep you and Jess going long enough for Gambit and Saifedean to reset the O blockchain.'

'Gambit?' Grace asked. 'Reset the blockchain? Jake, what the hell is going on?'

Astrid could see that Jake was trying to concentrate on the road, so she took over.

'Saifedean Burhan, the creator of the O blockchain, and Gambit are hacking it. They're going to fork it.'

'What does that mean?' Grace asked.

'It's a way to reset the entire blockchain,' Astrid said, turning in her seat to look at Grace. 'If they succeed, there will be no more Blue Oxygen and everyone will be given the same amount of oxygen.'

'Why do we have to have a quota? Why can't we have

no quota at all?' Jess asked, her eyes pleading. It was a child's question – obvious and yet true.

Astrid smiled warmly at her. 'You know that each of us has a tiny bit of technology inside us that protects us from illness? But the same thing also controls the amount of oxygen we're entitled to. There's no way to remove it.'

Jess didn't smile back. Instead, she crossed her arms and bowed her head.

'I'm sorry,' Astrid said. 'Resetting the O blockchain is the best we can do for now.'

'I don't see how Gambit can do that,' Grace said. 'How can he beat the government's computers? Carlisle is a powerful man.'

Jake steered the car through three tight bends that led them downhill towards a low bridge. The noise of the car engine echoed through the tunnel, making Jess cover her ears and close her eyes. Grace held her close.

'Gambit has Saifedean's help,' Jake said when they had exited the tunnel and were climbing the sharp incline on the other side. 'He created the blockchain. And if he has enough power, thanks to everyone Gambit and I have networked with, it will be possible.'

Grace looked unconvinced. But as she was about to speak, the rear of the car was illuminated by two lights. It was the Engineer's car.

'They're here!' Astrid shouted, leaning down to pick up the gun, unsure what she intended to do with it.

Jake sped up. In the back seat, Jess screamed. Astrid peered past them through the rear window, but all she could see were two bright headlights.

Jake weaved through the village's narrow streets, making people jump out of the way and duck into alleys and doorways. He always seemed to know which way to turn.

Astrid wanted to ask if he knew where he was going, but thought it best to leave him to concentrate on the road.

Two minutes later, as the car burst out onto an open road, Jake shouted over the sound of the engine. 'Up ahead is a bridge over the river. It's the only road out of the village for miles. The Engineer will have to use the bridge as well.' He checked the rear-view. 'We've lost them for now, but they will have to come this way.' He peered over his shoulder at Grace. 'Listen carefully. I don't want to argue. Go with Astrid. She can drive the car. Gambit will be hacking into the blockchain as we speak – but you will need to use the tubes of Blue.'

'No,' Grace said, tears in her eyes. She clearly understood Jake's intention.

'I'm not arguing,' Jake said. 'I'm going to stop them coming over the bridge.'

'But they'll kill you,' Astrid said.

'I don't have much oxygen left,' Jake said, his eyes on the road.

Grace leaned between the front seats and held out a tube of Blue. 'Take this.'

'It's for you,' Jake said. 'The other one is for Jess.'

'Take it!' Grace said, dropping it onto Jake's lap.

Then the bridge Jake had mentioned came into view up ahead. He stopped the car just short of the bridge, checked behind, then took a deep breath. He held up the tube of oxygen and spoke to Grace. 'You know how these things work. Only one person can use the oxygen inside; once used, it syncs with the blockchain. Your eyes are changing. And so are Jess's. There's a good chance that your oxygen won't last long enough for them to reprogram the blockchain. You have to take the Blue.'

Grace held Jess close. 'But ... I can't leave you here.'

Jake got out of the car, followed by Grace and Astrid. The air was still, the only sound the dull roar of the Engineer's car.

'I can't let you do this,' Grace said.

'You don't have a choice,' Jake said. He walked over to Astrid. 'Do you have the gun?' His eyes were almost totally black. He only had minutes left.

Astrid reached into her pocket and handed it over. She didn't want to leave him.

Grace ran into Jake's arms and held him. Jake held her away from him. 'You have to go.'

But Grace would not let him go, until Jess got out of the car and ran over to him as well. Jake stooped and hugged her.

'Bring me chocolate,' Jess said.

'I will, princess,' he said, and pushed her gently towards the car.

Grace ushered Jess back into the car and closed the door. She peered through the window. 'You always were stubborn.' She gave Jake a weak smile.

'Use the Blue when you need it.'

Grace turned away from him, tears in her eyes.

Astrid and Jake checked the street behind them. There was still no sign of the Engineer. They had lost them momentarily. But it was only a matter of time before they found them again.

'I want to stay with you,' Astrid said.

'I want that too. But I need you to help them.'

She stared at him.

'I'm sorry,' he said. 'For everything.'

Jake's dark eyes and deep frown made her chest ache. From the moment she saw him hiding in the shadows of the trees outside her apartment, a part of her knew he was about to change everything for her. He had no idea then, and didn't now, but he was the reason she was on the verge of freedom ... real freedom.

She kissed him.

'I'm not sorry,' she said.

Jake went to speak but then stopped. His expression told her everything she needed to know.

The growl of the Engineer's car grew louder, but still she stared at Jake.

'Hang on,' she said. 'For as long as you can. Saifedean and Gambit will hack the chain soon.'

'I will,' he said, but Astrid could see he didn't mean it. He had almost run out of oxygen, and he knew it.

They kissed again, then Astrid tore herself away and ran to the car. She got into the driver's seat, pressed the ignition button, shoved the gearstick into drive and stepped on the accelerator. She couldn't let herself stop to think, otherwise she wouldn't be able to do what she needed to do.

Grace and Jess turned to look out of the window. Astrid, in the rearview, watched Jake disappear in a cloud of dust.

# CHAPTER 53

## JAKE

THE CAR WAS on the bridge, powering away from Jake. He touched his lips, recalling the feeling of Astrid's against his. It had caught him by surprise. Only now did he realise how much he'd longed for it to happen. He watched the car until finally it turned right and vanished.

He spun around.

The Engineer's car appeared from the narrow street at the west of the village. Clouds of ash billowed up around the car as it headed for Jake.

The gun was loaded and ready to go. What was he going to do? The thought of stopping the Engineer and Cray had seemed straightforward. All that mattered was that he stopped the Engineer getting to Grace and Jess, as well as Astrid, Gambit and Saifedean. He would do everything he could to stop that from happening.

On the bridge, he peered over the wall at the river beneath. The river channel was manmade, concrete, collecting the water in a narrow, fast-running stream.

The Engineer's car picked up speed, its headlights blinding him.

Jake stood in the centre of the bridge, raised his gun and fired – once, twice, three times – but the car continued to hurtle towards him.

He fired again and hit one of the headlights. The car swerved left, then right, then straightened up, heading for Jake and the bridge. He took a step closer to the oncoming car, then stopped. He couldn't breathe...

No. Not now! He grabbed at his throat, but it was constricted. He couldn't swallow. There was no more oxygen. He opened his mouth wide and tried with all his strength to take one more gulp of air. But it was impossible. Heat suffused him. He was suffocating. He dropped to his knees, gasping. He'd have given anything for one more breath. Just one more.

The car was headed for him, its one headlight shining on him like a spotlight.

Jake lifted the gun. It took all his determination and strength. He pulled the trigger. And again.

The car kept coming.

He pulled the trigger again.

Just one more breath. But it was no good. His vision was blurred. All he could see was the dazzling light headed for him.

He pulled the trigger again and again. The car engine was deafening. It could only be metres away.

There couldn't be many bullets left in the gun. He waited, his arm outstretched, and collected the energy to shoot one more time.

The car made a strange sound, like a wounded animal, then a high-pitched whine. It skidded to the left, then to the right, sending the car spinning sideways. The car was so close, Jake thought he heard the cries of fear from the men inside. The car shot over the bank just short of the bridge, then tumbled down the bank into the river.

Jake dropped the gun. He gazed up at the sky, where scattered clouds moved from left to right.

He wanted it to end quickly; the tightness in his throat and chest was unbearable. A spot of rain hit his cheek.

## *CHAPTER 54*

ASTRID

From the back seat of the car, Grace directed Astrid. 'That way.'

Astrid turned the steering wheel, constantly checking in her rear-view for the Engineer's car. There was no sign of it. Could Jake have stopped him? She hated leaving him at the bridge, but she knew that he would never have changed his mind. She could have stayed with him ... but that would have meant sacrificing Grace and Jess. She'd had no choice, but that was no consolation.

'The next left,' Grace shouted.

The front wing of the car grazed a wall before Astrid nudged the car back onto the street, which ran through a market.

'No one drives a car out here,' Grace said. 'We're going to draw attention to ourselves.'

People ran to avoid the car.

'I think it's a little late to worry about that,' Astrid said.

'Stop here,' Grace said, pointing to a house. Astrid recognised it – it was Gambit's place. Astrid stopped the car and got out. They all jogged to Gambit's house. Astrid pushed open the front door. A startled-looking Gambit appeared from the room next to where the computers and terminals were hidden.

'Quickly,' Gambit said, waving them in.

The three of them ran into the computer room, where Saifedean was typing furiously at a terminal.

'Where's Jake?' Gambit asked.

Astrid didn't know what to say. She waited for Grace to speak, but she said nothing either.

'He stayed,' Jess said, pointing to the doorway. 'Uncle Jake stayed.'

Gambit's face twisted with confusion.

'He was nearly out of oxygen,' Astrid said. 'He wanted to stop the Engineer from following us here.'

Gambit bowed his head, his shoulders slumping.

'How close are you to resetting the blockchain?' Astrid asked him. 'Maybe he can make it.'

Gambit fell into a chair, shaking his head. 'I'm not sure. We only have around eighty coders. There are others on their way, but we need more time. The more coders we have, the wider the new network is, and the more chance we have of forking the O blockchain.'

'Jake doesn't have more time,' Astrid said. 'And they know.'

Saifedean paused. 'Who knows?'

'Cray and The Engineer,' Astrid said. 'They're coming here. To stop us.'

'They won't be the only ones,' Gambit said. 'If The Engineer knows, then Carlisle will know too.'

'How much longer will it take?' Astrid asked.

'At least another half hour,' Saifedean said, returning to typing.

'He won't make it,' Astrid said.

Jess was by her side, so Astrid tried not to appear concerned.

'It's going to be okay,' Jess said, smiling up at her. Astrid didn't understand what she meant. Jess reached into her pocket and handed Astrid a tube of Blue.

'Where's the other one?' Grace asked her.

Jess bowed her head and muttered something Astrid couldn't hear. Grace dropped to a crouch beside her. 'What did you say?'

'I gave it to Uncle Jake,' Jess said, tears in her eyes. 'Did I do a bad thing?' She looked up at her mum.

Grace ruffled her hair. 'No, sweetheart. You did a good thing.'

'So Jake has it?' Astrid asked.

Grace smiled. 'I never thought any girl would fall for my little brother.'

'Go after him!' Gambit said. 'Go!'

Astrid ran out of the house and jumped into the car.

## CHAPTER 55

JAKE

JAKE LAY ON THE GROUND, waiting for it to end. His chest and stomach convulsed involuntarily. His vision swirled. The sky spun and he felt as if he was falling. He was cold and alone, and he needed it to stop.

His hand fell to his side. There was something in his coat pocket.

A tube.

It couldn't be. He'd given them both to Grace. Then he remembered Jess hugging him and asking for chocolate. It was Jess ... she'd done it.

He fumbled through the folds of his coat and rolled onto his side, finally gripping the tube. He held it to his lips.

The first inhalation made him choke. He rolled onto his back, gripping the tube in a clenched fist. It took all his strength to lift the tube to his mouth a second time and inhale. His throat opened up and he wheezed. He inhaled, over and over, until he tasted the Blue Oxygen. He gasped, holding the tube between his teeth. Shakily, he got to his knees. Maybe there was still a chance that he could make it back to Gambit. He hoped that Grace and Jess had made it.

He got to his feet and leaned forward, gulping the Blue. The bridge looked even longer now. He took one, then two steps, before stopping to take more oxygen. He would never make it.

'You're a tough bastard!' a voice said.

Jake spun around, almost falling. It was Cray, his face bloody, his arm shaking, aiming a gun at Jake.

'It's too late,' Jake said. 'It doesn't matter if you kill me.'

Cray's brow furrowed and he stumbled. He steadied himself and gripped the gun tightly, raising it so it was level with Jake's chest.

'We're going to take back the blockchain,' Jake said. 'Everyone ... even you ... will have a full quota again.'

Cray smiled. 'The Engineer knows all about Gambit and Burhan, and what they're doing. Don't worry – we'll stop them before they get close to doing something stupid. The Engineer has had his eye on Gambit for some time. Never thought he'd be stupid enough to try anything like this, though.'

Jake held the tube to his mouth and inhaled deeply.

Cray came closer, his gun waving side to side. He was hurt badly, but his determination was clear. Jake breathed in as much Blue as he could.

Cray's gun was close enough to reach, but Jake had no strength left.

'It really does taste different,' Jake said. 'Don't you think?'

'You're a fool, Jake. You know that? I've wanted to do this for a long time.'

Jake closed his eyes and felt the barrel of the gun press against his forehead. He swallowed.

The sound of an engine made him open his eyes.

'What the hell?' Cray said, spinning around to point the gun at the oncoming car.

With the last of his strength, Jake pushed Cray. The car veered towards Cray, who was trying to regain his balance. Then the car hit Cray, sending him over the bridge and into the river below. Jake fell backwards and lay on the cold ground.

## *CHAPTER 56*

ASTRID

THE CAR SKIDDED to the right. Astrid's eyes had been closed when she hit Cray. Now she didn't want to open them. She'd stalled the car, leaving only a ticking sound coming from the car bonnet.

'Get out of the car,' she told herself. 'Get out!' She reached over, opened the door, and fell out of the car. She jogged over to Jake, who was lying on his back on the bridge. She had been relieved to see him alive when she reached the bridge, but when she saw Cray holding a gun to his head, she was filled with rage. There was no time to think twice about hitting Cray.

'Jake!' she shouted, dropping to her knees beside him.

He could barely speak. 'What ... are ... you doing ... here.'

'Your sister told me about the Blue Oxygen.'

Jake raised a fist, the tube stuck out the top. He held it to his mouth and inhaled.

'We have to get you back to Gambit's,' she said.

Jake tried to get to his feet, but needed Astrid's help. With her arm around his waist, they stumbled to the car.

'What happened?' she asked, peering over the edge of the bridge.

He spoke in a hushed whisper. 'I shot ... the car.'

Making him talk was stupid. 'Save your breath.' She helped him into the passenger seat then ran around the front of the car and got into the driver's seat. She pressed the ignition button but the car moaned several times without starting.

Jake leaned his head against the window and closed his eyes.

'Start, goddamn it!' She thumped the steering wheel. This time, the car started. She turned the car around to head back across the bridge.

At the far side of the bridge, two figures appeared.

'It's the Engineer,' she said. 'And Bear.' She put her foot down on the accelerator and drove past them.

'They'll follow us,' Jake said.

Two gunshots rang out, making Astrid duck. 'We'll get back to Gambit's and work out what to do from there.'

Jake looked as though he might argue, then gave up and leaned his head against the window again.

In her wing mirror, Astrid watched Bear start to jog after them. 'Gambit and Saifedean will have re-coded the blockchain by now,' she said, wanting to convince herself. She powered the car towards Gambit's house.

## *CHAPTER 57*

JAKE

Jake swung open the car door, got out and hobbled through the garden at the front of Gambit's house. Every part of his body hurt. He pushed his way through the front door.

'How close are you?' he asked, falling to the floor. He inhaled from the tube of Blue.

Grace and Jess ran to him. Then Astrid came through the door.

'You're alive!' Grace said, trying to help him sit up.

Jake held her and then reached for Jess. 'Thank you.'

Jess wrapped her arms around his shoulders. It hurt, but he wasn't going to tell her so. He held her shoulders and looked into her eyes. They were dark blue.

'Jess's eyes...' he said to Grace.

'We have time,' she said. 'It's going to be okay.'

'Help me up,' Jake said, still inhaling from the tube of Blue. Astrid and Grace helped him up so he could go and see Gambit and Saifedean. When he entered the room, they were both typing urgently.

'They can't stop us now,' Gambit said, glancing over his shoulder. 'Not unless they destroy these terminals.'

'The Engineer is coming,' Jake said. 'He knows what we're doing, and where we are.'

Saifedean's fingers paused. 'How long do we have?'

'They have no car, so they will have to walk. Maybe another ten minutes?'

'You need to buy us as much time as you can.'

'Your eyes,' Jake said to Saifedean. 'They're turning Blue.'

'That's no surprise,' he said without turning around.

Jake wanted to say the right thing, but didn't know what that was. Saifedean had sacrificed himself, and Jake was the one who had asked him to do it. He faced Grace and Jess. 'You need to leave. As soon as the blockchain is reset, you will be safe.'

'We're not leaving,' Grace said.

'Then hide,' Astrid said, pointing to a narrow door at the other end of the room.

Grace hesitated, before glancing down at Jess. 'Be careful,' she said to Jake, then led Jess to the far side of the room and the door. Jake helped them inside the small cupboard and closed the door.

'I'm coming with you,' Astrid told Jake.

Jake wanted to tell her to stay with the others, but he knew she'd not take no for an answer. Besides, he wanted her with him.

'Me too,' Gambit said.

'You have to keep coding,' Jake said.

Gambit hesitated. He looked at the terminal screen, then back at Jake.

'Once it is done, you can help,' Jake said.

'Goddammit!' Gambit said. 'Don't die.' He took a gun

from a drawer on the far side of the room and placed it on the table, then returned to his computer.

Jake took the gun and pushed it into his pocket. As Jake was about to leave the room, the sound of coughing came from the cupboard. It was Jess. Her oxygen was out. He hobbled over to the door and opened it. Grace had already taken the tube of Blue and pushed it into Jess's mouth. Jess inhaled deeply. She'd be okay for as long as the tube lasted.

'We have no more Blue,' Jake said, inhaling from his tube yet again.

'I have enough,' Grace said. 'Go. Stop them.'

Jake closed the door, and with Astrid's help, made it to the doorway outside.

'What are you going to do?' she asked.

Out in the garden, waiting for the Engineer and the other man to appear, Jake straightened his back and clenched his fist. He could barely stand up, but he would do everything he could to stop them.

He inhaled from the tube. 'I'll kill him if I have to.'

## CHAPTER 58

ASTRID

ASTRID HEARD the helicopter before she saw it.

'Who is that?' Jake asked.

She stumbled across the garden, a hand shielding her eyes, peering at the horizon. 'It's my father.'

'Your father? How does he know you're here?'

'Sometimes I think he knows everything. There's nowhere to hide.' She turned and headed back to Gambit's house. 'We're not going to make it.'

Jake inhaled from the tube of Blue. 'We will. Gambit and Saifedean are nearly there.'

Astrid shook her head, then pointed to the left, across to where two men were headed their way. It was the Engineer and Bear.

Jake raised his gun.

'It's no good,' she said, grabbing his arm and pulling him backwards. 'My father will have armed men with him.'

The helicopter swooped left and right, before hanging in the sky and then descending more slowly, landing somewhere close to the market on the other side of the tunnel.

'Hurry,' she said, dragging Jake towards the steps and

into the house. 'We can slow them down.'

She got Jake inside and closed the door, then reached for a chair and slid it over to block the way in.

'Help me,' she said.

Jake was clearly struggling with injuries and the lack of oxygen. She saw the effort it took for him to lean against the chair and push it. When they had done it, Jake inhaled deeply from the tube of Blue.

'There ... isn't much ... left.'

Astrid helped him to the other side of the room and helped him rest against the wall.

'We're going to make it,' she said, but heard the uncertainty in her own voice. 'Hang on.'

Jake's eyes closed and then opened lazily. He couldn't stand without the help of the wall.

Banging at the door.

'Open up!' someone shouted. It wasn't her father, the Engineer or Bear. 'We have been notified of illicit coding on these premises.'

Astrid didn't know what to do.

'Don't let them in!' Gambit shouted from the other room. 'We're nearly there.'

As Astrid was about to respond, the glass shattered and men clambered through the windows.

Jake was almost out of it, but still he raised his gun, ready to shoot. But Astrid stopped him, taking the gun from his hand and dropping it to the floor. It was over. There was no way out of it.

Two soldiers removed the chair from the door, unlocked it and pushed it open. Light streamed into the room, blinding Astrid. An enormous figure blocked the light and entered the room. It was her father. Then more people entered. The Engineer, Bear, and even more soldiers.

# CHAPTER 59

## JAKE

JAKE INHALED from the tube of Blue, wary that at any moment, he would try to breathe in and find nothing left inside the small silver tube. He shook his head and took in the room as if for the first time, or waking from a dream.

'It's over,' Astrid's father said, glancing over at the Engineer and the man Astrid had called Bear.

'Stay away from him,' Astrid said, moving between Jake and her father.

Her father stopped, taken aback. 'What has got into you?' His voice wavered.

The soldiers headed for the next room and pointed their guns at Saiferdean and Gambit, who were no longer typing, but had their arms in the air.

Jake's vision swirled, but he did his best to check on the door behind which Grace and Jess were hidden without giving them away.

The Engineer arranged his jacket, now dirty and ripped in places from the crash on the bridge. 'You have done a good job of running from us. I'll give you that.'

'You're too late,' Astrid said. 'There are coders all over the villages, resetting the O blockchain.'

The Engineer pointed to Jake and mimicked his deep and heavy breathing. 'The blockchain looks to be working perfectly fine to me.'

Astrid took a quick step backwards, seemingly defeated.

'She's right,' Jake said. 'You're too late.' He wanted to back up what Astrid had said, even if he wasn't sure he was right.

Astrid's father approached Astrid, shaking his head, his face bright red. 'That's enough of this foolishness. You are coming with me.' He reached to grab Astrid's arm. She pulled away and retreated so she was standing behind Jake.

'Shoot the computers!' the Engineer said. 'Take them out!'

Gambit spread out his arms, defending the computers. 'The moment the other coders see our signal is down, they will finish what we started.'

'You're lying,' the Engineer said. 'You'd have done it by now if you could.'

'They'll be ready any minute.' Gambit lowered his hands and offered the computers. 'Go ahead. Destroy them. It won't stop them. They will reset the blockchain soon.'

The Engineer glanced over to Astrid's father.

'How do we stop it?' her father asked Saifedean.

Saifedean crossed his arms. 'You can't.'

The Engineer took a rifle from one of the armed men and aimed it at Jake. 'You can stop it. You can stop the reset.'

Jake shook his head. 'No. I can't. Not now.'

The Engineer strode towards Jake and struck him in the stomach with the butt of his rifle.

Jake keeled over, gripping his stomach with one hand,

and gripping the tube of Blue with the other. Winded, yet again.

The room spun. There was a scuffle, with Gambit and Astrid attempting to tackle the Engineer and the armed men. Jake's vision swirled, and he struggled to keep up with what was happening. More noise and movement, and then finally it all stopped. Someone was helping him stand. The Engineer faced him. Astrid and Gambit were restrained by the armed men.

The Engineer gripped Jake's chin. 'Take your last breath.'

Jake did as the Engineer said, lifted the tube to his mouth, and inhaled.

'How does it taste?' the Engineer asked. 'Make the most of it. This is your last chance. Either you stop the reset, or you die here and now.'

Jake held the oxygen in his throat, then swallowed.

The Engineer waited.

Jake enjoyed the desperation in the Engineer's eyes. He smiled, then shook his head. He didn't care what happened to him. All that mattered, was that his sister and niece were okay, and that they had reset the blockchain.

'You're a fool,' the Engineer said, pushing Jake up against the wall and pointing his rifle at his chest.

Jake waited, ready for the Engineer to pull the trigger.

But then, from the other side of the door that hid Grace and Jess, came stifled choking.

The Engineer's head turned quickly. He let go of Jake and headed for the door.

Jake stumbled towards the Engineer, desperate to stop him. But he was too late. The Engineer and Bear were already opening the door to reveal Grace and Jess. They were both out of oxygen.

## *CHAPTER 60*

ASTRID

Astrid tried to wrestle free from the man holding her, but she couldn't loosen his tight grip.

The Engineer reached into the cupboard and pulled Grace out. She was choking – out of oxygen. Jess, clinging onto her mother, was trying not to cry, the tube of Blue in her mouth.

'Let go of her!' Jake said, trying to push past Bear.

'Who the hell is that?' her father snapped, his face twisted in disgust.

Grace's face was pale, her hands reaching for her throat.

'This is Jake's sister,' the Engineer said in a teasing voice. 'And his niece.'

'Help her!' Astrid snapped.

The Engineer reached into his pocket and took out a tube of Blue.

'Please,' Jake said, no longer trying to get past Bear. He could barely stand. 'Help her.'

The Engineer laughed. 'It's remarkable how quickly a situation can change, isn't it? Now you need *my* help.'

'Stop the reset,' her father said, pointing to Gambit and then Saifedean.

'It's too late,' Gambit said.

But his tone was not definite enough and Astrid noticed how the Engineer's back straightened and his eyes lit up.

'Do it!' the Engineer snapped at Jake. He then pushed the tube of blue to Grace's mouth.

She inhaled, and then spoke quickly to Jake, 'Don't listen to him. Reset it.'

The Engineer took away the oxygen, and a moment later, Grace was suffocating.

Jake inhaled from the tube. It would soon be gone. 'There's nothing ... I can do.'

'He's lying,' her father said.

The Engineer stooped beside Grace and Jess. He smiled at Jess, who recoiled, her eyes filled with tears. The Engineer then looked up at Jake with a smug expression. 'You know what will happen to them if you don't stop the reset. You can pretend all you want that there's nothing you can do. But I think there is.'

Bear gripped the back of Jake's shirt and pushed him towards a terminal.

'Don't listen to him,' Saifedean said.

Jake leaned over the terminal, his two hands set on the table either side of the keyboard, one of them still holding the near-empty tube of Blue.

He was going to do it. Astrid wanted to help him, to make everything better. But there was nothing she could do. It was no good telling him not to do it. She couldn't imagine being in the same position.

'You can't stop it now,' Gambit said to Jake, trying to go to him. The armed men stopped him. 'We're nearly there.'

Jake turned his head to the Engineer, standing next to

Grace, who was on all fours, suffocating, Jess next to her, trying to give her mother the tube of Blue.

'That won't help your mummy,' the Engineer said to her. 'It is synced with you, little one.'

'Get ... away from ... her,' Jake wheezed.

But the Engineer edged closer to Jake's niece and whispered. 'The only person who can help your mummy is Uncle Jake. If he does what I want him to, I can give your mummy all the Blue she needs.'

Jess's eyes, wet with tears, opened wide, pleaded with Jake to help.

The Engineer strolled towards Jake. 'If you stop the reset, I will give your sister and your niece a way out of this. All the Blue they will ever need.'

Astrid struggled to break free one last time. It was no good. Jake bowed his head. She saw he was beaten ... he was ready to stop the reset.

## *CHAPTER 61*

### JAKE

If only Grace and Jess weren't there...

Jake rested his hand on the keyboard. Stopping the reset would be easy enough. But all that work would be for nothing. There would be little chance, now that Astrid's father and Carlisle knew it could be done, that taking down the O blockchain would ever be possible again. Yet, he couldn't let his sister and niece suffocate and die...

But he couldn't trust the Engineer either. Even if he did it, what would stop him from killing them?

He inhaled enough Blue to speak. His chest and lungs burned with the beatings he'd taken. 'How do I know ... you will give them ... the Blue they need?'

'You have my word,' Astrid's father said, before the Engineer could speak. 'You don't understand what you're doing, young man. Taking down the O blockchain would cause chaos across the globe. In stopping this, I will reward you for your good deed.'

'Good deed?' Jake said in disbelief.

The Engineer gave Grace another shot of Blue oxygen.

'It's up to you, kid. Either you stop this, or your sister and niece run out of oxygen.' He shrugged.

Jake glanced over at Astrid, hoping she would tell him what he should do. 'I will make sure your sister and niece get the oxygen they need.'

Even Gambit and Saifedean stared back at him, helpless, appearing to have also given up.

It was impossible. He knew he should let the reset happen. But if he did, his sister, niece, Gambit, Saifedean – they would all be dead. The only way his sister and niece had any chance of leaving the place alive was if he stopped the reset. But all those people around the world... He had the chance to reset the blockchain for everyone. Ten billion litres of oxygen for everyone. And no more Blue oxygen. The same for every person, no matter how many credits they had.

He typed on the keyboard. The option to stop the code was there in front of him. He stopped typing and stared at the screen.

## *CHAPTER 62*

ASTRID

Astrid wanted to help Jake, but she was powerless. Her father watched on, his face covered in a sheen of sweat. She couldn't understand how he could do what he had done. All those people, dead, their oxygen taken and sold to those who could afford it.

Jake was hunched over the computer, his fingers hovering above the keys. He didn't have a choice. Not really. And yet, he was about to contribute to the shortening of millions of lives.

'I can't do it,' Jake said.

'You don't have a choice,' her father said to him. 'You have to trust me. This is the right thing to do.'

Jake shook his head slowly.

A low muttering to Astrid's right drew her attention. It was the Engineer. He had spoken to one of the soldiers, who tightened his grip on his rifle. In that simple movement, Astrid knew what was about to happen. Neither Jake, his sister and niece, Gambit, or Saifedean were going to make it out of that place alive. The Engineer and his soldiers were going to kill them all the second Jake stopped the reset.

## CHAPTER 63

### JAKE

JAKE RESTED his finger on the keyboard. This was it.

'I should never have trusted a villager,' Astrid said.

Jake took his hands from the keyboard. How could she say something like that?

'What?' he asked, unsure whether he'd heard her right.

'You gave me your word,' she said. 'You said you would do anything to reset the blockchain.'

Even the Engineer and her father stared at her, confused.

Jake couldn't work out why she would say such a thing. But then something changed in her eyes.

'What good is anybody's word?' she said, and with her eyes, motioned for Jake to look to his right.

He didn't understand.

'You need to stop the code from running now,' the Engineer said, edging closer to Jake, pointing a gun at Jake's chest.

Jake turned to the computer screen, then back to Astrid.

Again, Astrid moved her eyes, telling him something he couldn't understand. It was too confusing.

'She doesn't have long left,' The Engineer said, glancing over at Grace.

Jess was holding on to her mother. Jake had no choice.

'I'm sorry,' Jake said to Astrid, and took a long inhalation of Blue.

Astrid's eyes opened wider, and then he glimpsed what she was signalling to him. It was one of the soldiers next to her. He was gripping his rifle tightly, making it tremble. Then, one of the other soldiers took a small step forward, his hands gripping his rifle too. The Engineer wasn't going to let his sister or his niece get out alive. That's what Astrid was trying to tell him. He resisted the anger stirring inside him. If he had any chance of getting his sister and niece out of this, he would have to give nothing away.

He glanced over at Grace who was doubled over, her arms around her stomach, choking for air. Jess was crying. The world around him slowed down until somehow he could hear his own heart beating.

He inhaled from the tube of Blue. It was now or never. He typed on the keyboard.

'What are you doing?' Astrid's father asked.

'You want the reset stopped don't you?' Jake stopped typing and stared at the screen. It was done. 'You can trust a villager's word.'

'It is the right thing,' Astrid's father said.

Jake tried to inhale Blue, but it was gone.

'Do it!' The Engineer said.

With two hands on the table, Jake pushed backwards and propelled himself into the Engineer, sending both of them to the ground. Jake was falling. There was a gunshot. Then a second. A burning in his stomach.

## *CHAPTER 64*

ASTRID

The gunshots caused total confusion. Astrid kicked out, making connection with the shin of the soldier who was holding her. She spun around and pushed the man against the wall. The back of the man's head struck the wall, knocking him out instantly. She stooped down and grabbed his rifle, all the time waiting for some kind of contact from behind. But she had the advantage and was aiming the rifle at the Engineer, who was struggling to stand.

Jake was on the ground at the Engineer's feet, blood coming from his stomach.

'Astrid!' her father shouted. 'Put it down!'

Grace was breathing. Jess too. Jake had activated the reset.

'It's done,' Astrid said to the Engineer. 'You're too late. The oxygen has been reset.'

'No!' the Engineer kicked out at the computers.

'Is she right?' her father asked, turning in a circle, his eyes wide with panic. 'It can't be reset. It can't!'

'You're not getting out of here alive,' the Engineer said to Astrid, then to her father. 'None of you.'

'Now, wait a moment,' her father said.

'Shut your mouth!' the Engineer said, spitting as he turned on her father.

'Carlisle will hear about this,' her father said. 'You're going to have to answer to him.'

The soldiers surrounded her father.

'Jake!' Grace shouted, hunched over him, crying desperately.

The Engineer stumbled to the door.

Astrid was ready to shoot him, but knew if she did, it would trigger a flurry of gunfire.

'Bear,' the Engineer said, 'do it.'

Bear lifted his rifle and swept it around the room, backing away towards the door and the Engineer. The soldiers followed him.

'No!' her father said to Saifedean. 'You have to put this right. There can be no reset.'

Saifedean gave him a wry smile and shook his head slowly.

Astrid strode towards the Engineer.

'Stop there!' Bear shouted at her, and turned to face the Engineer.

The Engineer froze. 'What are you doing, you idiot? Shoot them!'

It was as though everyone in the room was holding their breath.

'Bear?' The Engineer said. 'I've told you what to do. Now do it.'

'I think I'm done with you telling me what to do.'

'Put the gun down,' the Engineer said, fear in his voice.

Breaking the silence, Bear opened fire, sending the Engineer flying backwards and into the wall. He toppled to the floor, dead.

'Don't move!' one soldier shouted at Bear.

'Stay right there!' another one growled at him.

But Bear continued backing away, his rifle again sweeping the room. He hesitated by the door and looked at Astrid. There was a glint in his eye and the gentle rise of his top lip into a smile. There was no way the soldiers were going to take him on. Now the Engineer was dead, there was nothing in it for them. Better to let him go. Bear burst through the door and was running. She knew where he was going. He was headed for the Barren Sea.

'Come with me!' her father said to Astrid, gripping her arm.

'Let me go!' she snapped back at him, heading for Jake.

He was still alive, but in pain. Grace, Gambit and Saifedean carried him to another room and onto a bed.

'You're coming with me,' her father said.

'I know what you've done,' she said. 'And soon, everyone else will know.'

The soldiers in the room moved uncomfortably, glancing at one another and then at her father.

'I don't know what you're talking about,' he said, wiping sweat from his forehead. 'You've lost your mind.'

'I suggest you go now,' she said. 'Before it's too late. Once the villagers find out what you have been doing, they are going to come after you.'

Her father turned in a circle, then pointed to the soldiers. 'Take her. She is coming with us.'

But none of the soldiers followed his orders. Her father hesitated, before backing away towards the door. Moving slowly at first, he ran to the door and out.

'We have reset the blockchain,' Astrid said to the soldiers. 'It's true. Your loved ones now have maximum oxygen. And so do you.'

The soldiers looked at one another, unsure.

'That's impossible,' one of them said.

'See for yourself.' Astrid pointed to Grace and Jess. 'You saw their eyes. And you saw how they couldn't breathe.'

The soldiers appeared unconvinced, but all the same, their confusion was enough to make them leave without taking Astrid or the others away.

'Go and see for yourselves,' Astrid said, watching them leave.

They had done it. They had actually reset the oxygen for everyone. And the rich could no longer exploit the poor through the sale of Blue.

## CHAPTER 65

JAKE

JAKE OPENED HIS EYES, the world a kaleidoscope of shapes and colours.

'We stopped the bleeding,' someone said.

'Gambit?' Jake asked, then realised he was breathing freely. 'Jess? Grace? Are they okay?'

'We're here,' Grace said.

Jake reached out and felt two hands grip his. One of them was Jess's hand.

'You did it, Uncle Jake.'

'Astrid?' he asked. 'Is she here?'

The room was silent for a moment. 'No,' Grace said. 'She saw you were okay and then had to leave.'

Jake rested his head back into the pillow and told himself that as long as she was okay, that was all that mattered. Yet, he wanted to see for himself.

'She has gone to see Tom Carlisle,' Gambit said. 'His father has disappeared, along with Astrid's father. Everyone knows what they did. Things are going to change. Thanks to you.'

He should have been happy. But something was stopping him from feeling it. He couldn't stop thinking about all the people who had gone missing and who had died because of what they had done. Even now, the oxygen they were inhaling was being measured. The O blockchain still existed.

'Get some rest,' Grace said. 'Gambit says you were lucky to survive.'

Jake closed his eyes and thought about Astrid.

## *CHAPTER 66*

ASTRID

ASTRID, standing in front of her mother, bowed her head. She never thought she would see inside her father's home again. She felt like a four-year-old all over again. 'I'm sorry I left like that.'

Her mother, with tears in her eyes, smiled weakly. 'And I am sorry you felt you had to disappear in that way. You must have been very unhappy.'

'Do you forgive me?' Astrid asked.

Her mother opened her arms and Astrid walked into her embrace.

'And what about father?' Astrid asked. 'What will you do?'

Her mother's face took on a serious expression. 'Your father and I have had problems for a long time. I can't say I'm not surprised by what he has done. Even so, if I had know, I'd have done something about it.'

'I know,' Astrid said, unsure her mother would have had the courage. Nevertheless, she understood.

'What will you do now?' her mother asked. 'You have a home here, with me. You know that, don't you?'

Astrid looked around the large room. 'I can't stay here.'

'Where will you go?' her mother asked.

'I'm not sure.' Astrid's skin pricked and a shiver made its way through her whole body. She really didn't know what she was going to do. The world had opened up in a way that was unbelievable. Each passing second and minute felt like a dream. So many possibilities. And yet, now she had her quota like everyone else, her life became even more important somehow. Each moment needed to be lived and enjoyed. That was all that mattered.

'Goodbye,' she said, and once again hugged her mother.

'Come back and see me,' her mother said.

'I will,' Astrid said, and turned to leave.

## *CHAPTER 67*

JAKE

JAKE SAT on the chair outside Gambit's front door, beneath one of the trees. It had been a week since he had taken the gunshots to the stomach, and a week since he'd seen Astrid.

Gambit came down the steps and sat on the wall beside Jake's chair. 'Both Carlisle and Solomon are denying it.'

'I expected nothing else,' Jake said. He looked up at the branches drooping over his head. Now and then, when the branches swayed in the breeze, sunlight hit his eyes. The air was fresher now, somehow. It was an illusion. Even so, breathing felt different now everyone had the same amount of oxygen. No matter who you were or how rich you were, everyone was the same.

'The O blockchain is becoming more centralised every day,' Gambit said. 'We're up to ten thousand nodes. There are coders cropping up all across the villages, and now, even in the city.'

Jake stared up through the branches and leaves. The light turned the leaves shades of yellow, brown and gold.

'You miss her, don't you?' Gambit said.

Jake twisted his head. 'Who?'

'You know who,' Gambit said, smiling. 'You like her. It doesn't take a genius to see that.'

Jake didn't know what to say. It was true, and to say otherwise would have been foolish.

'Well,' Gambit said, standing, then walking back up the steps to the house. 'You can tell her how much. Here she comes.'

Jake's stomach lurched when he recognised Astrid walking towards him.

'Astrid?' he said. 'You're back.'

She took off her jacket and sat on the wall where Gambit had sat. 'You're up and about, I see.'

'I'm sorry,' he said. 'I shouldn't have-'

'Don't,' she said. 'I'm glad you did what you did. If you hadn't, then none of this would have happened. I won't lie – things got pretty crazy. But you made a massive difference. To everyone.'

Relief filled him. He still couldn't come to terms with what had happened. He should have been happy, relieved, but something was stopping him.

'I want to help you reach Moscov City,' he said. 'Like I promised.'

Astrid pulled her feet up onto the wall and wrapped her arms around her knees. 'You do keep your promises, then?' she asked, smiling.

'Yes,' he said seriously. 'I owe you that much.'

Astrid shuffled off the wall and stooped beside Jake's chair. 'Is that what you want?'

Jake struggled out of the chair

'Be careful,' she said.

'I'm fine.' He stood. The stitches in his stomach, as well as the pain from broken ribs, made him wince.

She stood in front of him, offering her hands to help him stand.

He held them. 'Do you want to go to the city?' he asked.

On tiptoe, she reached to kiss him.

'What do you want me to do?' she asked.

'I think you should stay with me,' Jake said, and kissed her again.

'I think so too,' Astrid said.

Jake smiled and thought to himself how no one he'd ever met, until then, had the power to take his breath away quite like Astrid.

The End

## *THANK YOU!*

Thank you for being a reader and taking the time to read *Oxygen*.

As I'm an indie writer of speculative fiction, I'm very much dependent on reviews. If you could spare the time, I'd be hugely grateful if you could leave an honest review of *Oxygen*.

And please visit sethrain.com if you'd like to stay in touch. I'd love to hear from you.

For now, all the best.

Seth.

SETHRAIN.COM

SETH RAIN

Printed in Great Britain
by Amazon

26468135R00179